Windward Secrets

K.A. Davis

ALL RIGHTS RESERVED

No part of this book may be reproduced or transmitted in any form or by any means, electronic or mechanical, including photocopying, recording, or by any information storage and retrieval system, without permission in writing from the author, except in the case of brief quotations embodied in reviews.

Cover Art:
Michelle Crocker

http://mlcdesigns4you.weebly.com/

Publisher's Note:

This is a work of fiction. All names, characters, places, and events are the work of the author's imagination.

Any resemblance to real persons, places, or events is coincidental.

Solstice Publishing - www.solsticepublishing.com

Copyright 2015 K.A. Davis

Windward Secrets

By

Kathleen Andrews Davis

**For
brave
women
everywhere.**

A woman is like a tea bag –
you can't tell how strong she is
until you put her in hot water.
Eleanor Roosevelt

Windward Secrets

Chapter One
Friday
Claire

Claire McPherson turned the faceted, glass doorknob... nothing. She twisted harder and rammed her shoulder into the door. It didn't budge. "Damn it!" Leaning her back against the door, she slid down and sat cross-legged on the floor. *Damn, damn, damn,* she thought as she banged her head gently against the door with each word. *Why would anyone lock a room in a rental house?*

"Oh well, too bad, too late, I'll worry about it when they get here," she mused, out loud, getting to her feet.

Claire and her three best friends, Caroline Hudson, Diane Fuller, and Jill Stone, had been meeting for "girls' get-a-ways" every few years since they graduated from college thirty years earlier. As much as they would have loved getting away every year, there were new babies, sick children, new jobs, no jobs, no vacation time or any number of reasons making it impossible. In the beginning, they could only afford weekends but, the past few years, they had taken the plunge into full weeks; real vacations. They took turns choosing the destination and this year it was Claire's turn. She chose this big, old, Victorian cottage located on the outskirts of Haworth, a small Cape Cod town. "The Point," as locals called the small peninsula that jutted into the Atlantic Ocean, had been her favorite vacation spot as a child. She loved Haworth, the quintessential, picture postcard town with good restaurants and village shops. Most importantly, the beaches on The Point were pristine, and the neighborhood quiet, with no two houses closer than the length of a football field. Summer had ended for the tourists with the start of school, and the foursome were among the few who preferred the off-season on Cape Cod.

Feeling responsible, since the choice of location this

year had been hers; Claire had arrived early, picked up the key from the realtor, and gone grocery shopping. The cottage had four bedrooms, one for each of them, but when Claire stopped at the realtor's office, she was informed that one of the bedrooms was not to be used. Not wanting to make a scene, and besides it was too late, Claire stated that the cottage had been falsely advertised and for their inconvenience she expected an adjustment to their bill. The realtor, avoiding eye contact, mumbled a noncommittal reply as he handed her the key.

"Wimp," she muttered, under her breath on her way back to her car.

Unlocking the front door of the cottage, she entered a large parlor with a fireplace and comfortable looking furniture. Not fancy furniture, but certainly adequate. To the left of the parlor was a medium-size, dining room. The kitchen stretched across the back of the house.

The first thing Claire did was haul the groceries to the kitchen and call Spence, her husband, to let him know she arrived safely. The kitchen was good size; big enough to function well for a large family. There was an old, porcelain sink with an attached drain board like her grandmother's. Claire remembered stories of being bathed in a sink like this when she was a baby. There were two casement windows over the sink with blue and white, gingham curtains. The walls were faded blue and there were white, painted cabinets along the long, inside wall. An antique, Welsh cupboard filled with a mishmash of old china flanked the end wall. The countertops were made of thick, natural-stained wood scarred from many years of use. Hazy blue, marbled linoleum covered the floor. There was a round, oak table in the middle of the room covered with an old-fashioned, oilcloth tablecloth. A gray-blue crock sat in the middle of the table filled with plastic daisies.

Opening the old Kelvinator refrigerator, that hummed incessantly, Claire put away the perishables and then placed the dry goods in the cupboard closest to the stove. Standing back, she marveled at the stove, it looked like something out of a Good Housekeeping magazine from the 1950s. "Cooking on that could be a challenge," she said out loud. "Hmmm... no dishwasher, but at least there's a coffeemaker."

The back wall, facing the ocean, had a row of double hung windows that looked over the back porch and beyond to the ocean. *What a great kitchen even without modern appliances* Claire thought, as she folded the grocery bags and stuffed them into a drawer next to the refrigerator.

Still frustrated about the locked room on the third floor, Claire let out a sigh, filled a mug with black coffee, and padded bare-footed to the front porch. Sitting down in an old, white, Shaker rocker she propped her feet up on the porch railing. With her feet extending from the frayed hems of her jeans, she stretched her toes to take full advantage of the warm sun and gentle breeze. She smiled at her newly pedicured toes, a rare treat, but worth the splurge for vacation. Taking a long sip of coffee, she watched as seagulls dropped clamshells onto the macadam road. The shells broke open and every seagull within earshot scrambled to claim the coveted clam meat. The smart seagulls simply waited by the side of the road and reaped the profits of the others' hard work.

How does one test the IQ of a seagull? Claire thought marveling at their ingenuity.

Tilting her mug to her lips, she surveyed her surroundings.

Windward Cottage, proclaimed by the sign on the front gate, was a three-story, weather-beaten, Victorian with wide porches surrounding the first floor and a widow's walk on the roof. The wavy, grey, shingle siding and peeling, white paint of the gingerbread trim epitomized the long years of summer sun and winter storms off the

Atlantic. Late-blooming roses gentled the grand, old lady's façade as they spilled over the once white, picket fence that fronted the property while drifting sand greedily swallowed the fence as it ran the property lines toward the ocean. The old Victorian, almost in the middle of nowhere, was surrounded by high, sand dunes imitating beached whales. Tall pines and undergrowth contorted by the harsh, winter wind stood in mock fortification around the property.

It was quiet. Tranquil. Only the distant sound of waves colliding with the beach behind the house, the gentle rustle of the wind in the trees, and the occasional squeak of the rocker when she moved interrupted the serenity. That's what it was: pure, sweet serenity, a comfort like she had never felt before. No work. No phones. No jarring television.

Claire liked being alone. She didn't need to be entertained or to be entertaining. She was secure in her maturity, comfortable in her own skin. Silence was bliss. Reaching up, she pushed the tortoise shell headband farther back on her shoulder-length, brown hair.

Exiling the thought of the upcoming week to a dark corner of her brain, she closed her eyes and let the sun coax the dark pigment to the surface of her skin. Sunscreen was the furthest thing from her mind; peace and quiet were uppermost at the moment.

Diane and Jill would probably love the quaint, old Victorian; but now, with only three bedrooms, she wondered about Caroline. Caroline always chose an expensive spa when it was her turn to pick the destination. She was the prima donna of the group with her hair always perfectly coifed and makeup complete by eight o'clock. The others could give a rat's ass. The best thing about their getaways was NOT having to rush around in the mornings making themselves presentable. Years of blow dryers, curling irons, squeezing into panty hose, packing lunches, getting kids off to school and, hopefully, themselves to work on time, had taken its toll and they were more than happy to be ponytailed and barefaced on their days off.

Caroline had married a successful businessman enabling her to be a stay-at-home mom. Not that anyone was critical or jealous. Caroline had paid her dues raising three very active, if not spoiled, boys who somehow managed to turn out okay. She might be ostentatious with her designer clothes and handbags, but she was kind and generous, and they loved her. When funds were short, Caroline would dip into her "mad money" and graciously cover any deficits.

Diane was the professional. She had built a successful, advertising firm. She had really made something of herself; she had to, her husband died young and left her with two, small children to raise. Diane was not only smart, she was savvy. She always knew what was happening in every corner of the world and could handle any crisis with finesse. When there was a disagreement among the four, she was the mediator seeing both sides of every situation and resolving it with logical reasoning.

Jill was the clown. There was never a dull moment when Jill was around. Fun-loving, sharp-witted, Miss Congeniality. She loved everyone and everyone loved her. Jill was the survivor of an abusive marriage. Claire often wondered if the Little Miss Sunshine act wasn't a cover to hide the real Jill. She would never know because once Jill had gotten herself and her daughter out of the house, she never looked back, and never talked about it again. Jill was always the first one at your door with hot coffee and homemade cinnamon rolls when there was an emergency. More than any of them, she knew the value of friendship.

And then there was Claire. Who was Claire? She often asked herself this question. Claire always felt like she was on the outside looking in, never quite sure where she belonged. To this day, she was still amazed she had been included in this small cluster of remarkable women. She felt her education had been a waste because she never used it. Instead, she had taken any job she could get to help keep her family of four afloat. They weren't poor, just barely middle class, living in a depressed area where you were lucky to have a job, any job. However, of the classmates, Claire thought she was the luckiest. She had a great husband and two wonderful daughters but, somehow, she never felt complete; always waiting for something, but never knowing what.

The edges of her mouth curled into a smile when Claire thought of Spence. He was aging well, and still made her heart skip a beat when he looked at her. He was a loving husband and a wonderful father. Spence still surprised her with bouquets of wildflowers picked from the field beside their house, and caressed her cheek when he kissed her good night. Spence was an auto mechanic and, when he wasn't at his regular job he worked on cars, in their garage, on the side. He had the proverbial heart of gold, never charging enough for his services and even bartering if the car's owner was short on cash. Spence once took a broken down, tandem bicycle in trade from an elderly couple who desperately needed their car fixed. He worked hours restoring that old bike. It was his gift to Claire for their tenth wedding anniversary. Sure, her friends were going on cruises and getting diamond bracelets, but she and Spence still rode that bike almost every evening after supper. She preferred the years of happiness pedaling behind her husband to any overpriced piece of jewelry or being forced to sit at a dinner table with pompous bores on a cruise ship. Shaking her head slightly she didn't know how they managed to get the girls through school. There were a few grants, college loans of course, but they still had to pay part of the tuition and living expenses. Claire knew Spence sacrificed a lot to get them through the roughest years and, even now, he helped her save money for her getaways. Who could ask for anything more?

Hearing a vehicle approach, Claire opened her eyes to see if it was one of the others arriving but it was just a beat-up, red, pickup truck rattling slowly past the cottage. Claire took another sip of coffee before setting the mug on the porch floor and leaning back in the chair again. Closing her eyes she fell asleep.

***

Caroline

Tears of frustration ran down Caroline's face as she pulled her suitcase down the curving staircase of the pseudo-antebellum mini-mansion located on the outskirts of Atlanta.

"There's never anyone around when I need them!" she exclaimed, bumping the suitcase down another step.

"Thelma, are you here?" Caroline yelled, at the top of her voice. When the housekeeper didn't answer she sat down on a step bracing the suitcase behind her. Pulling a tissue from the pocket of her beige linen slacks, she laid it over her face so she wouldn't destroy the makeup she had spent forty minutes applying, and then wept into her hands.

After a full five minutes of self-pity, Caroline took a deep breath, dabbed gently at her eyes, and ferociously grabbed the handle of the suitcase. "I'll show them. I'll show them all. I don't need him." And, with that, she yanked the suitcase down the remaining stairs and onto the tile floor of the entry hall. Glancing in the full-length, antique, pier mirror she surveyed her appearance. Thankfully, her makeup only needed minor repairs. Flipping open her compact she covered the tear streaks with powder and then touched up her lipstick. Looking closer she saw the earlier application of under-eye concealer had not hidden the dark circles that had gathered like storm clouds around her eyes from months of unhappiness; she gave them a little extra pat of powder and snapped the compact closed. Then she tucked a stray strand of chin-length, auburn hair behind her ear and straightened her pink, silk blouse. Checking her watch, she had two hours to get to the airport and check-in for her flight to Hyannis; plenty of time for the puffiness from crying to disappear.

Reaching into her handbag she pulled out the envelope with Bill's name on it. She wasn't going to tell him where she was going, let him guess. The message inside the envelope was short.

GOING AWAY WITH THE GIRLS.

Leaning the envelope against the vase of flowers, on the round table in the middle of the foyer, she turned, extended the handle on the suitcase; and rolled it out the front door.

Words she didn't allow spoken in her house spewed from her mouth as she reached her boiling point wrestling the heavy suitcase into the trunk of the car. Slamming the trunk closed made her feel better and, with a skyward glance, she apologized for swearing. Seated behind the steering wheel of her new convertible, the annual upgrade from one of her husband's dealerships, she shifted into drive and pressed the gas pedal. She watched her lovely home shrink slowly in the rearview mirror as she drove away.

It was an easy drive to the airport and, as she drove, Caroline went over the events of the last few months. 'How could this happen?' she asked herself for the thousandth time. 'I thought we still loved each other. When did we drift apart? Bill worked hard to build the business and I thought I played a role in that by freeing him of any responsibilities at home, entertaining his clients, and taking care of the boys' needs. We had a good marriage, three great kids, and a beautiful home. I just don't understand what went wrong. When did he start running around? Why didn't I notice?'

Having to be told by a friend at the country club that Bill was having an affair with their dental hygienist was not only embarrassing, it felt like she had been punched in the stomach. She couldn't breathe; the wind was knocked out of her. She had made a mad dash for the ladies' room and hid in a stall until she got herself under control. She sat on the toilet holding her stomach and wanting to vomit. When she was sure there was no one else in the ladies room, she went to the mirror to see how bad she looked. It was BAD. After due diligence to her face, she returned to the dining room and tried to pretend nothing was wrong. Bill seemed fine, telling jokes and laughing. She wanted to spear him with her fork but, instead, she smiled and laughed at his stupid jokes she had heard a hundred times. She didn't dare look around because she knew every eye in the room was waiting to see what she might do.

Dental hygienist, my ass! There were three in their dentist's office, but she didn't need to ask for verification… she knew which one. Bridgette, the blond with the big boobs! The bitch made my gums bleed!

Following the signs to the valet parking, at the airport, Caroline pulled up to the curb and popped the trunk. The attendant removed her suitcase and handed her a ticket. In return, Caroline handed him a hefty tip and headed for the sliding glass doors and the ticket counter. Walking down the concourse, her iPhone played its ridiculously, cheery tune. *I really need to change that*, she thought. The caller ID glowed with Bill's name and office number. 'Fat chance!' Caroline glared at the phone, turned it off, and threw it into her handbag.

She took her place in line at the security area, removed her shoes and placed them in the plastic tub along with her handbag, and stepped up to the metal detector. The agent motioned her through and, of course, the bleeping alarm went off.

"Oh geez, what now!" Caroline exclaimed, as she backed out and took off her watch placing it in a tub on the advancing conveyer. "It has to be this bracelet," she said, to the guard holding up the humongous ornamentation for him to see. In her embarrassment, she neglected to place the bracelet into one of the plastic bins so it disappeared under the wavy flaps of the x-ray machine and got caught at the other end jamming the machine and setting off another alarm.

"Sorry, sorry," Caroline lamented, to the passengers waiting behind her. It took three security personnel to release the bracelet and get the conveyer moving again.

"Next time use a tray," the female guard said, dangling Caroline's bracelet with an indulgent look saved for naughty children.

"Yes, yes, of course," Caroline whispered, snatching her bracelet and hurriedly stepping into her shoes. Red-faced, she grabbed her handbag and made a run for it.

Embarrassed and flustered she plopped down in a seat in the waiting area at the gate. Her mind raced toward the danger zone again.

Mr. Bill isn't as smart as he thinks, she thought with a smirk. She never let him know that she knew about his little escapade. She had been killing him with kindness for two months while she transferred funds from their joint accounts to an account in her name only. She had even moved some stocks and bonds without him knowing. "If he thinks he's going to get away with spending everything we saved, for the last twenty-seven years, on some bimbo he's a freaking lunatic," she mumbled, a little too loudly.

The sound of someone clearing their throat made her look up. An elderly couple across from her was looking at her with raised eyebrows.

"It's been a long day," she said, sweetly, in her best southern accent and flashing them a big smile.

Finally, seated in first class, with a cocktail in hand and luckily an empty seat beside her, Caroline started to feel her stress begin to melt. She closed her eyes and put her head back against the seat. *What do I tell the girls?* Closing her eyes she thought, *Oh hell, I'll cross that bridge when I come to it.*

***

Jill

"Woo Hoo!" Jill exclaimed, as she kissed Carrie, her daughter, goodbye. "I'm off! Be good. No men in the house while I'm away and don't forget to check in on Gram at least once a day. Okay, sweets?"

"Sure, Mom. Don't worry about me, just have a good time," Carrie replied, grinning from ear-to-ear at her mother as she nearly lost her balance battling two suitcases, a tote, her purse, and a large pastry box from Patsy's Bakery.

"Here, Mom, let me help."

Carrie took one of the suitcases and the tote, and placed them in the trunk of her mother's powder blue, Volkswagen beetle. Laughing, she loaded the rest of the luggage and gave her mom a big hug. "Have fun and call me when you get there."

"Are you sure you'll be okay," Jill asked, looking up at her daughter's crystal clear, blue eyes.

Carrie was three inches taller than her mother with the same curly, black hair but her father's light, blue eyes. Jill couldn't help thinking *thank God that's all she got from her father.*

"Come on, Mom. I'm twenty-three years old. I'll be fine. Please don't worry."

"Okay, I'll try," Jill said, turning toward the car before Carrie could see the tears building in her eyes.

Carrie walked up the front steps of their tiny, red, brick house and waved as Jill pulled out of the drive.

Jill swallowed the lump in her throat. *How did I get so lucky? What a great kid. I miss her already*, she thought. Gripping the steering wheel tighter she turned left at the corner and headed for I-95. The three hour drive was a little daunting not to mention boring. She found an oldies station on the radio and began to sing.

Before long she tired of the music and switched it off. The GPS was re-calculating. "It's an interstate for crying out loud, what could I have done wrong? I must have missed a direction with the music drowning out Miss Happy Voice," as she called the GPS narrator. Pulling to a stop on the side of the road, Jill waited for Miss Happy Voice to get her act together. Finally, she was directed to turn right three times and left once and drive back the way she had come.

After driving a few minutes she realized she had exited the interstate without meaning to. "No worries. We're back on track," she declared, to Miss Happy Voice.

Traffic was light and she quickly accelerated to the maximum speed. "Let's go Lulu," she said, to her car as she settled in for the rest of the drive.

Several hours into the drive she began to think about how nice it would be to have a chauffeur to do the driving. "Better yet a MAN," she said, out loud. "Where did that come from?" she asked her reflection in the rearview mirror.

Anyone watching her as she carried on her one-sided conversation would have thought she needed to be institutionalized. In addition to talking, she gestured with her hands and made exaggerated head movements.

I haven't thought about having a man in my life for years. I love my job, well most of the time; and I have Carrie. Her mind suddenly felt like it hit a concrete wall. *Oh my God, Carrie! She just graduated from nursing school and will probably be leaving home soon. What if she takes a job far away? What will I do?*

Jill's skin grew clammy and her hands were slippery with sweat on the steering wheel. Her chest tightened. Her heart raced. She knew the signs of a heart attack and was afraid she was headed for one.

She slapped her cheek. "Get a grip! This is silly. There's no reason to worry. Take a deep breath! Carrie's a smart girl... I have to trust her judgment. I raised her to be independent and now I have to let her choose her own path. On second thought... crap on all that psycho-babble, I want her to stay home with me forever."

Another half hour of processing this information and she perked up. "This isn't a heart attack, it's a mid-life crisis. Mid-life if you live to be a hundred and six!" she chuckled. "Maybe it is time to think about a relationship."
***
Diane
It was already 4:45 p.m. and Diane felt a headache coming on. She was never going to get out of the office in time to beat the rush hour traffic leaving Boston, so she may as well stay and get a little more work done. Picking up the phone, she dialed Claire's cell. No answer. Voice mail picked up. "Hi Claire, it's Diane. I'm running behind and can't beat the traffic so I'm going to stay and work a little longer. Please, don't wait up for me. Just leave the key under the mat and directions to my room. I'll see you all in the morning. Love ya."

She ran her hands through her short, spikey, blond hair and then massaged her temples. Reaching into a side drawer of her mahogany desk she pulled out a bottle of ibuprofen. "Lord, I get tired of these headaches." Tossing two pills into her mouth she washed them down with a large gulp of water from the ever present bottle on her desk.

"Okay if I leave?"

Swallowing hard Diane looked up to see Karen, her assistant, standing in the doorway.

"Sure, go ahead. If you need me while I'm gone feel free to call."

"When pigs fly," Karen giggled, slipping into her navy, blue blazer. "Have a nice vacation and try not to worry about the office."

"Oh, we always have a great time," Diane smiled. "You have a good weekend and I'll see you when I get back."

Diane heard the outer door close and quiet invade the office, and said, out loud, "Okay, two hours is my limit! By then the traffic won't be as bad and I can make better time."

Swiveling her desk chair around, Diane surveyed the city skyline from the windows of her twenty-second floor office. The afternoon sun bounced off the west facing windows, of the surrounding buildings, winking at her.

"Gosh, where have the years gone? We have such different lives, yet are still friends after all these years." She thought back to their days at the University of Massachusetts. "What fun we had." That was where she had met her husband Tom. The old terror came back as she remembered the day he died. She still had a hard time believing he was gone, and so quickly. A brain aneurysm at thirty-two and that was it. She would never stop missing him. Deidra had been four and Tim only two. Taking a deep breath she rotated back to her desk.

Diane ticked items off the list on her note pad. Call the kids and remind them to stop by the house to feed the cat and water the plants. Finish up the Larson's Seafood account. Leave all the pending files on Karen's desk. Call Mom and Dad to remind them I'm going away. Set the alarm before leaving the office. Luggage was already in the car.

Turning her attention back to her computer she went to work.

Yawning, she glanced down at the clock in the corner of the computer screen. "Yikes. It's 7:53 already. Where did the time go?"

She logged off the computer, cleared her desk, got her handbag out of the bottom drawer, and laid files on

Karen's desk as she headed for the door. One last look around and she activated the alarm and pulled the door closed.

In the elevator Diane pushed "P" for the parking garage and leaned against the wall as the elevator descended. It felt good to be going away. When the doors opened she stepped into the dimly lit, underground garage and walked toward her silver BMW.

***

The crunch of car tires on the crushed shell driveway woke Claire. There was no way not to smile when she saw Jill. Hugs and kisses. Drag in the luggage. Jill always over packed. "Better to have it and not need it, than to need it and not have it" was Jill's motto. She would have made a great boy scout.

"Oh, I love it! Just love it!" Jill cried, walking in the front door. "This is a cottage? Are you kidding? It looks like something out of a movie. And The Point... The Point is soooooo 'Summer of '42.' You remember that movie, don't you Claire?"

Jill could say more in one breath than anyone Claire had ever met. "Yes. This is what the Victorians called a summer cottage. A bit bigger than what most of us think of, wouldn't you say? And, yes, I do remember the movie."

Before Claire could say any more Jill was halfway up the stairs. "Where do you want me?'

"Jill, wait," Claire said, lugging the second suitcase up behind her. "I'm sorry but I have some disappointing news."

"Please don't tell me something's wrong. I've been looking forward to this vacation for months."

"Well, not really wrong, just inconvenient. We can't use the fourth bedroom. When I booked the house it was advertised as four bedrooms but, for some unknown reason, when I picked-up the key I was told we can only use three of the bedrooms. Would you mind bunking with me?"

"Is that all? Gosh, you scared me; I thought there was a problem. No worries, it'll be like old times… as long as you don't snore."

"No, no, you're safe on that account," Claire replied, with a smile.

Claire took the lead up to the third floor and into the room with twin beds. It was a large room. There were two single beds, an oak dresser with a mirror, and two slipper chairs on either side of a small, round table between two of the four windows. The walls were covered with faded, floral wallpaper and lace curtains hung at the windows. The floor was painted white with braided rugs scattered here and there.

"Ah… pretty room," Jill said.

The other room on the third floor was the locked room. It was like a specter stretching out its gnarly fingers toward Claire every time she passed; punishment for not knowing about it when she booked the cottage.

"Hey, thanks, you made up my bed," Jill said.

"No. The beds were already made when I got here."

"I don't understand. You told us to bring our own sheets and towels."

Claire shrugged her shoulders. "That's what the confirmation said, but why not use what's here. We can wash the sheets and re-make the beds when we leave."

"Works for me. Now, which way to the beach?"

"Let's wait for the others. How about some coffee?"

***

By early evening Caroline had arrived and Claire had retrieved the message from Diane saying she would be late.

Caroline, as expected, had chosen the largest bedroom, on the second floor, closest to the bathroom. Diane would have the other room on the second floor.

"Sitting on the back porch waiting for Caroline, Jill whispered to Claire, "does Caroline look okay to you?"

"Funny you say that. I thought she looked beat up from the feet up."

Hearing footsteps approaching from inside the house Claire and Jill became silent.

***

Jill nominated herself as the official tour director and took over organizing the vacation with an emphasis on food and beverage. She prepared an easy meal of grilled burgers and vegetables, directed cleanup of the kitchen, and then suggested a walk on the beach.

"It's too cold," Caroline whined.

"Oh, come on Caroline, just a short one," Claire said. "We need the exercise and it'll help us sleep."

Bundled up against the September wind, the three set out. The sun appeared to set the trees on fire as it slid out of site below the horizon.

"It's cold, let's go back," Caroline shouted, over the wind.

"As much as I hate to say it, she's right," Jill called to Claire.

Turning around they started back toward the house walking against the wind with their heads down. Finally, at the steps leading over the dune to the house, they stopped to catch their breath.

"That was a workout," Claire said. "Hopefully, it won't be as windy tomorrow."

"Look," Jill said, pointing to the house. "Diane must have gotten here early."

Caroline and Claire looked in the direction Jill was pointing and saw the silhouette of a woman standing on the roof of Windward Cottage.

"She's on the widow's walk," Caroline said.

"What's a widow's walk?" Jill asked.

"It's an area on a roof surrounded by a railing, sometimes it's a glass-enclosed cupola. Women would watch for their husband's ships returning from sea. They were given the term 'widow's' walk because sometimes the husbands never returned," Caroline explained.

"Well, that's cheerful," Jill said, looking up at the roof again.

Hurrying up the steps, and into the house, they called Diane's name.

No response.

"Diane, we're down here," Caroline yelled.

Still no reply.

"She must not be able to hear us. I'll get her," Claire volunteered, striding up the stairs. "Diane, are you here?" she called at the second floor. No answer. "Come on Diane, don't make me climb those stairs, I've already done it more times than I care to count!"

No answer.

Surely Diane had seen them on the beach and would have come down from the roof, thought Claire as she climbed the stairs to the third floor. She checked Diane's and Jill's room. No one there. *She must still be out on the roof and can't hear me. How did she get up there?'*

Looking around Claire located a back hallway she hadn't noticed earlier. There was a set of narrow stairs leading up. 'Great. More stairs.' At the top of the stairs was a door, which Claire opened and stepped through onto the roof.

"Diane, are you up here?"

No answer.

Claire walked around the flat, mansard roof but there was no one there and nowhere for anyone to hide.

For crying out loud, this isn't funny Claire thought, as she retraced her steps down the stairs. Checking each floor again, she looked more carefully into the room designated for Diane. There was no luggage, nothing to indicate Diane had arrived.

"She's not here," Claire announced, entering the parlor where Jill and Caroline sat curled up with blankets in front of a crackling fire.

Caroline and Jill looked at each other and then back at Claire.

"How can that be when we saw her on the widow's walk?" Caroline asked.

"I don't know, but there's no sign of her."

Caroline got up and looked out the front window. "Her car's not here."

"Well, we must have seen something that looked like a person but wasn't," Jill offered. "Things always look different at night."

"Who started the fire," Claire asked, with a nod toward the fireplace.

"It was already laid. All we had to do was light it," Jill answered.

"Well, what do you want to do?" Claire asked.

Pointing to a bookcase on the far side of the room Jill suggested, "How about a game? There are some board games and a poker set on the shelf over there."

Caroline had a blank look on her face with her thoughts obviously far away. *If I'm going to tell them about my failing marriage I only want to do it once, I'll wait till morning when Diane is here,* she thought to herself.

"Caroline, do you want to play a game," Jill repeated.

"Oh sorry, I drifted... thanks, but if you two don't mind, I think I'm going to turn in early."

"No problem. We'll see you in the morning," Claire answered, with a mystified look. It wasn't like Caroline to be the first to go to bed. She usually liked to finish the last of the preferred beverage of the evening.

Caroline folded her blanket and laid it on the sofa. Without giving them another glance she walked up the stairs seeming to need the assistance of the banister to pull herself up.

"Oh yeah, there's definitely something wrong," Jill

whispered, snuggling deeper into the overstuffed sofa.

Claire sat down beside her and pulled Caroline's blanket over her legs. "I think you're right. You don't think she's ill do you?"

"I don't know. She never said anything to me and we talk every few weeks or so. Come to think of it, we haven't spoken since, I think… July. That's much longer than normal."

The two women talked quietly as the flames died and the embers slowly faded to gray.

"I'll leave the key and a note for Diane, you lock up the rest of the house," Claire directed.

***

Something woke Claire and she sat straight up in bed. The digital clock on the bedside table read 3:08. *Boy, Diane is really late,* she thought returning to her warm nest under the blankets.

Chapter Two
Saturday

Bright sunlight hit Claire directly in the face so she rolled over, away from the window. Opening one eye she looked at Jill's bed, it was empty. The deep, rich aroma of coffee hit her nostrils like adrenaline. Throwing back the covers she stretched and eased up into a sitting position. She grabbed her quilted, cosmetic bag. 'Hmmm...just like college...taking your toiletries down the hall to the bathroom.'

Freshly showered, and hair still wet, Claire entered the kitchen expecting to see Jill but the kitchen was empty so she helped herself to a mug of coffee and peeked into the pastry box in the center of the kitchen table which was set for four. 'Yum, I better wait for the others.' Pushing the wooden, screen door open she stepped to the edge of the back porch and sat down on the top step. It was a perfect day. The sky was pure blue and the bright sun sent diamonds skipping across the whitecaps.

Halfway through her coffee, Claire noticed two people walking on the beach and a dog running in the water with a stick in its mouth. Claire watched as a man and woman slowly walked up the beach toward her.

Without warning a giant, black lab was suddenly at her feet sniffing her. Not a great dog person, Claire sat perfectly still and quietly said, "Hello." A sharp whistle from the man and the dog bolted back to his master kicking up sand with his hind legs. *Whew. Thank you,* thought Claire as she looked down from the porch. The couple had stopped just below the house and she recognized Jill. 'What the?'

Jill climbed the steps over the dune. The man nodded up at Claire and then turned and walked back the way they had come. The dog quickly ran past his master and plunged into the waves.

"Good morning," Jill said, when she reached the porch.

"Well hello…and who was that?"

"His name's Drew Carson. I met him on the beach."

"Is that safe?"

Jill gave Claire a curious look. "Do you want me to run screaming back to the house every time I see someone on the beach?"

"No, of course not. You're right, I'm sorry."

"He seems very nice. His dog's name is Ike. He rented a cottage down the beach for a month. Lucky guy, a month would be wonderful."

"What's he doing out here all by himself…or isn't he by himself?" Claire asked, trying not to sound too suspicious.

"He IS by himself. He's divorced. He just wanted a change of scenery and some peace and quiet. He's a business strategy consultant and can work from anywhere."

"You got all that on one walk?"

"Well, sure. No sense wasting time if he's married," Jill grinned.

Claire rolled her eyes skyward in pretend annoyance. "You must be hungry. Let's see if the others are up yet."

The kitchen was still empty, so they returned to the porch to wait.

"Did you hear Diane come in last night or rather this morning?" Claire asked.

Jill shook her head. "What time was it?"

"Just after three. I'm thinking she might sleep in."

"Wouldn't doubt it."

The conversation had turned to what to do after breakfast when the screen door squeaked behind them. Caroline joined them looking like she had just stepped out of Vogue magazine in a black velour, jogging outfit. "Good morning, ladies."

Jill looked up annoyed. "Caroline, if you have a string of pearls around your neck I'm going to have to slap you."

Caroline smiled, "Don't be silly, they're diamonds."

Claire laughed and asked, "How did you sleep?"

"Better than I have in months, thank you. Are you two hungry?"

"Always," Claire replied. "But Diane's not up yet."

"She's not here," Caroline returned, surprised Claire didn't know.

"What do you mean? I heard her come in very early this morning?" Claire stated wrinkling her brow.

"Well, I looked in her room and she wasn't there and there's no luggage. Did you check for her car?"

Claire walked to the driveway side of the house. "I'll be darned. Her car isn't here, but I was sure I heard something last night."

"Must have been the wind," Jill injected. "Claire, check your phone to see if she called."

Claire hurried to the parlor for her handbag and pulled out her phone. No messages.

Returning to the kitchen with phone in hand she hit speed dial. While she listened for a connection they heard a car in the driveway.

Jill reached Diane first and threw her arms around her, "God Diane, we were just about to panic. Where have you been?"

Diane patted Jill's back. "Oh, just a nightmare trip. Left the office later than I expected and then, half way here I had a flat and had to wait over an hour for help. I don't know why I keep paying for AAA membership, they're so slow. Then, the guy took forever to change the tire. I swear I could have done it faster myself. Thank goodness for GPS. If I had gotten lost that would have been the icing on the cake."

As Claire reached into the back seat for Diane's

suitcase, she glanced over the roof of the car just in time to see the old, red pickup drive by again. "Come on Diane, you must be exhausted. Do you want coffee, shower, or sleep?"

"As much as I want to catch up with you all, I think I better sleep."

Once they had settled Diane in her room, Claire, Jill, and Caroline returned to the kitchen and sat down around the table.

Opening the box on the table Caroline asked, "Where did the pastries come from?"

"My favorite bakery," Jill answered, biting into a cheese Danish.

"Well, thanks," Claire said. "And, thanks for setting the table and making the coffee this morning."

Jill stopped in mid-chew and with chipmunk cheeks full of Danish mumbled, "I didn't make the coffee or set the table. It was done when I left to walk on the beach. I thought Diane had done it last night. Of course, that was before I knew she hadn't arrived."

Caroline and Claire both stared at Jill expressionless.

Winking and waving her index finger Caroline laughed, "One of you had too much to drink last night and forgot you did it."

Claire looked at Jill and shrugged her shoulders. "We did hit the margaritas pretty hard."

"And, maybe one of us did have one too many. It's happened before," Jill admitted, looking directly at Claire.

"Your secret's safe with me. I won't tell anyone," Caroline proclaimed. "What do you say we walk to town? I'd love to see what shops they have."

Finishing their coffee the women cleaned up the kitchen and grabbed their wallets.

"We better leave a note for Diane," Jill volunteered, grabbing a notepad and pen from the desk beside the front door.

The road to Haworth was narrow and followed the shore line. There were very few houses and not one car passed the trio.

"Gosh, this is great. Smell that sea air," Caroline said, with a big smile on her face.

Jill looked at Caroline. "You seem to be feeling better than you did last night."

"One hundred percent! I can't tell you how good it is to be here."

They were soon meandering down the sidewalks of Haworth looking in store windows. Huge, yellow, and red signs announced large reductions in prices in nearly every store they passed. Summer merchandise had to be moved to make room for cold weather gear. The main street of Haworth was not very long so it didn't take long to go up one side and down the other. Near the end of the street was a sign pointing down an alley, "Blackbeard's Tavern."

"Well, of course," Jill said, sarcastically. "Every shore town has to have a Blackbeard's or a Davey Jones restaurant. Let's see if we can get a cold drink."

Turning down the alley they found a picturesque, cedar-shingled pub with a hand-carved sign depicting a bearded pirate. Slipping inside the cool darkness of the tavern they waited for their eyes to adjust. The restaurant was fairly crowded. A waitress greeted them and escorted them to a small table in the far corner.

"This is darling," Caroline offered. "Are you eating or just getting a drink?"

"Just iced tea for me," Jill said. Claire nodded in agreement.

The waitress took their orders and returned promptly with tall glasses with wedges of lemon balanced on the rims.

"Should we take something back for Diane?" Caroline asked.

Claire lowered her glass and shook her head. "I stocked the frig pretty well, but we could use some wine."

Back in the warm sunlight the women found a liquor store and then started their return trip to the cottage.

With the wine stowed in the refrigerator, they donned bathing suits and walked down the steps to the beach. It was mid-afternoon when a shadow crossed their faces and made them look up from their beach towels. Diane was standing above them.

"Good day Sleeping Beauty," Claire said. "Pull up a chair, or rather a towel."

Spreading her towel on the sand, Diane sat down at the end of the row of well-lotioned cellulite and then eased onto her stomach. Propping herself up on her elbows she engaged the others in a description of their morning activities and updates on their families. Caroline was unusually quiet and lay with her sunhat covering her face. The conversation slowed to silence and the warm sand lured their bodies into oblivion. One by one they closed their eyes and slipped into sleep. A cool breeze and clouds crossing the sun woke them with a sudden drop in temperature.

"Yikes. It got cold!" Claire said, sitting up.

Gathering their beach paraphernalia they walked toward the house discussing what to do for dinner. They decided to try one of the restaurants in town to celebrate being together again. By six thirty everyone was showered and changed. Claire, Jill, and Diane wore jeans, sandals, and cotton sweaters. Caroline appeared in an expensive looking sundress, full makeup, perfect hair, and accessorized like a gypsy on parade.

"For heaven's sake, Caroline. Don't you ever dress down?" Jill asked, bluntly.

Diane and Claire looked at each other wondering if Caroline was insulted by the remark.

Caroline's smile vanished and she looked down at

her body. "I guess I am a little overdressed. Just give me a minute and I'll change?"

Ten minutes later she returned wearing white slacks and a cashmere sweater with only minimal jewelry.

"Much better," Diane complimented her, with a kind smile.

Exploring Haworth they found a small, seafood restaurant located next to the commercial fishing docks. They were treated to a window table where they could watch the fisherman unload their catch and wash down their boats.

"Some nice looking men out there," Jill announced, softly. "Yup, men sure love their hoses."

Diane laughed so hard she spit wine. Embarrassed, she grabbed a napkin and covered her mouth.

"You go girl," Claire said. "And take Diane with you."

"Oh no, no thanks," Diane replied, still laughing. "I'm not in the market."

"Well I am," Jill boasted, holding up her wine glass to clink the others'.

"Yes, you're long overdue," Claire laughed.

The waitress interrupted to take their orders. They all chose mixed, seafood platters and ordered another bottle of wine. Shared stories of their college days entertained them through dinner. Full of good food and wine they settled back in their captain's chairs and watched as the setting sun cast distorted outlines of the gently, rocking boats across the water.

"Dessert anyone?" the waitress inquired.

The four women groaned simultaneously and, with regret, declined.

Diane was the first to stand, "I'm sure glad we drove. I couldn't walk back to the cottage if I tried."

"I know what you mean, that's more food than I've had in a month of Sundays," Jill chimed in.

Back at the cottage it was a race up the stairs to change into pajamas. Gathering everyone in the parlor, Jill made an announcement. "I hereby declare that we are starting a tradition...nightcaps on the roof!"

"Jill, there's nowhere to sit up there," Claire said.

"Ah, but there is," Jill declared. Holding up a bottle of Moscato, and four wine glasses, she led the way up the stairs.

"Better grab some coats or blankets," Diane said. "I think she's serious."

Opening the door to the widow's walk, Jill bowed and waved her friends onto the roof. Four, aluminum, lawn chairs with green and white, plastic webbing were arranged in a semi-circle facing the ocean. A kerosene lantern glowed from its position, on the roof, in front of the chairs.

Laughing, Diane looked at Jill. "I remember chairs like these, my parents had them for years. When one of the webs broke Dad would re-weave it with a new piece. Unfortunately, the new piece never matched the old and, after a few repairs, the chairs were a kaleidoscope of color. Mom hated it. She said it made our yard look like a circus."

The women each took a chair and Jill poured everyone a glass of wine.

"Where did you find these chairs and how did you get them up here?" Claire asked, reaching for her glass.

"I found them in the shed out back this morning before I went for a walk. The shed was unlocked so I took a look and there they were. I brought them up while you all were sleeping. Cool, huh?"

Covering herself with a blanket Claire held up her glass. "Good find, Jill. Here's to you."

It was a beautiful night. Stars sparkled, by the millions, overhead and the man in the moon smiled down at them. The women chatted and laughed and poured more wine. Jill noticed Caroline hadn't said anything for quite a while and was quietly staring out over the ocean.

"Caroline are you okay?" she asked.

Diane and Claire stopped talking and looked at Caroline.

There was a long pause before Caroline turned to face her friends. "Well," she took a deep breath. "Not really... Bill's having an affair." There, she had finally said it out loud. It didn't hurt as much as she thought it would.

Claire, sitting next to her, reached over and took her hand. "Oh, Caroline, I'm so sorry."

"Thank you, but you know what? Telling you three right now felt good. I haven't spoken to anyone about it and it's been driving me crazy."

"Are you sure he's cheating?" Diane asked.

Caroline shrugged her shoulders and pursed her lips. "Did I catch them in the act? No. But, there have been signs, and Joan Gates seemed sincere when she told me." Caroline went on to tell them everything that had happened including how she had moved the money."

"Are you planning to leave him?" Jill inquired.

"I don't know. Until right now, I really hadn't thought that far ahead. I'm tired being someone's wife, someone's mother, a social director, everything but my own person."

Trying to lighten the conversation Jill asked, "Does that mean you won't have to look like a million bucks all the time Caroline?"

"Maybe," Caroline laughed.

"Do you even own a pair of jeans?" Claire asked.

"Of course I do."

"We've never seen you in jeans. Even at school, we wore cutoffs and you had coordinated Bermuda short outfits!"

The cumulative effect of the evening's wine was starting to loosen Caroline up and she let out a full belly laugh. "I wear jeans when I garden."

"You garden?" Diane asked, sincerely amazed.

"Yes! I garden! I even have my own garden tools. They're pink."

By now the other women were laughing out loud in spite of Caroline's unfortunate situation.

"You've got to be kidding. Pink garden tools?" Jill asked.

Caroline stood stretching her five foot five inch frame to its max and with great melodrama said, "Well, certainly, doesn't everyone? The Women's Auxiliary at the hospital sold them as a fundraiser for breast cancer. As the exemplary president that I am, I had to buy them which meant I had to take up gardening."

The laughter continued as they tried to picture Caroline digging in the dirt.

"Oh, you'd be surprised. None of you know the truth about me," Caroline added, sitting back down.

The laughter stopped abruptly and Claire, Jill, and Diane looked at Caroline. Caroline was glad it was dark and they couldn't see her face because she was afraid she would get emotional. Since she started, she was going to keep going and finally, after all these years, let it all out.

Diane spoke first. "What do you mean we don't really know you? We've known you for thirty-four years. We've grown up together. Are you okay? Is it your health?"

"I'm fine. And no, it's not my health. You know those cute Bermuda short outfits you just mentioned Claire?"

"Yes."

"They were hand-me-downs from the family my mother worked for. Every piece of clothing I had was a hand-me-down, until I married Bill."

"Big deal, we all had hand-me-downs at one time or another."

"Maybe, but I never had any new clothes. We were dirt poor. Mom worked as a housekeeper because my father was a disgusting drunk."

The women audibly sucked in their breath and waited.

"Yup, good old Dad. He would rather hang out all day in a bar swilling beer and doing shots than support his family."

"We didn't know your dad was an alcoholic," Jill said, sympathetically.

"Oh no, Jill, not an alcoholic… please, don't dress it up. Alcoholism is not a disease like all the do-gooders try to make us believe. It's a freaking choice that selfish, weak people make. He wasn't anything as nice as a disease, he was a falling down, sickening drunk who made our lives miserable. My mother worked her fingers to the bone trying to keep us from living in the street."

Caroline took a sip of wine and went on. "Didn't you ever wonder why I always accepted the invitations to your homes on school breaks, but never invited you to mine? We lived in a slum. I was too embarrassed to let anyone see how we lived. We had nothing. Mom worked hard and Dad would steal her pay and piss it down the drain. Arnie, my brother, quit school at sixteen and lied about his age to get into the Navy. Bless his heart, he's a good guy, and has a great job and family now. My sister, Bonnie, deliberately got pregnant so that Ralph would marry her and get her out of the house. Yup, that's the way it really was."

Stunned, Diane asked, "Caroline, how did you afford school?"

"I knew the only way to get out of the slums was education. So, I worked my ass off in high school and won a full math scholarship. Yeah, I bet you thought I was always a dumb, little, Southern gal, didn't you? Nope, I've got it upstairs," she said, pointing to her head. "But I learned that acting cute and dumb got me a lot further with the guys than being smart. College was the fast track to rich guys and I was not going to be poor ever again."

"I thought you majored in art?" Claire interrupted.

"I let you think that. My major was economics. My minor, and my passion, was art." she continued, taking a deep breath. "One year, for Christmas, Mom got me a sketch pad and some yellow #2 pencils. She wrapped them in plain, tissue paper tied with string. She pretended they were from Santa, but I knew better. She didn't know there were different pencils for sketching, not that she could have afforded them. That was the best Christmas of my life. I would go up on the roof of the tenement, it was not like this," she said, waving her wine glass toward the ocean. "Instead of a beautiful view like this, I had the smells and sounds of the inner city. Anyway, I would sketch up there for hours. When the weather was bad I would hide in the furnace room, in the basement, and sketch; anything to get away from Dad."

"Geez, Caroline, why didn't you tell us? I'm sure there were things we could have done to help you," Jill said.

"You were all so cool. I just couldn't make myself tell you. Stupid pride."

"Did Bill know?"

"Hell, no. Mom died shortly after graduation and I didn't meet Bill till later. I never told him details about my family."

Diane leaned a little closer. "May I ask what happened to your Dad?"

"Don't know. Don't care. As far as I'm concerned he killed my mother and should have served time."

The night air had become thick with emotion. For once, no one could think of anything to say. Finally, Claire asked, "Caroline, if you could do anything you wanted, what would it be?"

Caroline thought for a few seconds and then looked at Claire like she had given her an expensive gift.

"I would paint. Do nothing but sit in a garden, or at the beach, or on a mountain top, and paint."

Caroline got up from her chair and leaned over Claire. Lifting Claire's head up with her hand she kissed her on the cheek. "Thank you."

"For what?"

"You just did more for me in one sentence than my shrink has done in ten years."

"Well, hell, Claire," Jill laughed. "You've missed your calling."

"Holy shit. Think of the money I could have been making all these years!"

"Ya know what else?" Caroline asked.

"Afraid to ask," Diane replied.

"This isn't even the real me. Somehow, we all drifted apart during those years when we married and had children, and you never met Bill. He was all about status. I had to be the best wife, the best mother, the best hostess… he even dictated what I wore and how to look. What you see is not me, my hair isn't auburn; it's frizzy, strawberry blond with streaks of grey and I have freckles all over my face! And, I wear contacts and Spanks! So there!"

This was the last straw, the women were laughing so hard they couldn't see. Wiping her eyes with her pajama sleeve Jill suddenly jumped up, ran to the stairs, and disappeared.

"Her bladder," Claire said. "Wine and laughter always do that to her."

Chapter Three
Sunday

    Morning came way too quickly for all four women. Claire woke with what felt like a mouth full of cotton and looked at the clock. "Oh Lord. Jill, wake up it's after eleven."

    Her eyeballs felt like they were going to fall out of her head. Easing herself up to a sitting position she focused on the other bed. Jill was already gone. Claire fell back onto her bed and covered her eyes with her forearm. "Holy crap. I drank way too much last night. I'm going to have to take this slowly."

    Forfeiting a shower in favor of a glass of water and some aspirin she willed her muscles to cooperate. Leaning on the banister for support, she slowly moved down the staircase. The scene in the parlor was less than attractive. Caroline was lying on the sofa with one foot on the floor, sunglasses over her eyes snoring like a drunken sailor. Diane was half sitting, half laying in a recliner with a washcloth over her eyes and her mouth wide open. Claire made the sign of the cross toward her friends and continued to the kitchen.

    On the kitchen counter she found an array of vitamin and aspirin bottles. There was a note in Jill's handwriting.

To Whom It May Concern,
Take one of each vitamin, 2 aspirin, a full glass of water, and go back to bed.

    It hurt to smile. Claire followed the directions and turned to go back upstairs when the screen door opened behind her.

"Hey, you're up," Jill whispered.

"You don't have to yell," Claire said, putting her

hands over her ears.

"I haven't seen you this bad since that kegger at Lambda Chi."

"And, hopefully, you never will again."

"Where are the other two?"

"Splashed all over the parlor, and they don't look any better than I do. Where were you?"

"Walking on the beach with Drew."

Claire was too tired to quiz Jill, she just raised one eyebrow and grabbed the sink to steady herself.

"I need to get my phone and take some pictures. This will make good blackmail someday," Jill said, heading for the parlor.

Claire followed her holding onto the wall as she went.

Jill, good to her word, was shooting pictures when Diane woke up and pulled a throw pillow in front of her face. "You show those to anyone and I'll sue."

"Oh, come on Diane, be a sport. We'll laugh at these next year."

Caroline started to stir. Keeping her sunglasses on, she sat up. "What time is it?"

"It's going on noon," Claire replied.

"Shouldn't we be getting cleaned up?"

Claire looked at Diane. Diane looked at Jill.

"Don't look at me," Jill laughed. "I'm fine. You three are the ones who need showers."

"Yeah, yeah, I'll go first," Caroline said, stumbling toward the staircase.

"Thank God," Claire replied, heading for the sofa. "I need a little more time."

Diane laid her head back down, placed the washcloth back over her eyes, and mumbled, "I'm so glad our kids aren't here."

Caroline

The hot shower started the healing process and encouraged life back into her body. Caroline looked into the mirror, over the dresser, in her bedroom. She felt better but her reflection wasn't convincing. The white bathrobe, and white towel wrapped tightly around her head, made the sunburned face and bloodshot eyes look like a caricature of the woman she thought she knew.

Her eyes felt dry and gritty. "Oh hell, I forgot to take my contacts out last night." Locating her makeup bag hanging on the back of the bedroom door, she retrieved her glasses and a bottle of Visine. Returning to the dresser she carefully removed the contacts and liberally squirted drops into each eye.

Bending over, she released the towel and rubbed her hair briskly. Standing up she combed her fingers through her hair and placed her glasses on her nose. Again she looked in the mirror. She looked pretty bad... to be expected after the night they had. She knew the woman in the mirror. She recognized the face, the throat, the hair. She reached up and touched the laugh lines around her eyes and traced the furrows that led to the corners of her mouth that now drooped slightly with age. What she didn't see, was the soul. *Where was this woman's heart? Where were her dreams?*

Movement in the mirror caught her attention. The breeze coming through the open window behind her was gently blowing the lace curtain. The curtain beckoned. Caroline studied it. Beautiful in its delicate design, it flew gracefully free on the wind anchored only by the curtain rod at the top. Years of guarding the room from the sun had turned the curtain yellow. *What had that curtain seen over the years? A family growing up in this house and playing on the beach?* It probably had watched a life similar to Caroline's and although aged and losing its beauty, like her, it was still free to fly on the wind.

Crossing the room Caroline pushed the curtain to one side. She turned a large wingchair to face the window and sat down. Closing her eyes she tried to clear her mind. When she opened her eyes there was no longer a window before her, there was a masterpiece framed by the window frame with a beautiful banner of lace flowing down one side. She studied every detail of the scene. She saw the billions of sand particles covering the earth like a lush carpet. She saw the sea grass swaying on the breeze like the dancers in a Jean Beraud painting. She saw the endless, blue sky with magnificent, white, cloud horses galloping across it. Finally, she saw the waves marching up the beach and then retreating.

Each wave touched her heart, as it receded back into the ocean it took with it a piece of her unhappiness. Slowly, each wave came and went. Slowly, she let herself heal. Slowly, she found herself. Slowly, tears ran down her cheeks as a voice inside her told her it was going to be okay. "And, it will," she said, out loud.

Caroline wiped the tears away with her hands and stood up. She patted the back of the chair and walked back to the mirror. "It's time girlfriend," she whispered. Her hair was almost dry and looked like spiral pasta twists it was so curly. Normally, she would have reached for the flatiron to straighten her hair into its chic style, but instead she turned away from the mirror and started dressing.

Turning the doorknob to leave the room, Caroline looked at her well-manicured hands with the long, artificial fingernails. She noticed her makeup bag hanging on the back of the door; it held as much inventory as a Nordstrom's cosmetic counter. She didn't want to guess the dollar value tightly zipped into each clear plastic compartment. Shaking her head she left the room.

Caroline could hear the water running in the bathroom and the old pipes rattling with the effort. She sent a message to the person in the bathroom. "Hope that shower does as much for you as it did for me."

Diane was still asleep in the chair in the parlor and there were sounds of someone moving around in the kitchen. Caroline opened the front door and left the house.

***

Seeking shade on the north porch Diane, Claire, and Jill sat in the Shaker rockers with tall glasses of orange juice lined up on the porch railing in front of them.

"Is this what it's going to be like?" Jill asked.

"Like what's going to be like?" Diane countered, turning to her friend.

"Us, in our old age, sitting in rockers too tired to do anything fun."

Claire chuckled, "Speak for yourself. Last night was just a bump in the road. We may not be able to handle our booze like we used to, but we have lots of good years left."

"I agree," Diane added. "We're just out of shape and a little overwhelmed with busy lives."

"Exactly," Claire said. "Starting this evening, we're going to get back into shape."

Jill stopped rocking and leaned forward to look past Diane who sat between her and Claire. "If you're talking about exercise, I already had mine for today, thank you."

"How about you Diane? Should we start doing exercises or rent some bikes?"

Always the diplomat, Diane replied, "I think that's a wonderful idea. However, I'd like to suggest we research the matter in depth in the morning."

"I second that," Jill said.

"Okay, tomorrow is soon enough. By the way, did Caroline tell either of you where she was going?" Claire asked.

"Not me," Jill replied.

"Me neither. I didn't even hear her leave," Diane answered.

"Do you think we need to worry? She was pretty upset last night."

Diane took a sip of juice. "I'm sure she's embarrassed and just wanted some time to herself."

The afternoon slowly progressed with seagulls flying overhead, going about their work of bombing the road. Jill hummed an old 80s tune while Diane and Claire rocked in time to the beat.

Claire's stomach growled. "Is anyone getting hungry?"

"Sure am," Diane answered. "We better start thinking about dinner."

"No worries. I have a chicken casserole in the oven and a garden salad in the frig," Jill smiled.

"Dear Martha Stewart, what would we do without you," Diane asked.

"Probably starve," Jill grinned.

The sound of a car drew the three pairs of eyes toward the road. Caroline's rental car pulled into the driveway.

Diane squinted. "Who's that in Caroline's car?"

The trunk lid flew up and the driver's door opened. A woman in stone-washed jeans, a white T-shirt, and flip flops stepped out of the car. She had short, curly, light red hair and wore sunglasses.

"What the?" Jill declared. "I recognize the sunglasses, but not the woman,"

The woman waved and walked to the trunk of the car.

"Oh my God, it's Caroline," Claire exclaimed, in disbelief. "What happened to her?"

"I'd say, the shuttle has landed Houston," Diane offered.

Caroline leaned into the trunk and removed a wooden easel, a leather case that resembled a small suitcase, and a large, shopping bag. Walking toward the porch she called out. "Hi, everyone."

The women on the porch could only stare with their mouths agape.

Caroline walked up the steps, leaned the easel against the porch railing, and set the case and shopping bag on the porch floor. She replaced her sunglasses with her regular glasses and asked, "Isn't anyone going to say anything."

Diane found her voice first. "Caroline, what have you done?"

Holding out her arms she twirled around. "It's the new me. The real me. What do you think?"

The women sitting in the rockers examined her from head to toe. She had had her hair cut and lightened, if she was wearing makeup it was so light you could see her freckles, and the artificial nails were gone revealing short, clean nails.

Claire was the first one to say it. "You look ten years younger and wonderful!"

"Did you get all that done in Haworth?" Jill asked.

"Sure did. Amazing little town."

Reaching into the shopping bag Caroline pulled out three, pink T-shirts and handed one to each of her friends.

Diane held up her T-shirt and read the large blue message on the front, "Old Broads Rock!" Underneath the words was a row of white, rocking chairs exactly like the ones they were sitting in.

"Thank you, Caroline. You didn't have to do that."

"I know, but I wanted to thank you all for helping me last night. This is going to be the best vacation ever and I want us to remember it."

"Oh, no doubt about that," Jill said, pulling her phone out of her pocket and pointing to it. "I've got the proof."

"What did I tell you about those pictures?" Diane interrupted, with a glare.

Claire changed the subject to Caroline's purchases. "It looks like you're going to start painting again."

"I'm going to try. It'll take some time, but I plan to make the time. And, I want to take some classes to get the old, artistic juices flowing."

The timer on the oven rudely interrupted. Claire held the door for the others to enter. Before going in herself, she took one last look around. The old, red pickup was slowly passing Windward Cottage. Claire closed the screen and inside doors, and made sure they were both locked.

***

Jill

Nightcaps on the widow's walk turned into warm mugs of cocoa.

"That was a great dinner Jill. Thank you," Caroline said, wrapping her hands around her hot mug. Claire and Diane nodded in agreement as steam from their mugs carried the smell of the sweet chocolate to their noses.

"You're a great cook Jill. Do you cook much at home?" Diane asked.

"No, not much. Carrie's not home for supper very often so I usually grab fast food on my way home from work. Can you tell?" she asked, standing and squeezing the roll around her middle.

"That's nothing," Caroline said, taking up the gauntlet. "Look at the size of these thighs!"

"Stop it you two. We are what we are. We're all blessed with good health and a few extra pounds doesn't matter," Claire declared.

"I know, but with the whole world so focused on youth it's depressing. What chance do women our age have of attracting a man?" Jill asked.

Lowering her mug into her lap Diane looked at Jill. "Are you seriously looking for a man?"

Thoughtfully, Jill answered Diane. "I don't know.

I'm starting to feel old and with Carrie probably leaving home soon I think I might be afraid of being alone. I actually do like to cook and take care of someone. If I had had my way, I would have been a stay-at-home mom and doted on my husband."

No one said a word. Jill had never expressed these feelings or talked about her marriage.

After a long silence Jill looked at her friends. "What's wrong? Why isn't anyone saying anything?"

"We didn't know you were unhappy," Claire said.

"I wouldn't say I'm unhappy. I just feel like I missed something without a man around. I like men. I sometimes worry that I made Carrie too independent and that she won't give a man a chance because of my leaving Ray. You think you're doing the right thing, but then you look back and ask if it was really as bad as you thought at the time. Did I cheat Carrie out of having a dad? How is she going to feel about men not having a dad or brothers? She never even got to know my dad because she was so little when he died. He was a wonderful man. I think I resent his death more than I do Ray for being such a bastard. He was a bastard, wasn't he?"

"I didn't really know him," Diane said.

Caroline shrugged her shoulders. "We were already living in Atlanta when you were married and I never got to know him either."

Jill looked at Claire who was sitting motionless with her mug held up to her mouth.

"Claire?"

Claire looked at Jill and lowered the mug slowly. "Oh, he was a bastard alright. You can rest assured you did the right thing. Do you remember the night Spence and I had to pull the SOB off you? You were black and blue from your head to your toes and poor Carrie was screaming in fear. Oh no Jill, don't you dare question leaving him."

"Sometimes, I just need some reassurance that I did

okay with Carrie."

"Carrie is a wonderful girl, Jill. I don't' think anyone could have done a better job than you."

Diane, who had been listening quietly, finally spoke up. "You know Jill, you and I are kind of in the same boat. I think you have been alone long enough. If you would like a man in your life I think you should go for it.

"I think I do Diane. I really think I want someone to come home to, to cook for, and to snuggle up with on the couch and watch old movies."

"Well, you're wrong about one thing," Caroline interjected.

"What's that?"

"It won't be old movies you watch… it'll be football."

Jill looked out over the ocean. "I think I could handle that."

Caroline stamped her feet on the roof and wiggled in her chair. "It's getting cold. Let's go down, start a fire, and play some games."

"Great idea," Diane said.

"How about I call Drew and we make it strip poker?" Jill suggested, walking down the stairs.

Claire shook her head and laughed. "I don't even want to try to picture that!"

When the foursome reached the second floor hallway it felt much warmer. Continuing down the stairs, to the first floor, they stopped midway. There was a blazing fire in the fireplace and the poker set was set-up on the game table.

"Who started the fire?" Claire asked.

The women all looked at each other and shook their heads.

"None of us," Diane answered.

"Well, then, who did?" Caroline asked.

"This is strange, very strange," Claire said,

continuing down the steps. Walking to the front door she tried to open it. It was locked. So was the screen door, just as she had left them before dinner. "We need to check the back door."

All four women went into the kitchen together and Claire reached for the doorknob. The door was unlocked. "Okay, who left this door open," she asked. Without waiting for an answer she continued. "Someone probably came in and started that fire to try and spook us. We're going to have to be more careful and make sure all the doors and windows are locked when we go upstairs."

Turning, suddenly, she faced Jill. "Do you think Drew would have come into the house and done that?"

"I don't think so, but if he had it was probably only to be nice because it was getting chilly. I'll ask him tomorrow."

No longer interested in playing a game they double checked all the windows and doors, and made their way up the stairs to their rooms. Their faces were set in stone as each one went over in her head what had happened. Questions pushed into their minds uninvited. *Had someone really come into the house? Was one of them playing a trick on the others? Were they safe?* Their unusual silence created a vacuum in the old house.

***

Claire brushed her hair off her face and looked at the clock; 2:49 a.m. Someone was crying.

Chapter Four
Monday

Caroline set her coffee on the kitchen table and took a seat between Claire and Jill. "So, did either of you get any sleep?"

"Not much," Jill answered. "We were just discussing last night. It's rather unnerving isn't it?

"Yes. I'm a little worried, actually. Have you been out for your walk with Drew yet?"

Jill emptied her mug. "Nope. It was foggy so I thought I'd wait until it lifted. It's almost gone now, so I think I'll walk down and ask him if he came to the house last night."

"Good," Caroline said. "I sure hope he says yes, because I would feel a lot better knowing it was him and not some weirdo."

Claire picked at a rough spot on the tablecloth and looked up. "Who says he's not a weirdo?"

"Oh, Claire, stop it. You don't even know him," Jill declared.

"Well, geez, Jill, he could be. You've only walked on the beach with him a few days and you're ready to hand him the keys to the vault. Okay, that was a bad analogy. Forget I said that."

"You can be sure I will," Jill said, slipping into her windbreaker.

Claire blushed and looked at her friend. "I'm sorry Jill. That was out-of-line. Please forgive me. I'm tired and out of sorts."

"Ah, forget it. It was actually pretty funny!" Jill laughed, closing the kitchen door and stepping onto the back porch.

"Claire! What is wrong with you? That WAS out-of-line," Caroline said. "You're just darn lucky Jill has a sense of humor."

"I know. I really am sorry. I never should have said that. I can't explain it, without even knowing the man he bothers me. There's something about him. I just can't put my finger on it."

"Well get over it," Caroline said, taking a sip of coffee.

"Get over what?" Diane asked, entering the kitchen and heading for the coffeemaker.

"Oh, I put my foot in my mouth," Claire said. "Let's not talk about it."

Diane leaned against the sink and crossed her arms with her coffee mug in one hand. "Probably a good idea since we have a problem."

Claire jerked her head toward Diane. "What now?"

"The drain in the tub is clogged. I couldn't get the water to go down."

Claire relaxed. "Oh crap, Diane, I thought it was something serious. I'll call the realtor and ask him to send a plumber."

When Claire left the kitchen to get her phone Diane looked at Caroline. "Is something wrong?"

"Not really, Claire is just a little testy this morning. It'll be fine."

Shortly Claire returned to the kitchen. "They're sending Wendell's Plumbing. Didn't give me a time, just said he would fit us into his schedule."

Before Claire could make another move there was a knock at the front door. "I'll get it," she said, retracing her steps to the parlor.

Opening the front door Claire faced, rather looked over the head of a short, stout man, with at least three days' stubble on his face, and a tool box in his hand.

"Wendell's Plumbing. Here to fix the tub."

Claire tried to make eye contact but she couldn't because the man never looked directly at her. He was wall-eyed.

"Oh... Gee... Ah... Okay... Good... That was fast."

The man mumbled something about a cancellation.

"Follow me," Claire said. "I'll show you to the bathroom."

"Know where it is," Wendell replied, pushing past Claire and starting up the stairs.

Claire stared in surprised. "Well, okay then."

Turning to close the front door Claire saw the old, red pickup parked behind Caroline's car. "Wendell's Plumbing" was hand-painted on the driver's door.

"Oh shit!"

Rushing back to the kitchen Claire closed the door between the kitchen and the parlor.

"Who was it?" asked Diane.

"It's wall-eyed Wendell," Claire whispered, spewing spittle as she laughed.

"Claire, what is wrong with you?" Caroline demanded, looking disgusted.

"I'm sorry. You know I would never make fun of someone with a disability, but this is just too weird. The plumber is this little guy who's been driving past here every day in an old, red pickup and now he's upstairs unclogging the tub. I'm sorry, I'm really sorry, but this is just getting crazier by the minute. Are we in the twilight zone?"

Pipes rattled and banged overhead.

"You need a little Jack in your coffee Claire. You're losing it," Caroline said.

Claire started to laugh uncontrollably and sat down at the table. She rested her forehead on the table and held her stomach as waves of laughter possessed her body.

Diane looked at Caroline and lifted her hands as if to say, what now?

Claire finally looked up and wiped her face with a napkin. "Oh, it's nothing, really. Ignore me. Jill's off with an axe murderer, we have someone coming into the house at night without us knowing, and now we have a wall-eyed stalker fixing the tub. There is absolutely nothing wrong here, it's just me being paranoid." She sipped her coffee between giggles.

"Well, if you'll excuse me, I'm going up to the roof to sketch," Caroline said, getting up and tilting her head toward Claire. "She's all yours, Diane."

The banging overhead continued while Diane cleaned up the breakfast dishes.

"Claire you should eat something. Can I make you some eggs?"

"No thanks, Diane. I really am fine. I don't know what got into me…all of a sudden everything seemed funny… weird… but funny. I'll just have some cornflakes.

In an effort to achieve normalcy Diane asked, "Were you serious about renting bikes?"

Claire finished chewing a mouthful of cereal. "Sure. I think it would be fun, don't you?"

"Well, the truth is I'm not very coordinated, but I'll give it a try." Squinting and wrinkling her nose she added, "I seem to remember riding a bike in my youth."

"I noticed a bike rental in town the other day. We can go there when Jill gets back and wall-eyed Wendell is finished," Claire laughed, with a maniacal look on her face and gazing up at the ceiling from where the banging emanated.

Diane shook her head and turned back to the sink. Looking out the window she said, "Here comes Jill now."

Leaving her damp windbreaker on the porch, Jill entered the kitchen and poured herself a cup of coffee.

"Well?" Claire asked, anxiously.

Turning from the sink to see if there was going to be fireworks from Claire, Diane waited.

"No," Jill paused, and looked directly at Claire. "Drew did not come to the house last night."

"Oh swell," Claire replied, pushing her chair back and taking her bowl and spoon to the sink. "I was so hoping it was Drew."

"WHAT DO YOU THINK YOU'RE DOING?" Came Caroline's raised voice from the direction of the parlor.

Claire, Diane, and Jill ran to the parlor to see Caroline chasing wall-eyed Wendell down the stairs. "I caught him coming out of Diane's room!"

Before anyone could stop him, Wendell was out the door.

"But... is the drain working?" Claire inquired, in a business-like fashion.

Diane pushed Claire. "For Christ's sake Claire, will you stop?"

"What in the name of God is going on, and who was that man?" said an astonished Jill. "I leave for an hour and you all go to hell in a handbag."

Caroline continued down the steps. "Diane you better go see if anything's missing from your room?"

As Diane walked up the stairs, Jill repeated, "Who was that man?"

"That was wall-eyed Wendell," Claire said, dead serious.

Ignoring Claire, Jill turned to Caroline. "Caroline, what's going on?"

"That was the plumber. The tub wasn't draining properly so the realtor sent him to fix it. In the meantime, Claire has lost her mind."

Diane stood at the top of the steps motionless.

"What is it Diane," Caroline called.

"The only thing missing is a pair of panties."

"Sweet Jesus," Claire cried. "He's a freaking, wall-eyed pervert."

***

Silence prevailed as the four women walked to

town, hands in their pockets and looking straight ahead. Finally, Claire broke the silence. "Do you think we should move out of the house? I saw a nice little B&B in town."

Diane was the first to respond. "I think we have just had a few strange things happen all at once. Let's not panic. What do you think Jill?"

"I agree. Let's just be more careful locking up. Caroline?"

"I really like it here and would hate to leave just because we were probably a little careless. Back to you Claire."

"The majority rules. I feel guilty because I chose Windward Cottage. I'm sure everything will be fine. We'll just have to get Diane some new panties."

"Oh God, here she goes again," Caroline laughed.

***

At Claire's suggestion, it was decided to rent bikes for three days. "I'm telling you, you are going to enjoy this so we may as well take them for three days. There's no sense coming into town if we want them again, and besides it's cheaper."

"Ah, the voice of reason," Jill smiled.

"Easy for you to say, Jill, you didn't see her this morning," Diane whispered, as she tried to balance on one of the bikes.

The bicycle rental man did the paperwork, fitted them with helmets, and gave them a map of the area. "Have fun ladies. If you decide to keep the bikes longer no problem, we'll just square up when you return them."

Diane wobbled back and forth across the road as Claire and Caroline expertly pedaled ahead.

"Look at them. Show-offs!" Jill squealed, barely avoiding the ditch on the side of the road.

Claire and Caroline were waiting for them in the driveway when they got back to the cottage.

"Good job, everyone. Let's lock up the bikes and go

to the beach," Claire said.

"Great. I'm going to try a little watercolor," Caroline declared.

Once settled on their beach towels Jill opened a picnic basket and passed out fruit and cheese. She handed Claire a bottle of water and uncorked a bottle of white wine. Filling two glasses, she handed them to Caroline and Diane.

"Where's mine?" Claire asked.

"You're shut off," Jill answered, taking a sip from her glass.

"Oh, come on, one little incident and I'm being punished?"

Jill smiled and handed her a glass. "Just kidding, you can have some." Continuing she said, "Drew asked me to dinner tonight. Does anyone mind if I go?"

"Who's going to cook for us?" Diane asked.

***

Drew and Ike

Claire, Diane, and Caroline sat in their rockers, on the front porch, like a firing squad awaiting their victim. It wasn't long before a sleek, black Mercedes turned into the drive.

"Looks like the consulting business is booming," Caroline said.

The driver stepped out of the car wearing khakis, a pale blue, button-down, collar shirt with the long sleeves rolled up, Docksiders with no socks and dark sunglasses.

"If there's a Ralph Lauren emblem on that shirt I'm going to puke," Claire whispered, from behind her glass of lemonade.

Drew opened the back door of the car and Ike, his black lab, jumped out. Reaching into the back seat Drew withdrew a large canvas bag. "Ike. Come."

"Do you think he deliberately color coordinated his

car with his dog?" Claire asked, snidely.

"Don't start, Claire. Give the man a chance," Diane whispered.

Wagging his tail so hard it seemed it would disconnect from his body the dog followed his master up the sidewalk as the women scrutinized Drew. He was average height, probably five feet ten inches with sandy hair graying at the temples.

"Not bad," Diane said, out of the corner of her mouth.

"I'm thinking approaching sixty but, with that bod, he works out regularly and looks younger than he is," Caroline volunteered. "I see this type at the country club all the time."

"Is that a good thing or a bad thing?" Claire asked.

Caroline shrugged. "Depends on what you like."

Drew walked up the steps and removed his sunglasses. His eyes were hazel and he had perfect teeth. "Good evening, ladies. I'm Drew Carson." Setting down the bag he shook each of their hands. When he took Claire's hand she squeezed his so hard he almost flinched.

Without a reaction to Claire's bone crushing hand shake he smiled and turned to Ike. "Stay."

Ike ambled to the end of the rockers were Claire was sitting and laid down beside her. Claire inched closer to the opposite side of her chair and looked at Drew.

"Looks like he likes you."

"Really? I can't imagine why."

"Neither can I," Drew said. Covering quickly he added, "I thought you all might feel safer if Ike spent the night. He's a great watch dog and if anyone tries to enter the house he risks losing a leg."

"That's very thoughtful," Diane said, standing up with the pitcher of lemonade. "Would you like some lemonade, Drew?"

"Thank you, but no." Pointing to the bag he said, "I

brought food and Ike's bowls. You won't have any trouble with him."

The screen door opened and Jill walked out wearing a soft, flowing, floral dress that reached just below her knees. She had a simple, gold chain around her neck and gold, hoop earrings. On her feet she wore strappy, heeled sandals. Her hair was shiny and curly. Anyone who didn't know her wouldn't recognize the signs that she had tried to straighten her hair without success. She wore a little eye makeup and just a touch of lipstick. With her newly, acquired tan she looked young and lovely.

Drew's eyes sparkled. "You look beautiful, Jill."

Jill blushed and reached for his hand. "Thank you."

"What time will you be home?" Claire inquired, sounding almost rude.

"No clue. Don't wait up," Jill said, with a wink.

Leading the way down the steps Drew looked over his shoulder and smiled. "Nice meeting you."

Opening the passenger door, Drew helped Jill into the car and then walked to the driver's side and got in. He backed slowly out of the drive and Jill waved as they drove down the road.

"Did you see that?" Claire said, rocking faster. "He opened the car door for her. Nobody does that any more, not even Spence."

"Claire you are acting like the mother of a sixteen year old going out on her first date," Diane said. "I think he's nice."

"Me too," Caroline added.

"I take the fifth," Claire said, taking a long drink of lemonade.

"Why don't we head into town and see what the special is at Blackbeard's. Maybe there's music." Diane stood up and stretched.

"Great idea," Caroline said, collecting the pitcher and glasses on a bright yellow, plastic tray.

Windward Secrets

"What do we do with Ike?" Claire asked, holding the screen door open for Caroline.

"We'll leave him in the house. He'll be fine."

***

At Blackbeard's, the special was fried clam sandwiches with coleslaw and French fries. Claire and Diane opted for the special and Caroline chose a Cobb salad. They were disappointed there was no live music, but there was an old jukebox they loaded with quarters and stacked with their favorite oldies.

"Gosh, it's strange without Jill, isn't it," Claire observed.

"It is," Caroline agreed. "Do you think it will turn into anything with Drew?"

"Too early to tell, but if he's as nice as he seems I hope it does," Diane offered.

"Diane, what about you?" Claire asked. "Isn't there anyone special?"

"Interesting that you asked that Claire. Listening to Jill talk about Drew has me thinking. There is a friend who has been there for me for quite a while. He does the occasional, odd job around the house and when I need an escort for a special event he goes with me."

Lowering her fork, Caroline asked, "Really? You've never mentioned anyone. What's his name?"

"Ed. I've never really thought of him in any way other than just a friend. Now, I'm wondering if I've missed something, and if I've been taking advantage of him."

"If he's been hanging around this long, you really need to take a closer look," Claire said.

"You know, I think I will." Claire took a sip of iced tea and smiled with a faraway look in her eyes.

"Maybe our vacations are going to turn into couples vacations," Claire thought, out loud.

"Don't count on it," Caroline said, a little too quickly.

Changing the subject, Claire asked, "do either of you find it strange that wall-eyed Wendell turned up at the house so fast and knew where the bathroom was?"

"Not really," Diane said, putting down her glass. "This is the slow season, and he probably has been in that house lots of times. Old houses always need repairs."

"Well, I think I'll ask some questions at the real estate office, and let them know about the missing panties."

Caroline looked up from her salad. "Although I am totally convinced you're paranoid Claire, I do think his behavior was strange and should be reported. What if there had been children in the house? You can't be too careful these days."

"I agree," Diane added. "I just wish you didn't have to mention my underwear."

***

Back at Windward Cottage the women found Ike curled up on the braided rug in front of the fireplace. He lifted his head and then placed it back down on his crossed paws.

"Some watchdog," Claire declared.

"It's too cold to go to the roof, how about some cards?" Caroline asked, taking off her sweater.

Claire closed and locked the door and started up the stairs. "I'm going to change into my pajamas, what about you two?"

Ike got up from his rug and followed Claire up the stairs.

Dressed in pajamas and bathrobes they gathered around the game table and Diane started to shuffle the cards. "What are we playing?"

"Hearts?" Caroline suggested.

"Works for me," Claire agreed. "Why is this dog sitting beside me?"

Knowing how she felt about dogs Diane and Caroline were amused.

"He loves you," Caroline said. "Animals seem to want to win over people when they know they don't like them."

"It's not that I don't like him, I just don't love dogs. I never had one."

"I do feel safer with him here, don't you?" Caroline asked.

Claire reached down and patted Ike's head. "Actually, I do and I think he's already growing on me."

After a few hands of hearts Claire yawned and pushed her chair away from the table. "It's been a long day. I'm going upstairs to read. Are you going to wait up for Jill?"

Diane looked at Caroline and shrugged her shoulders. "If we're up, we're up, or not. She's a big girl."

Ike started to follow Claire to the stairs when she said, "No Ike. Stay." pointing to the rug near the fireplace. Ike lowered his head and slowly walked to the rug and laid down. "Look at that, he listened," Claire said.

***

Once in bed, Claire opened her book and started to read. She had only read a few chapters when she heard Diane and Caroline moving around on the floor below. A few more chapters and her eyes started to close. The book slowly lowered to her chest and she fell asleep only to be interrupted by a bad dream. She felt cold, it was dark and raining. There was little girl with curly, blonde hair standing at the foot of her bed reaching toward her. Claire felt the sweat of fear soaking the mattress. She shook her head and tried to wipe the rain off her face but it kept getting wet. The little girl looked directly at her and whispered, "Help me."

Frightened by the dream, Claire rubbed her eyes and finally opened them. Two, big, brown eyes and a black nose were only inches from her face. It wasn't a little girl, it was a dog. And, the rain was Ike licking her face. One more lick and she was wide awake. He was standing next to the bed nudging her with his nose.

"Geez Ike. You startled me. Do you have to go out?" She would swear the dog nodded his head yes so she got up and felt around for her flip flops and robe. Searching the bed she could not find her book. 'Must have fallen under the bed. I'll get it later.'

Jill was snoring in the other bed.

I should wake her and make her take him out. After all, he's more her dog, Claire thought, indignantly.

"The sun's not even up you crazy mutt. Come on, I think your timing stinks," she moaned, glancing out the window.

Ike followed Claire to the kitchen where she opened the door and let him out. "Am I supposed to go with you or what?" she asked Ike as he brushed passed her. "Oh darn, what if he runs away. Ike, come." Ike immediately returned to her. Taking the belt off her robe she slipped it through his collar and walked onto the porch and down to the beach holding onto the belt tightly.

"I can't believe I'm walking a stranger's dog in the middle of the night. This is insane." She proceeded to lecture Ike on having more consideration and timing his needs better. When she was sure he had taken care of business she turned him back toward the house. The sky was turning the color of a ripe eggplant, with a faint gold arc at the horizon, fading upward in a halo promising daylight. Claire could see the glint of the white caps. Taking a deep breath she smelled the salt air and listened to the sound of the waves hitting the beach. Ike moved closer and rubbed against her leg as they walked. Involuntarily, Claire reached down and scratched his head. The calm of her first day sitting on the porch returned and she soon reveled in the solitude.

Watching the stars disappear into the morning sky Claire glanced toward the house. Someone was on the roof.

"Look at that Ike. I think Caroline is painting the sunrise."

Claire fed Ike, started the coffee then went up the stairs. Ike followed closely behind. When they passed the locked room Ike stopped and sniffed around the door. Lifting his right front foot he pawed at the door.

"No, Ike. We can't go in there."

Claire could hear Jill still snoring and quietly worked her way to her bed. Sitting down on the side of the bed to remove her flip-flops she sat on something hard. Reaching back she felt her book. *Hmmm, where did that come from? It wasn't there when I left* she thought.

Ike nuzzled her hand and she laid the book on the bedside table.

"Lay down and be quiet," she whispered, patting Ike's head.

Chapter Five
Tuesday

Claire came out of the bathroom to find Ike sitting at the door. "Are you my shadow or what?"

Ike moved to the locked room and whined softly.

"What is it you like about that room," Claire said, trying the door handle. "See. Locked. Now come."

Claire entered the empty kitchen and poured herself a cup of coffee. She was bothered by the dream and couldn't help wondering if her daughters were okay. They were certainly older than the child in her dream, but the little girl reminded her of them when they were small. Going to the parlor she retrieved her cell phone from her handbag and hit the speed dial number for Spence.

"Hi hun," Spence answered, recognizing Claire's number on the caller ID.

"Good morning. You at work?"

"Yup, been here an hour already." There was a pause and then Spence asked, "Everything okay?"

"I had a strange dream last night and just wanted to make sure you and the girls were okay."

"We're good, but what about you? You don't usually call when you go away."

"I'm fine, Spence, really. The dream just bothered me."

"You sure?"

"Yes. Yes. I'm sure. Give the girls my love and I'll see you Saturday."

"Bye, love."

As Claire returned to the kitchen, voices drifted in from the back porch through the open windows and screen door.

"Good morning all," Claire said, holding the door open for Ike.

"Looks like it's going to be a beautiful day," Diane

said.

"How was the sunrise Caroline?" Claire asked.

Caroline looked up from her coffee in surprise. "I don't know. Why would you ask that?"

"I saw you on at the widow's walk when I took Ike out before dawn."

"Not me," Caroline said. "Claire, are you okay?"

Jill and Diane turned toward Claire and waited.

"Yes, I feel fine. Ike had to go out. I went with him because I was afraid he'd run off. I saw you up on the roof and thought you were waiting to paint the sunrise."

"No... honestly Claire, I didn't go up on the roof this morning. I was in bed."

"Do you remember the first night we were here? We thought we saw someone up on the roof that time too. It's probably some kind of an optical illusion caused by the changing light," Jill interceded.

"But it was nearly light and I could see clearly," Claire responded. "It was a woman standing at the edge of the railing looking toward the sun."

Claire looked at Diane and Jill. "Were either of you up there this morning?"

Jill and Diane slowly shook their heads.

Claire sat down in a rocker. "I'm starting to get those strange feelings again. And, I had a very strange dream of a little girl in our room."

"I didn't see anyone," Jill said.

"Jill, you were snoring so loud you couldn't have seen or heard anything," Claire retorted. "Did you put my book on my bed?"

"What book? I never saw a book."

"I fell asleep when I was reading. I couldn't find the book before I took Ike out, but when we came back the book was on the bed."

"Claire," Diane said, softly. "I think maybe you were overtired and just didn't see the book. You were pretty stressed yesterday."

Claire sat quietly and looked at her friends. "Do you think I'm losing my mind?"

"No," Diane said, delicately. "I just think you were tired and upset from that strange encounter with Wendell."

Claire let out a nervous giggle. "That was weird, wasn't it? Don't let me forget to call the realtor today and complain about that little weasel."

"I whipped up some pancake batter," Jill said, getting up from her chair. "Let's have breakfast."

"Aren't you walking with Drew this morning?" Caroline inquired.

"We were out so late we decided to walk later."

Diane, Claire, and Caroline looked at each other and winked.

"Just exactly how late is late?" Diane asked.

"Late enough that you were all asleep, and it's for me to know and you to find out!" Jill laughed.

Jill served a filling breakfast of blueberry pancakes and sausage.

"You cooked, Jill. We'll clean up," Caroline said, getting up and gathering plates.

"Thanks. I need to take Ike back to Drew."

"Do you think we can have Ike again tonight?" Claire asked.

"I thought you didn't like him," Jill said, tilting her head to one side and raising her eyebrows.

"Well, he does grow on you. I felt more comfortable last night, didn't the rest of you?"

"Actually, yes," Diane said.

Caroline nodded in agreement.

"Okay. I'll ask Drew. Come, Ike."

Ike, who had been sitting beside Claire, laid down on the floor and looked up at Jill with sad eyes thumping his tail on the floor.

"Ike come," Jill repeated, more sternly. "Geez,

Claire what have you done to him. He doesn't want to go home."

"I didn't do anything. I don't know why he likes me so much."

Claire got up, went to the screen door. "Ike. Come."

Slowly, Ike got to his feet and ambled to the door with his head down.

Claire reached down and lifted his head up. "It's okay, sweetie. We'll see you later."

Jill gathered Ike's bowls and food, and pushed the screen door open. "I'll be back shortly."

Caroline scraped the remnants of food off the plates into the trash can and Diane filled the sink with hot soapy water while Claire called the realtor.

"So," Diane asked, when Claire returned to the kitchen. "What did they say?"

"Exactly what you would expect. They have never had any complaints about Wendell in the past."

"And you said?" Caroline asked.

"I said he was a pervert and he had just not been caught before."

"That was it?" Diane inquired, suspiciously.

"Well, not quite. I suggested they keep an eye on him before he did something really serious. I officially put them on notice that we better not see him around here again."

Caroline laughed. "Now, that's our girl. No nonsense Claire."

In the background, Claire was sure she heard the old red truck rattle by the house.

***

"What are we going to do today?" Diane asked.

"Let's get the map and go for a bike ride," Claire suggested.

"I'd like to go somewhere scenic to draw," Caroline added.

Claire looked at Caroline. "Is a lighthouse scenic enough for you?"

"Perfect."

By the time Jill returned from Drew's, a lunch was packed and a route mapped out to a lighthouse on the tip of the peninsula.

"Come on Jill, we're going on an adventure. Get your sunblock," Diane said, pulling a ball cap over her short hair.

"Oh Lord, do you think I can make it that far," Jill asked, looking at the map.

"Sure. It's not as far as it looks," Claire said. "We used to ride our bikes there all the time when we were kids. Besides, you should be in pretty good shape from all of your walking on the beach."

"You have been walking, right?" Caroline asked, with a grin.

"Oh, please, of course. Don't be silly," Jill said, flushing red from her neck to her hairline.

"What about Ike for tonight?" Claire interrupted.

"It's fine," Jill answered. "I hope you don't mind, I invited Drew to dinner tonight to thank him for last night and for letting us borrow Ike."

"His dog's nice, so he can't be that bad," Claire said, poking Jill in the ribs. "But, Drew's not allowed on the roof. That's our special place."

***

It was a gradual, uphill ride to the lighthouse. Red faced and legs burning the women couldn't get off their bikes fast enough. Caroline promptly found a shady spot among a cluster of scrub pines where she had the best view of the lighthouse.

Claire, Diane, and Jill set off to explore. The lighthouse sat on a high cliff overlooking the Atlantic. Only a rickety, split rail fence kept sightseers from falling over the sixty foot drop to the rocks below.

"Whew, kind of makes you dizzy doesn't it?" Jill said, peering over the cliff edge.

"Jill, get back. That fence wouldn't hold a bird let alone one of us," Diane said, pulling the back of her friend's shirt.

Closer inspection of the lighthouse revealed a sign on the door stating the lighthouse was open for tours on weekends only.

"Darn. We'll miss seeing the view from the top," Claire said, standing back and looking up with her hand shading her eyes.

"Maybe another year," Diane offered.

Claire turned. "Would you really come back here?"

"Sure. I think it's great. I love the sea, the beach, and the peace and quiet."

"What about you Jill?"

"Yes. I like it too, especially since it's off-season and there are no crowds."

Diane walked around snapping pictures with her iPhone while Jill and Claire joined Caroline in the shade. When the time came to return to Windward Cottage they packed up the bikes and started the journey back.

"Thank God, it's mostly downhill," Jill squealed, as she pushed off stretching her legs out from the pedals and coasted away from the lighthouse.

***

Caroline and Diane set the picnic table in the yard for dinner. Claire prepared a peach cobbler while Jill marinated steaks, put potatoes in the oven, and cleaned asparagus.

Drew and Ike arrived promptly at six o'clock. Ike ignored Drew's commands to heel and ran to Claire sitting down directly in front of her waiting for her greeting.

"Well, hello there Ike," she said, bending down and roughing his jowls with both hands.

Drew handed Diane the bottle of wine he had been

carrying and turned to Claire.

"This isn't going to work you know."

Claire froze not knowing what she had done to offend Drew. "Excuse me?"

"My dog appears to like you better than me."

Claire grinned, "You have nothing to worry about. It's only puppy love." Then with emphasis she added, "WE'LL be gone at the end of the week, so no more puppy love."

"His heart will be broken," Drew said, leaning down to pet the top of Ike's head letting Claire's comment pass without a response.

Diane returned from the kitchen with wine glasses. Drew uncorked the wine and filled the glasses. Jill grilled the steaks and asparagus to perfection. "Let's eat everyone," she announced, arranging the meat and vegetables on a large platter.

In spite of Claire's earlier feelings toward Drew, she found herself warming toward him during dinner. He seemed genuine and appeared to care for Jill. *Ah, probably just the wine getting to me* she thought to herself. The shriek of the oven timer brought her out of her trance and she quickly untangled herself from the picnic table bench and ran toward the house with Ike at her heels.

"What is with that dog," Jill asked.

"I have no idea," Drew replied. "He has never taken to anyone like he has to Claire."

Claire returned with the hot cobbler and made an exaggerated presentation setting it down quickly as it started to burn her hands through the worn oven mitts. "Ouch! Hot! Hot! We almost had cobbler a la sand."

Caroline, Diane, and Claire took the dirty dishes to the kitchen and returned with clean bowls and vanilla ice cream.

"Oh, wow," Drew said. "I haven't had cobbler since my mother died. This is a real treat."

Diane pulled her phone from her back pocket. Let's look at the pictures I took at the lighthouse today. She passed the phone to Jill. "Looks good, Diane. Nice work."

"Look at this shot of the waves hitting the rocks below the lighthouse," Jill said, passing the phone to Claire.

Claire took the phone and studied the photo. Advancing through the pictures, Claire stopped at another picture and squinted her eyes. Reaching over the table she pointed to the photo and asked, "Diane, what's this in the background?"

Diane looked where Claire was pointing and then took the phone to get a better look. "Holy crap," she said, slowly. "That looks like a red truck in the trees behind Caroline."

Caroline quickly reached for the phone. "What? Let me see that."

Jill looked over Caroline's shoulder to see the object of interest. "Sure looks like Wendell's truck," she said, looking at Claire.

"You three left me alone with that pervert?" Caroline declared.

"We didn't know he was there; if it is his truck," Diane responded.

"Maybe it wasn't him. There's certainly more than one red pickup," Jill interceded.

Drew reached for the phone. "Who are you talking about?"

Caroline handed the phone to Drew holding her finger on the spot in question.

Drew looked at the photo. "I see a red spot, but can't be sure what it is."

Claire rudely snatched the phone from Drew and looked at the picture again briefly.

"You know I think it's just the trees starting to change color." She turned the phone off and handed it to Diane who looked at her curiously.

"Well, let's get these dishes taken care of," Claire said, getting up from the table.

Drew looked from one woman to another. "Pervert? What's she talking about?'

"Oh," Claire said, quickly, "just an old joke."

Claire gave Jill a warning glance and very slightly shook her head no.

Jill gave an almost undetectable nod to acknowledge she understood she was not to tell Drew about their experience with Wendell.

Drew and Jill remained at the table while the others cleared the dishes.

In the kitchen, Diane turned to Claire. "Why did you grab the phone from Drew?"

"We don't know him. He could be a friend of Wendell's."

"Claire, you're being paranoid again," Diane said.

"Oh, I don't know Diane. If that is Wendell's truck, what would he have been doing there? I doubt he was fixing the toilet at the lighthouse," Claire said, in Caroline's defense.

"Let's just hope it wasn't him," Diane commented.

Caroline mixed up a pitcher of sangria and the three headed for the roof.

A loud "woof" at the screen door brought Claire back to the kitchen. "Come on boy," she said, opening the door for her new best friend.

As they passed the locked room Ike again pawed at the door and looked up at Claire. "Sorry Ike. I don't know what you like about that room, but we're not going in."

Settled in their lawn chairs on the roof, the three women could see Jill and Drew still seated at the picnic table below.

"Okay, who's going to be the one to break this up?" Diane asked, pointing to the couple.

"I'm the bad guy, I'll do it," Claire said, getting up

from her chair. Standing near the edge of the decorative railing that bordered the roof, she placed two fingers in her mouth and gave a shrill whistle that could wake the dead. "Yo! You down there. Curfew!"

Jill looked up and waved.

Drew helped Jill to her feet. With the roof dwellers watching he bent and kissed her. "Thank you for a wonderful evening. You're a great cook."

"Good night, Drew. I'll see you in the morning."

Claire watched Drew walk down the beach toward his cottage and then turned back to Diane and Caroline. Ike was working his way around the perimeter of the roof sniffing feverishly and whining. "I know I don't know anything about dogs, but I think Ike's behavior is peculiar."

"He's got a scent of something," Diane replied. "My dad's hunting dogs used to do the same thing."

Jill suddenly burst onto the roof. "Really, Claire, did you have to be so obvious."

"It's my job dearest," Claire replied, lifting her glass toward Jill.

***

The Confessional
Diane

"Diane is thinking about a man thanks to you Jill," Caroline volunteered.

"Really, Diane? Is that true?"

"I like watching you and Drew, and I wonder if maybe I have been taking advantage of an old friend. That's all, nothing serious."

Jill looked down at her lap a little embarrassed and then back up at Diane. "It's nice, Diane. I like being with him. I like his smile, his smell, and most of all, I like seeing my reflection when I look into his eyes."

Diane smiled at her friend. "Claire seems to think that Ed has had an ulterior motive for hanging around all these years."

"She's probably right. How long have you known him?" Jill asked, looking at Diane.

"Since about five years after Tom died."

"Diane, why didn't you figure this out sooner?"

Diane was pensive. "I hurt so badly when Tom died that I couldn't see anything but my grief. When you lose the love of your life it's truly devastating. I think I was semi-comatose for years. I didn't feel anything but emptiness. I felt barren... vacant... without purpose."

Suddenly, Diane set down her glass and doubled over in her chair. Holding her knees, she closed her eyes and took several deep breaths.

Claire spoke up. "You don't have to talk about this Diane."

"Yes. I think I do. This roof is our confessional and this vacation our cleansing. It's way past time to move on."

Anticipation hung in the air like an unseen priest behind an opaque divider.

"I remember it like it happened yesterday," Diane finally murmured. "Tom came in the back door after mowing the lawn and walked toward me. He got a look of surprise on his face and then collapsed to the floor. I knew he was gone even before I reached him. I knew. I just knew."

Tears filled her eyes and rolled uncontrollably down her cheeks. Diane sniffed and wiped her tears with the corner of her blanket.

"The kids didn't just lose one parent, they lost both of us. There was no insurance. I wasn't working. My parents were our saviors. We moved in with them and they watched the kids when I found a job. It was like they were raising all three of us. I started as a secretary at an ad agency and was lucky to work for a wonderful woman who mentored me. I threw myself into work. It was like a drug, it numbed my senses." Diane picked up her glass and took a sip of sangria. "Have you ever heard of lost limb syndrome?"

"No," the other three answered, in unison.

"Well, when a person loses a limb, for whatever reason, it feels to them like it's still there. Even after the pain is gone their mind thinks the limb is there. Of course, when they try to use the limb it's gone. That's how I felt. Only I still had the pain and refused to believe Tom was gone. I expected him to walk in the door any minute. I listened for his car. I waited by the phone for his call." Tears starting rolling down Diane's cheeks again, but she continued. "I was catatonic. I don't know why my parents didn't have me committed. I wasn't a mother. I wasn't a daughter. I wasn't anything. Because I was hurting so badly, I couldn't help the kids with their grief. I let my parents do all the work. I was selfish. I wanted Tom back at any cost."

Claire pulled a box of tissues out from under her chair and handed them to Diane.

"Where did those come from?" Jill asked.

"The way things have been going up here, I thought it might be a good idea to be prepared… like you and your luggage Jill."

Diane laughed and went on. "I finally came to my senses and realized I had to stand on my own two feet. I saved enough money for a down payment on a house and the kids and I moved out of Mom and Dad's. I met Ed when I went to a convention in New York City. He's an attorney and lives in Boston. He was single. We started running into each other more often. Before long we were having lunches and he was stopping by the house when I needed help fixing something. It's gone on like that all this time."

Caroline was dumbfounded. "He has never made a pass at you in all these years?"

"Caroline, I don't know if I would have noticed. To me, he was the brother I never had. When I think of him now, I see what I never saw before. He is a loving, caring, and definitely attractive man, who has truly blessed me with his friendship. He loves my kids and they love him. I think maybe Tim saw it, because there was a time when he didn't want Ed around. I wasn't smart enough to figure out why he felt that way."

"So, now what?" Jill asked.

"I like seeing the potential of something developing between you and Drew." Then looking at Claire, she said, "and I want what you and Spence have had all these years."

Caroline was quiet and looked thoughtful.

"I'm sorry Caroline," Diane said. "I shouldn't be talking like this with what you're going through."

Caroline leaned toward Diane and looked her straight in the eyes. "Diane, our situations are entirely different. You have suffered terribly from a life-shattering event beyond your control. You've made me realize I have nothing to complain about. I had a good marriage for a long time. I never had the fear of not being able to support my children or worrying about holding down a job. If my marriage ends, it ends because my husband is an ass with a capital 'A'. There's a huge difference."

"And, that might not be such a bad thing," Jill interrupted.

Three sets of eyes snapped toward Jill.

"What do you mean," Caroline asked.

"If it hadn't been for Bill's actions you would not have found yourself this week. You'd still be running around in high heels, worrying about your grey roots showing, and dripping jewelry."

Laughter burst out that could be heard the whole way to Haworth.

Ike finally settled down beside Claire's chair with his head on her left foot.

Diane looked at her friend. "Well, Claire, we've all had our time in the confessional except you. What's your deep dark secret?"

"Hell, Diane. You all make me feel like Rebecca of Sunnybrook Farm. Compared to the three of you, my life is boring."

Jill wasn't about to let Claire off that easy. "Come on Claire. You have to have had some problems over the years. Isn't there anything you yearn for?"

Claire thought for a minute. "The only thing I want is to keep on going the way we have. We don't have a lot of material things or even much savings, but we have had a great life. I love the way we have grown and matured. We're better friends and lovers now than we ever were. You only get that with time. I can tell you, I wouldn't want to go through what you three have faced."

"You're not leaving this roof until you give us something to think about," Caroline injected.

"Hmmm. I guess there is something. I would like to make life easier for Spence. He works like a dog." Looking down at Ike, she added, "No offense, Ike."

Jill interrupted. "So do you Claire. You've been a working mother and kept home and hearth together better than anyone I ever knew."

"Oh, thanks Jill, but I haven't done anything that millions of women don't do every day."

Diane brought the conversation back to Claire's statement. "How would you like to make life easier for Spence?"

"I worry he'll have a heart attack from the stress of working day and night. I've tried for years to find a better paying job but there's nothing where we live. My work is okay, I'm not complaining about the work. My boss is okay too, but he knows he can get away with paying us less because there are no other jobs in the area."

"What do you want to be when you grow up Claire?" Diane pressed.

"You pushed me. Now, it's your turn Claire,"

Caroline added.

"You know I majored in business. I've always been ashamed that I never used the education my parents worked so hard to give me. If there's anything, I guess it's that I want to use my education, what little I remember; and, my life experiences to a profitable end so that Spence can slow down."

"Have you been thinking of anything in particular?" Jill asked.

"Well, don't laugh, but I have been thinking about something for several years. There's an abandoned sweater factory in our town. It closed about ten years ago and that's when our town took a real nose dive. Over four hundred people lost their jobs. Homes were foreclosed on and our downtown has been closing up shop one business at a time ever since."

"And...," Diane encouraged.

"I would love to bring another industry into that building to provide jobs and start rebuilding our town."

"What kind of a business?" Caroline asked.

"Oh, I don't know, Caroline. I never really researched it because I don't have the money to pursue it."

Diane sipped her sangria. "That's a wonderful idea Claire. I think you should follow your dream."

Ike suddenly jumped up bumping Claire's chair so hard she spilled her sangria in her lap.

"Ike!" Claire yelled, catching her glass before it hit the roof.

The dog ran to the door to the house barking at the top of his lungs.

"What in the world is wrong with him?" Jill asked, annoyed.

"He probably has to go. I'll take him down," Claire said.

Diane got up and folded her blanket. "It's getting cold. We may as well move to the parlor."

As soon as Claire opened the door, Ike bolted down the steps. He was in the parlor barking when the women reached the bottom of the stairs. There was a fire burning in the fireplace and Ike was sniffing the room.

"Oh damn, here we go again," Diane said. "Who left a door open this time?"

Jill checked the front door. It was locked.

"I'll take Ike out and check the kitchen door," Claire volunteered.

"Not by yourself you won't," Caroline declared. "Nobody goes anywhere alone from now on. Something fishy is going on around here and we're not taking any chances. It's two-by-two from now on. Buddy system."

"I'll go with her," Jill said, getting her jacket out of the closet by the door.

Diane looked at Caroline. "Let's all go. We could use the walk."

Jill reached the kitchen door first. It was locked. Four sets of worried eyes looked at each other.

Claire snapped the leash on a reluctant Ike who wanted to continue his investigation, but an authoritative command from Claire brought him to attention and he followed her dragging on the leash.

Walking along the water's edge, the four were deep in thought.

Claire finally broke the silence. "I guess I have to make another call to the real estate office."

"I think it's more serious than that," Diane said. "I think we need to call the police."

Jill looked at Diane with concern. "You really think it's that serious?"

"Yes. I do. I can't think of any reason someone would be coming into the house, except to scare us."

Claire stopped walking. "But why?"

"That's the sixty thousand dollar question," Diane answered.

"I think she's right," Caroline said.

"Do we call them tonight or in the morning?" Jill asked.

"We'll let Ike search the house and if he doesn't find anything then we can wait until morning," Diane said, giving Ike a pat on the head.

Turning back toward Windward Cottage Ike started pulling hard on the leash.

"Ike. Heel." Claire commanded, tugging on the leash. "What in the world has gotten into him?"

"I don't know but he sure is agitated tonight," Jill said.

Back at the house Diane locked both the screen door and the kitchen door while Claire released Ike from his leash. Ike immediately went into his sniffing routine.

Jill and Caroline checked the front door and made sure all the windows were locked.

Finished with his first floor search, Ike trotted up the steps to the second floor. While Claire, Caroline, and Jill followed Ike, Diane went into her room and pulled something from her purse. Returning to the hallway she held up a handgun.

"Diane, for God's sake, what is that?" Caroline blurted out.

"It's a Beretta 3032 Tomcat. Don't worry, I'm licensed and trained on how to use it."

"Holy hell, Diane. How long have you had that?" Claire inquired.

"Over ten years. I travel alone a lot and decided I didn't want to be on the road without some kind of protection."

"Guns scare me," Jill said, looking uneasy and taking a step back.

"It's really okay, Jill. I'm quite experienced. I shoot at a range every month to make sure I don't get rusty. I just want to make sure, if there's someone in the house, we're protected."

Finding nothing on the second floor, Ike continued his quest on the third floor. His only interest was the locked room.

"Do you think we should break the lock and see what's in there?" Caroline asked.

"No. I don't want to be arrested for destroying someone's property," Claire answered. "We've never heard any movement, so there's no reason to think someone's in there."

"Well, Ike sure thinks there's something funny about it," Jill said.

"Look, he's not carrying on, he's just doing his sniffing thing," Claire pointed out.

With all the doors and windows secure, the foursome decided to double up in the large beds on the second floor with Ike standing guard at the top of the stairs.

"Ike, stay," Claire ordered, before saying goodnight and going into Diane's room.

Caroline and Jill closed the door to their room and all four settled in for a restless night.

Chapter Six
Wednesday

Ike announced dawn with a loud woof.

Claire rubbed her eyes wishing she had gotten more than two hours sleep. Carefully, not to wake Diane, she moved to the edge of the bed and stood up.

"Where do you think you're going?" Diane asked, in a throaty whisper.

"Ike needs to go out."

"Wait for me," Diane said, throwing back the quilt and hastily pulling on jeans and a sweatshirt.

"Diane, really, do you think that's necessary?"

Diane looked at her friend and nodded. "Yes, Claire, I do. It's easier to go with you now than to explain to Spence later why we let you go out at the crack of dawn, with a stranger's dog, and never came back."

Lacing up her sneakers, Claire shook her head. "Okay, then, come on."

In the kitchen Diane started coffee. "Do you think the bakery in town is open this early?"

"I don't know, but I could sure go for some cinnamon buns. We have to walk Ike anyway, so let's go that way."

"I'll leave a note for Caroline and Jill," Diane said, pulling paper and a pencil out of a kitchen drawer.

Claire snapped Ike's leash to his collar and retrieved slickers from the hooks beside the back door. The early morning fog crept into the house as they let themselves out the front door and locked it behind them.

Ike, anxious to get to the grass tugged hard on the leash pulling Claire off balance. The porch was slippery from heavy dew and Claire had to grab the back of one of the rockers to stay upright. "Geez, Ike. Slow down. Diane, be careful the porch is slippery."

Diane looked at the porch floor and pointed. "Look

Claire."

Claire's gaze followed Diane's finger to footprints in front of the windows. "Oh crap. It's not our imaginations. We've had, at the very least, a peeping Tom."

"Diane, Ike needs to go. You follow the footprints around the porch… I'll come along on the ground with him."

Thinking it was a game, Ike took off with a jerk and received a swift snap of the leash from Claire in response. "Damn dog, slow down."

Following Diane around the side to the back of the house Claire asked, "Do they go the whole way around, Diane?"

"No. They fade out right here where the dew isn't so thick," Diane answered, at the back porch.

"Can you tell anything about the footprints?"

"Well, they're not Jimmy Choo's, that's for sure."

Claire couldn't help laughing. "Seriously, Sherlock, are they men's or women's?"

"Definitely men's. My feet fit inside these with a good inch to spare the whole way around."

"Look," Claire said. "They come down the steps and head toward the beach."

The wet sand held the impression of the prints making it easy for Claire and Diane to follow.

"They're going in the direction of Drew's cottage," Diane noted.

"Maybe he came by to check on us," Claire said.

"Let's hope that's it."

"Diane, are you suspicious of Drew?"

"Right now, I'm suspicious of anyone who has a foot bigger than mine and had no business being on our porch."

"Whoever it was, had to have been there within the last few hours when the fog rolled in."

"How far do you want to follow the prints," Diane asked, glancing at Claire and then back at the footprints.

"Well, we're this far, we may as well see where they go."

Heads down, they followed the prints halfway to Drew's cottage before the incoming waves erased them.

"Dead end," Diane announced. "Let's go to town and see if the bakery and the police station are open."

"We can probably kill two birds with one stone," Claire said. "They're usually one and the same."

Diane laughed. "You're probably right. I didn't see a Dunkin' Donuts so that only leaves the bakery."

The bakery's red neon, open sign was a blinking beacon in the mist guiding the two women and canine to "The Corner Bakery" located dead center on Main Street. As predicted, two squad cars were parked in front.

Claire bumped Diane with her elbow. "Told ya."

Laughing as they approached they found two policemen sitting at one of the sidewalk café tables with coffee and donuts.

"Diane, you go get something good and I'll talk to the officers."

Claire watched as Diane entered the bakery, and smiled at the tinkle of the old-fashioned bell that sounded every time the door opened. Tightening her grip on Ike's leash, she approached the men.

"Good morning," she smiled.

The two policemen nodded and warily looked at Ike.

Must have had a few run-ins with dogs thought Claire as she walked closer. When she reached the table she commanded, "Ike. Sit." Instantly, Ike obeyed but not without just the hint of a snarl and a curled lip.

"Hi. My name is Claire McPherson. My friends and I have rented Windward Cottage, out on The Point. We were wondering if you have had any reports of break-ins in that area."

The officer closest to Claire stood up. Claire thought he was going to offer his hand in introduction, but instead he put both hands on his hips and said, "I'm Hank Peterson, Chief of Police here in Haworth, and this is Deputy Kevin O'Reilly."

Chief Peterson was six feet four inches and a good forty pounds past his fighting weight. Claire guessed his age to be just south of sixty.

Peterson glanced from Claire to Ike, and back again to Claire.

"Why do you ask?"

Claire was five feet eight inches tall but a man this size still made her feel small. Tilting her head back to meet his gaze she responded. "We've had some strange things happening over the past few days and, this morning, we found footprints going around the porch as if someone was looking in the windows."

Peterson looked at O'Reilly with what could easily be interpreted as a smirk. "Na, we never have any trouble out there. Good neighbors and they're careful who they rent to."

His tone and demeanor left Claire with the distinct impression he was inferring she may not be up to snuff for the neighborhood. Refusing to be put off, she continued. "Well, there's a first time for everything isn't there?"

Ike inched a bit closer to the officer. Claire took up the slack in the leash letting Ike know he needed to stay where he was.

Chief Peterson nervously shifted his weight to his other foot farther away from Ike. "We're just changing shifts. After O'Reilly and I review the night calls, I'll stop out and take a look around. Windward Cottage you say?"

"Yes. We'll look forward to your visit," Claire said, with just a touch of irony in her voice to let him know she hadn't missed his innuendo.

Diane exited the bakery with a large, white box just in time to hear the tension in Claire's voice. "Hello," she said, sweetly extending her hand to Chief Peterson. "I'm Diane Fuller. I see you've met my friend."

Reluctantly, the chief took her hand and gave it a mushy squeeze. "Understand you think someone was on your porch this morning."

"Why... yes," she said drawing out the short sentence to its fullest. "There were very, distinct footprints that we followed down to the beach. We would appreciate any insight you might have."

"Like I just told her," tilting his head toward Claire, but not looking her in the eyes. "I'll be out after I finish up here with O'Reilly."

Diane bent to the side and looked around Peterson's bulk to smile at the deputy. "Hello. Nice to meet you."

Kevin O'Reilly, was considerably younger than the chief and considerably better looking. The junior officer reminded Diane of her son, young, strong, and good looking. His hat lay on the table in front of him revealing blond hair streaked by the sun and warm, brown eyes. Kevin looked like he spent his off time either surfing or working out in a gym; Diane decided it was both.

Officer O'Reilly stood and smiled. "Nice to meet you, ma'am."

Claire was starting to get impatient when Diane took her arm and gently pulled her toward the street. "You too officer." Looking back at Chief Peterson she added. "We'll see you later then."

When they were out of hearing range Diane said, "Claire, the air was so thick back there you could cut it with a knife. What in the world did you say to piss him off?"

"I guess I threatened his authority, or his ego, simply by asking if they had had any trouble out at The Point. For crying out loud, what's wrong with that?"

"I don't know but he sure was exhibiting a crappy attitude, wasn't he?"

"I thought so. I don't think he believes there's anything going on. Or, he's just fat and lazy, and doesn't want to be bothered. You did a good job smoothing his feathers."

"It comes naturally in my line of work. You try to make a good impression, make the client feel important, then you give your presentation and go in for the kill."

"Apparently, it works with policemen too," Claire said.

***

Back at Windward Cottage, the four friends sat around the kitchen table savoring the delicacies from the bakery. A sudden rap on the back door made them all jump and Caroline slosh hot coffee down the front of her T-shirt.

Drew Carson stood at the door with a wide grin on his face. "Oh. Sorry. Didn't mean to startle you."

Diane walked to the door and unlocked it. "Come in Drew. Would you like some coffee and pastries?"

"Thank you, but I can't stay. I need to go to Boston on business and was wondering if I could leave Ike with you?"

"Sure," Claire answered, quickly. "We like having him as our guest."

"I was hoping you would agree, so I brought extra food for him."

Jill's face dropped as she took the bag of dog food from Drew and asked, "How long will you be gone?"

"I should be back tomorrow evening. If I have to stay longer I'll give you a call and make further arrangements since you'll be leaving on Saturday."

"Oh," Jill said, dejectedly. "I'll walk you back to the cottage."

Shortly after Jill and Drew left there was a knock at the front door.

"Geez, this is like Grand Central Station today," Caroline said, soaping up one of the breakfast dishes.

"It's probably Chief Peterson," Claire said, cleaning the coffee maker. "You go Diane, he likes you better than me."

"Who doesn't?" Diane snickered, walking through the kitchen door to the parlor.

"Ike does," Claire yelled, at her friend's back.

When Caroline and Claire had finished cleaning up the kitchen, Caroline picked up her sketch pad and walked to the back door. "I'm going down to the beach."

"Okay, but don't go far. We'll join you when Peterson leaves."

As hard as it was going to be, Claire decided to be as pleasant as possible with Chief Peterson. She locked Ike in the kitchen and set a fake smile on her lips before entering the parlor.

Diane looked up from her seat opposite the policeman. "I've explained to Chief Peterson about the foot prints and the fires."

"And?" Claire asked, looking at the officer.

"We haven't had any calls from out here about prowlers or break-ins this year. Probably just some neighborhood kids playing pranks."

"We haven't seen one kid since we've been here," Claire responded, quickly.

Diane intervened. "Chief, perhaps you could look around the house for us and see if you pick up any clues?"

Claire made a face at Diane and mouthed the word "clues?"

Diane shrugged her shoulders and raised her eyebrows as if to ask, "What did you want me to say?"

Chief Peterson had a little trouble getting his mass out of the over-stuffed sofa prompting Claire to turn away to hide her pleasure in his discomfort. Once on his feet, he slowly examined the parlor and then moved into the dining room. "Well, here's your problem ladies," he said, pointing to a lock on one of the dining room windows. "This here lock's broken. Someone has access to this house any time they want. You better get that fixed. Now, if you don't mind, I need to get back to work."

Claire rolled her eyes and somehow found the will power to keep her mouth shut.

"Thank you, Chief," said Diane. "I bet you're right. We'll call the real estate office right away and get that window fixed."

"Diane," Claire said, sharply, "did you tell him about Wendell."

"What about Wendell?" Peterson asked.

"He drives past here at least two or three times a day and...."

Before Claire could finish her sentence Peterson looked at her strangely, "I should hope so. He lives down the road and has to pass here to get to town and his customers."

Claire decided they were beating a dead horse so she shut her mouth and let Wendell's peculiar behavior go unmentioned.

Returning to the parlor Diane was the peacemaker once again. "Thank you very much for coming, Chief. We'll get that lock fixed. I'm sure everything will be fine."

"Sure hope so," Peterson said. "I have more important things to do than come out here."

Just to annoy the officer, Claire opened the kitchen door and Ike burst into the room and went straight for the policeman. Claire grabbed Ike's collar, ruffled his neck, and spoke to him as if she was talking to a baby. "Isn't he a sweetheart?" she said, looking up at Chief Peterson with a dumb-witted look.

Peterson was already on the other side of the screen door with his foot braced against the bottom of the door. "Keep that dog under control. If I get any reports that he's been a nuisance I'll have him taken away."

Claire opened her mouth to say something but Diane quickly clamped a hand on her arm to stop her.

"No worries, Chief. He's just playing. Thanks again for coming."

Waving as the officer backed his patrol car out of the driveway Diane said, through a clenched smile. "What the hell is wrong with you Claire? You deliberately let Ike out to antagonize that man."

"Yeah, well. He's a moron."

"That may be, but he's the law around here."

"Diane, you know very well he was just patronizing us. He didn't take one thing we said seriously."

"And that, my friend, is why I let him out of here so quickly. He wasn't going to help so there was no need to waste any more time with him."

"Diane, do you remember that lock in the dining room being broken?"

"No, and we've been checking the doors and windows every night."

"Strange. I'll get a hammer and nails from the shed and make sure no one opens that window again."

"Don't you think it would be better to call the realtor?"

"Nah, they might send another Wendell and you're running low on underwear," Claire chuckled.

Chapter Seven
Discovery

Claire and Diane walked down to the beach to find Jill sitting next to Caroline as she sketched. Ike searched the dunes for a stick returning to lay one proudly at Claire's feet.

"How did it go?" Jill asked.

"Waste of time," Claire answered, throwing Ike's stick into the water.

Caroline looked up from her work. "Really? No answers."

Diane sat down next to Caroline and looked at her sketch. "That's good Caroline! Nope, no answers. He wasn't taking us seriously."

Leaning back on her elbows Jill looked up at Claire. "What do you make of it?"

"Diane's right. He wasn't interested. I got the distinct impression he thought we were just menopausal maidens with nothing better to do than interrupt his day."

"What do we do now?" Caroline asked.

"We only have a few more days here, let's just continue to be cautious and keep Ike as long as we can," Diane answered.

The morning passed with the four taking turns throwing the stick for Ike while Caroline sat sketching. Each woman remained quiet, lost in her own thoughts.

Shortly before noon Jill stood up and dusted the sand off her clothes. "Let's pack a lunch and go for a bike ride. There are plenty of places to explore."

"Good idea," Caroline agreed. "My butt's sore from sitting so long."

Ike pushed past Claire as she opened the kitchen door, and raced through the kitchen and up the steps barking loudly.

"Oh geez, what's wrong with him now," Caroline

asked.

"I don't know," Claire said. "Just ignore him."

Jill opened the Kelvinator and removed meat and cheese for sandwiches while Diane packed the picnic basket with napkins, apples and the leftover pastries from breakfast.

Ike barked even louder.

"I'll take my painting things up and see if I can get Ike to come down," Caroline said, leaving the kitchen.

"Jill, does Ike bark this much when he's with Drew?" Claire asked, as she removed the breakfast dishes from dish rack and put them in the cabinet.

"No. He rarely barks."

"Do you think there's something about us he doesn't like?" Claire asked, turning to face Jill.

"No. I think there's something about this house that bothers him."

Ike suddenly ran into the kitchen and slid across the linoleum to Claire's side. Grabbing her pant leg with his teeth he pulled her into the parlor.

"Oh Ike, what is it?"

"Girls, come up here!" Caroline shouted. "The door to the locked room is open."

Claire pried Ike's teeth off her pants and started up the stairs. Ike scrambled past her nearly knocking her down.

Caroline met them at the second floor landing and together they climbed the stairs to the third floor. They could hear Ike already inside the room sniffing and whining.

Slowly opening the door the whole way the women cautiously peered inside the room.

"It's just another bedroom," Jill said.

Claire walked farther into the room. "Let's look around. There has to be some reason Ike is so interested."

The room was definitely decorated for a little girl. It

was large with two windows overlooking the sea and two facing the driveway. An ornate, iron bed with a once frilly, pink bedspread held an assortment of tired looking, stuffed animals. There were pictures of ballerinas on the walls. The furniture, once white, was now grey from years of dust permeating the paint. The windows had the same lace curtains as the other bedrooms, and there was a window seat in an alcove under one of the windows facing the ocean. At the foot of the bed was a wicker settee with an old fashioned scrapbook propped against its back.

Claire sat down on the settee and a mushroom of dust floated into the air. She picked up the scrapbook and examined the brown leather cover now cracked and brittle with age. When she opened the book and started to turn the pages, they nearly disintegrated. Carefully she studied the old snapshots held in place with black triangular holders at each corner.

Opening the closet Jill pulled out a little girl's dress. "Look at this. The closet is filled with little girl's clothes and shoes. These styles are at least forty years old."

Diane examined the top of the bureau, which held a mirror on a stand, hairbrush, comb and miscellaneous bottles and hair barrettes. Pulling open the top drawer she said, "Old clothes here too."

Caroline was standing next to a bookcase containing books and dolls. "This room looks like nothing has been touched in years."

Claire suddenly gasped. "I can't believe this."

Diane quickly crossed the room and sat down beside Claire. "What is it?"

Claire pointed to a picture of five children playing on a beach. "This is me."

"What?" Jill said, returning the dress to the closet and hurrying to stand on the other side of Claire.

Caroline moved beside Diane and they all looked where Claire was pointing.

"Look. This is me. This is my brother Will, and the other three children are Betsy, Patty and their brother David. We played with them every year that we came to The Point."

"Did they live in this house?" Diane asked.

"I don't remember that, but they must have. We were always on the beach, playing games, or riding bikes. If we came to this house I don't remember. That's so weird, how could I forget this big old house?"

"How old were you?" Caroline inquired.

"I think I must have been about eleven. Will would have been fourteen. He and David were the same age. Patty was a year older than me; and Betsy was, I think, about three years younger."

"What was their last name?" Jill questioned.

"I don't know. I'm sure I knew their name. I believe Mom stayed in touch with their parents over the years. I can't remember much else. I think this was the last year we came to The Point," Claire said, slowly turning the pages. There were more pictures of the children digging for clams, building sandcastles and in front of the house sitting on bicycles."

The corner, picture holders were dried out and no longer secured many of the pictures. Claire studied each picture closely before moving onto the next page. Halfway through the scrapbook were two old, yellowed, newspaper articles, one of which had a picture of Betsy and a headline that read, "Local Child Missing."

"Oh God," Claire declared, as she quickly scanned the articles. "Oh no. Something happened to Betsy. She either wandered off or was kidnapped and they never found her… or, at least, by the second article several months later there was no trace. I never knew this. I wonder if this is why we didn't come back after that year. Will and I never understood; we loved it here. If Mom and Dad knew about this they never told us." Finishing the article she looked up

Windward Secrets

at Jill, "Carter. Their last name was Carter."

Claire slowly worked her way through the book again, this time from back to front. Leaning forward, and looking closer, she picked up one of the pictures and walked to the window for better light.

"What is it?" Diane asked.

"Take a look and tell me what this is Diane," Claire requested, pointing to the side of the photograph.

Diane squinted and studied the photo. "It's an old truck. You can barely see it camouflaged among the trees and scrubs."

"Look at the door," Claire encouraged.

"It looks like W-E-N-D. That's all I can make out. Are you thinking it's Wendell's truck?"

"Well, of course it's not the same truck, it would be too old, but it's a pickup. I bet if we could see more of the lettering it would say Wendell's Plumbing."

"What are you saying?" Caroline interrupted. "Do you think Wendell may have had something to do with Betsy's disappearance?"

"Maybe. I'm going to study every one of these pictures."

"Surely, the authorities would have picked up on that?" Caroline offered.

"Not if they had the same attitude as Chief Peterson," Claire said.

"Claire, don't jump to conclusions," Diane stated.

"Diane, look at the way the truck is positioned. There are no houses around and no other cars or people. This truck looks as if it was being hidden on purpose. Someone could have easily been watching us without us knowing."

"You could be right, Claire. Do you recognize the beach location?"

"These rocks," Claire said, pointing to another section of the picture. "I remember them but I don't know where they are. They're probably totally covered with sand or totally exposed by now; could go either way after all this time."

Ike had finally settled down and was lying on the floor next to the bed.

"Look," Caroline said. "Ike's calm. It's like he needed to show us this room."

"This is all too weird," Jill replied. "I'm hungry. Let's go down and have some lunch."

***

Claire sat at the kitchen table studying the scrapbook as she ate a sandwich. The other three women looked at each other anxiously waiting for Claire to say something.

Getting up from the table Claire started opening kitchen drawers. Finally, she pulled out an old telephone book and paged through the yellow pages. "Here's what we're going to do."

"Why am I afraid of what she's going to say?" Caroline asked, nervously stirring her iced tea.

"Because it's probably not going to be good," Jill replied.

Diane waited in silence and then nodded at Claire to continue.

Claire looked at each as she spoke. "Wendell lives at 29 Beach Haven Road, that's farther down this road, a mile or so. Jill, you will take your phone and your car to the edge of Haworth. Caroline you will take your phone and car a mile past Wendell's house. You two are going to be the lookouts. Diane and I are going to ride our bikes down to Wendell's and see what we can find. If either Jill or Caroline see Wendell coming in our direction they will call us. It will be easier to hide the bikes than a car and if we get caught we can say we were just taking a rest from biking."

"Claire, you're nuts. This is dangerous. We have no business snooping around Wendell's," Caroline said.

"Well, he had no business stealing Diane's underwear. If my suspicion is correct, he's a sicko and might have had something to do with Betsy's disappearance."

Diane finally spoke up. "I'm game."

"Diane, you can't be serious," Jill said, surprised at Diane's statement.

"I am. I'm sick and tired of creeps getting away with all kinds of crap because honest citizens are afraid to do anything. We're only going to look around. We won't break and enter. We're not planning on stealing anything."

Caroline still looked apprehensive. "Who takes Ike?"

"Ike stays here," Claire said. "He'll keep anyone out of the house who might try to come in while we're gone."

"If we're going to do this, let's get it done," Jill said.

Claire took Ike outside to take care of business while the others got their cell phones and car keys. After doing a final check of the doors and windows to be sure they were locked the women adjourned to the driveway. Jill and Caroline backed their cars out of the drive and headed in opposite directions as Claire and Diane casually rode their bikes toward Wendell's. Approaching his driveway, they nonchalantly looked for his truck.

"Looks like he's out," Claire said, jumping off her bike and pushing it toward the tall grass beside the road. She walked the bike deep into the weeds and laid it down. Diane did the same.

"I say we just act like we are looking for Wendell to do some plumbing," Diane said. "No one can object to that."

"Unless they ask why we hid our bikes," Claire said, with a grin.

"Minor detail."

The drive curved to the right slightly and they could

see a small cottage sitting deep among the pines.

"Geez Louise," Claire said. "It looks like a puff of wind could blow it down."

"What a mess," Diane said.

The house was in bad need of a coat of paint. Some of the shutters were hanging precariously from their hinges. There was litter and unrecognizable pieces of junk scattered around the yard. An old sofa, with its stuffing hanging out, sat on the front porch.

Claire tapped Diane on the arm and pointed to the far side of the house. "Look over there Diane."

"Holy hell," Diane whispered. "That looks like the truck in the picture."

The truck was nearly rusted beyond recognition. The tires were gone, the windows were broken and someone had tried to scrape the lettering off the door.

Claire was about to step up on the porch when Diane stopped her. Pulling a Zip-Lock bag from her pocket she opened it and handed Claire a pair of surgical gloves.

"What the heck?"

"Okay, so I'm a germaphobe. I always carry gloves and Clorox wipes in my suitcase for cleaning hotel bathrooms. In this case, we won't leave any fingerprints."

"You're a genius, Diane."

Stretching the gloves over her hands Claire walked onto the porch and tried the front door. Locked.

Diane tried to see in the front window but dark colored drapes covered the window.

"Let's go around back," Claire said.

The back door was locked as well.

"That only leaves the windows," Claire announced.

"You're kidding, right?"

"Heck, no. He's probably the one who's been breaking into Windward Cottage. Turn-about is fair play."

Walking to a window at the side of the house, farthest from the driveway, Claire tried reaching it from the ground but it was too high. Looking around she found an old, wooden box and set it under the window. The box gave her just enough height to reach the window, which to her surprise pushed up easily.

"Look at that," she said, over her shoulder to Diane. "But I still can't get up high enough to crawl in."

"Move over a little," Diane said, mounting the box with Claire. Leaning against the side of the house and lacing her fingers together she made a stirrup with her hands. "Step in my hands and I'll lift as you pull yourself up."

It worked. Claire pushed the curtain out of the way, swung her free leg over the windowsill, and stepped into the room. Looking back out the window she whispered, "Diane, get rid of the box and go to the back door. I'll let you in."

Claire closed the window and looked around. She was standing in a bedroom. It was a small room with a single bed, dresser and a small closet. The bed was made and the room was neat as a pin. "Hmmm, weird."

Hurrying to the back door she unlocked it and Diane entered the kitchen.

"This kitchen is spotless," Diane said, swiftly scanning the room.

"So is his bedroom," Claire added, with a curious look. "Diane you search the kitchen and living room. I'm going to look for other rooms."

The kitchen cabinets revealed nothing but dishes and the expected dry goods. Frig and stove were clean. Wendell liked TV dinners, applesauce, pickles, and sour milk that needed to be thrown away. Under the kitchen sink were the normal cleaning supplies one would expect to find.

In the living room, Diane looked behind the furniture, under the sofa cushions, and in the TV cabinet that held Wendell's big screen TV. Nothing.

Claire found a spotless bathroom and several closets with clothing. A search of the pockets of his clothes revealed nothing unusual. She found a second bedroom a little larger than the first with a double bed and just as tidy as the first. There were no stairs leading to a second floor or attic so Claire tried the only door she had not investigated.

"Bingo!" she called to Diane.

Hurrying to her side Diane joined Claire looking down into the dark. "Where's the light?"

Claire felt around and found a switch. A quick flip and the stairs were bathed in bright light. "Hurry Diane. I'm getting nervous."

Diane followed Claire down the stairs to a damp-smelling basement. The basement was unusually well lit and clean. There were shelves lining two walls with miscellaneous tools and neatly lined-up canned goods. The furnace and water heater were tucked under the stairs. The fourth wall was stone.

"There has to be something here," Claire said. Not willing to give up, she moved to the shelving and started pushing and pulling. Diane did the same on the other wall.

Suddenly there was a creaking sound and the shelving unit Claire was pushing started to slide to the side. A little more effort and Claire had an opening large enough to step through. Without waiting for Diane she felt around and found the light switch. She was nearly blinded by the light.

Standing behind Claire, Diane let out a sharp cry. "Dear God, what is this?"

The room was like a national security control center. There was a wall of monitors over a table with several computers and a keyboard. Walking into the room Claire touched the space bar of the keyboard and the monitors sprang to life. Four of the monitors showed views from different sides of the cottage.

"This isn't good," Diane said. "He can see anyone approaching the house, and that would include us."

Diane's panties lay on the table beside the keyboard.

On the wall to their right was a bulletin board with a large map of the eastern seaboard of the United States with colored pins stuck at numerous locations. On the wall to the left hundreds of pictures were taped to a white board.

"Get out your cell and start taking pictures," Claire ordered.

As Diane started snapping pictures of the map, computer area and room in general, Claire walked closer to the wall with the pictures. "Sweet Mother of God," she whispered, as she felt the vomit rising in her throat. The pictures were of young girls; some clothed, some in underwear, and some nude. Some of the children appeared not to know they were being photographed while others stared at the camera in terror. Some were tied up, while others cowered against a wall trying to escape the person behind the camera.

Claire pulled her cell from her pocket and started snapping as fast as she could. When she got to the bottom right corner of the wall she froze. Her own eleven year old face was looking directly at her. There were photos of the Carter children and Will. They were playing on the beach almost directly in front of Wendell's cottage. As she moved lower she gasped. There was Betsy, dirty with a tear-stained face, and her once innocent blue eyes wild with terror. She was dressed only in underpants. Her blond curly hair was tangled and matted with dirt. Her body was scratched and dirty. Her little hands looked like they had been digging or clawing at something hard. Her nails were broken and bleeding. Claire grabbed her stomach and bent over. She had to get out of here before she was sick.

"Diane, run!"

Diane reached for her panties.

"Leave them. Evidence. Turn out the lights," Claire yelled, as she ran through the doorway.

The two women pushed the shelves back into place and ran up the stairs.

Claire in the lead yelled, "Lights."

They tore through the house and slammed the back door closed. They didn't care if they made noise. They didn't care if anyone saw them. They ran for their bikes as fast as they could.

Diane felt her phone vibrating in her pocket. "Yes!"

"Diane, he's coming. Get out of there," Jill yelled, frantically.

"We're on our way," Diane responded, as they reached the bikes. "Claire, he's coming from town."

The women dragged the bikes to the road and peddled as hard as they could toward Caroline's location. Caroline was parked on a pull-off overlooking the ocean and saw them coming. Getting out of the car she waited.

Claire and Diane turned the bikes into the pull-off and collapsed. Both women fell to the ground lungs ready to explode and legs that felt like they were made of burning rubber. Claire burst into uncontrollable sobs. Diane reached over to comfort her. Caroline rushed to their sides and dropped to her knees. "What's wrong? What happened?"

Claire held up her hand to stop Caroline and then crawled to the edge of the road and vomited. Lying down on the hard-packed sand she curled into the fetal position and wept.

Shaken, Caroline looked at Diane.

Diane shook her head and held her index finger to her lips. "Give her some space," she whispered.

***

Jill was waiting on the porch when they pulled in the drive at Windward Cottage. Claire walked past Jill like a zombie. Jill watched her pass and then hurried to the car to help with the bikes. "What happened? What's wrong with Claire?

"Let's go inside and I'll tell you everything," Diane said.

Ike was excited to see Claire, but she barely acknowledged him. He followed her up the stairs and laid down beside the bathtub as she lowered herself into the steaming water. She washed her hair vigorously and scrubbed her body with soap and a stiff brush in an attempt to rid herself of the invisible filth. The harder she scrubbed, the harder she sobbed. Finally, lying back in the tub she closed her eyes and tried to erase the images of the children seared into her brain. It was no good. Her muscles would heal but she knew her mind never would. *All those children. Their terror and pain. What about their families? She vowed she would make him pay.*

***

Claire didn't come down for dinner.

Diane told Jill and Caroline everything they had seen in Wendell's house.

"Dear God, she must be devastated," Caroline said, pushing her plate of half eaten food away. "I can't imagine what she's going through."

Jill stood up and started to clear the table. "Where do we go from here, Diane?"

"I don't know. We have to wait until Claire's ready to talk and then decide."

Ike wandered into the kitchen head down and dragging his feet.

"Oh, poor guy," Caroline said, reaching down and rubbing his back. "He really loves her."

"Do you think we should call the police," Jill asked, opening the back door for Ike.

Diane responded sharply. "Surely, you don't mean the local police? Chief Peterson is totally worthless, and I'm sure poor, Deputy O'Reilly isn't allowed to take on any responsibility for fear of upstaging Peterson. No, we'll wait and see what Claire says."

"What about Spence or her brother Will?" Jill inquired.

"I think that's Claire's decision. She has to be a wreck after seeing those pictures."

"Did you look at them Diane?" Caroline asked, meekly.

"I only got a glimpse before Claire charged out of the room. I'm pretty sure she got most of them on her phone. It took real strength to keep shooting when she saw what the pictures were. And so many, my God, I can't believe it."

Ike pawed at the screen door. Jill let him in and locked both doors behind him. The women followed him into the parlor. Ike slowly climbed the stairs while the women took seats; each picked up a book, or a magazine, in a useless attempt to occupy their minds.

Finally, Diane threw her book on the coffee table with a slap that made Jill and Caroline jump. "Jill, have you heard from Drew?"

"No. Not a word," Jill answered.

"How much do you really know about him, Jill?"

Jill looked up wearily and answered. "He has been divorced for over ten years. He says he and his wife parted friends; they had grown apart. Her name is Melinda. She's a nurse. She blamed him for working too much and he thinks she was probably right. They have two grown kids, a girl and a boy; and three grandchildren. She remarried about five years ago, a doctor from the hospital where she worked, and apparently is happy as a clam now."

"What about him personally?" Caroline asked.

Jill looked like she was ready to cry.

"This is ridiculous. There is nothing strange about Drew. He's very nice, as normal as we are."

Jill closed her eyes and then opened them suddenly and looked directly at Caroline.

"I don't know what you want me to say, Caroline. We like being together. It's comfortable. We like the same music, the same jokes, some of the same movies and books." Looking up she added, "If you're asking if he's acted inappropriately in any way, the answer is no. There's definitely an attraction but neither one of us has acted on it. Come on…we're mature adults, not teenie boppers with raging hormones," Jill giggled, "Well…maybe there's a little elevation in hormones."

"Have you seen anything at his cottage that may be out of character for a consultant?" Diane pushed.

"Like what? I don't know what's normal for someone who does his kind of work," Jill replied, defensively.

"What's his cottage like?" Caroline asked, using a lighter tone.

Feeling less under attack Jill looked at Caroline. "He's a very neat person. Let's the dishes pile up a bit, but other than that it looks fine."

"What about the bedroom?" Diane quizzed.

Jill glared at Diane. "I have not been in his bedroom. I have no clue what it looks like."

Caroline perked up and with interest asked, "Have you been in his bathroom?"

"Honestly, you two. Yes, I used his bathroom once. What are you after?"

Diane moved forward on the sofa and rested her forearms on her thighs. "I think we need to be sure he can be trusted."

Caroline thought she saw a flicker of doubt sweep across Jill's face for just a split second. "What did you see in the bathroom, Jill?"

Jill curled the edges of the magazine in her lap and then looked up. "There were a lot of pill bottles. More than you would think a healthy man would have."

"Did you read the labels?" Diane asked.

Jill hesitated looking guilty. "Yes."

"Well...?" Caroline insisted, impatiently.

"There were a lot of vitamins, blood pressure medicine, an anti-anxiety, eye drops...and several prescription sleeping pills. I thought it was unusual to have so many sleeping pills."

"Maybe we better pay a little visit to his cottage tomorrow," Diane suggested.

"No. Diane really," Jill said, in earnest. "Drew's okay. I'm sure of it. What could he possibly have to do with the children, or Wendell, for that matter?"

"I don't know," Diane admitted. "But, I think we have to suspect everyone in the area. How could that many children disappear and nobody knew about it? There were so many pictures that you would think it would have made the national news. I have a real bad feeling about this."

"I need a drink," Jill said, getting up and going to the kitchen. She returned with a bottle of wine and glasses. "Let's go to the roof and try to enjoy the rest of the evening."

***

It was a calm evening as Jill, Caroline, and Diane sat quietly sipping wine and looking at the ocean.

Caroline interrupted the quiet. "Since we appear to be into solving mysteries... how do you think the fire in the parlor gets started?"

"Good question. I wish I knew," Jill said.

Diane took a sip of wine and looked at her friends. "I know this sounds paranoid, but I wonder if Wendell somehow has it rigged. Nah, that can't be because it's real wood and not a gas fireplace."

"But how can anyone get into this house long enough to prepare a fire when we have been so careful to lock up, and we have Ike who hasn't caught anyone?" Jill returned.

Diane shook her head and yawned.

"Your guess is as good as mine Jill. The realtor has a key. Maybe someone else has keys. Secret passage?"

Hearing the door from the third floor open the women turned to see Claire and Ike step onto the roof. Claire was wrapped in a blanket from her bed. With Ike following her she slowly walked to the edge of the roof and took a deep breath. As her friends watched, she paced the perimeter of the roof just as Ike had done. When she got to the side of the house that faced in the direction of Wendell's cottage she stopped. She stood still for a few minutes and then started walking again.

"You okay, Claire?" Diane asked.

Claire turned and approached her friends. "Hi. Sorry I missed dinner."

"No problem," Jill answered. "It was just beef Wellington, twice baked potatoes, green beans almandine, and baked Alaska for dessert."

Claire smiled. "Funny, it smelled like beans and franks."

Getting the result she wanted, Jill stood up from her plastic webbed, lawn chair and hugged her friend. "We're so sorry about what you found."

Claire nodded and sat down, adjusting her blanket more closely around her body. "So, where's the wine?"

Jill poured a glass and handed it to her.

"Claire, have you eaten anything?" Caroline asked.

"Yes, thanks. I made myself a sandwich."

"What's next Claire?" Diane asked, knowing her friend well.

"I can't let this go. I have to find the answers."

"I didn't expect anything less," Diane replied. "I can't speak for Jill and Caroline, but I'm with you all the way."

"I'm worried I've put us in danger."

"What do you mean?" Diane asked.

"The cameras. Do you think they recorded us when

we approached the house today?"

Diane tensed. "I suppose, if they were recording. No sense having cameras and not using them."

"Then we're going to have to be extremely careful. I think it's up to us to solve this. For whatever reason, he's gotten away with it for over forty years. I want him to fry."

Caroline's voice shook with emotion. "I'm in Claire."

"Me too," Jill said.

"Do you have a plan?" Diane questioned.

"You mean besides cutting the bastard's balls off?" Claire asked.

"Well, yeah, but maybe something within the law."

Claire took a huge gulp of wine and turned her chair to face her friends. "We need to get as much background on all those children as we can. We have no computer service here so we're going to have to see where we can get it in Haworth; probably the public library. If you don't mind spending the time, I'd appreciate your help researching. Once we have collected as much data as possible we'll decide what to do next."

"Why can't we just go to the authorities with what you found?" Jill asked.

"Two reasons. One, we, in essence, broke into his house; and number two, because I don't trust them. How could they have not suspected something all these years? How could that many children disappear without someone being suspicious? There are too many unanswered questions."

Jill's cell phone rang. Looking at the screen she smiled. "It's Drew. Hello. Good and you?" Jill walked to the edge of the roof for privacy.

Caroline swirled her wineglass and looked at Claire. "Are you still uneasy about Drew?"

Claire took her time answering. "I really hate to sound neurotic… but, right now, I don't trust anyone. Drew has given us no reason to be suspicious. I was overprotective of Jill in the beginning, but now I'm more frightened of the unknown. And, let's face it, we don't know him from Adam, and he IS moving fast with Jill. Do you agree or do you think it's just me?"

"I think Drew and Jill found a real connection. I hope he's sincere because I don't want to see her hurt. Until we have something on him, I'm in his court. On the matter of what you found today, I think you had an incredible shock and especially when one of the children was a childhood friend. That has to be traumatic." Caroline leaned toward Diane. "What do you think, Diane?"

"I agree with both of you. I think, for peace of mind for all of us, we have to do something even if all we do is draw attention to this to get the authorities involved. Claire's right about Chief Peterson, there's something not quite right about him. Either he doesn't really care or he's just plain stupid. I can't really get a handle on it. Maybe it's nothing more than he's close enough to retirement that he just wants to get through his last years without any problems. At any rate, I think we have to help Claire."

Jill was walking back and forth along the roof phone to her ear.

"Looks like it's going to be a long conversation," Diane noted, ruffling her short hair.

"You do know, I only wish the best for her don't you?" Claire said, looking from Diane to Caroline.

"Yes, of course we do," Caroline answered.

Diane shifted in her chair. "Claire, would you like me to ask Ed to investigate Wendell?"

"Would he do that?"

"I think so. I should check in with him anyway. I'll give him a call first thing in the morning."

Jill finally re-joined the group.

"Well?" Claire asked, raising one eyebrow.

"Oh Claire, you're so silly. He just called to see

how we were getting along and if Ike was giving us any trouble. He's genuinely concerned about us."

Claire suddenly sat up straighter and blurted out, "You didn't tell him about us going to Wendell's today did you?'

"No, you don't need to worry, I didn't mention it. I didn't think you'd want me to."

"Thank you. Right now I think the fewer people who know the better."

Jill covered her legs with a blanket and picked up her wine glass. "What did I miss?"

"Nothing really," Diane said. "We were just talking about what to do next. Claire do you have any more ideas?"

"Only that I think two of us should go to the library to do research in the morning and the other two should search this house from top to bottom to see if we can figure out how someone is getting in."

Diane broke in. "Claire, I think you should let someone else do the research. You had enough of a shock seeing those pictures. If we turn up anything you need some time to prepare mentally to deal with it."

"Good idea," Caroline said, pushing her glasses up on her nose. "I volunteer to go to the library. Who wants to go with me?"

"I'll go," Jill offered. "I like research."

"Good. Claire and I will stay here and search the house," Diane said.

The wind picked up and clouds swiftly moved across the sky. Within minutes rain drops were pelting the women.

Ike ran for the door and barked.

"We better take these chairs downstairs in case we get high wind," Jill said.

Stashing the chairs in the third floor hallway, the women continued down to the first floor. In the kitchen they washed the glasses, discarded the wine bottle, and let

Ike out for his final bathroom break. Splitting up they checked all the windows and doors and met in the parlor.

"Did any one notice?" Diane asked.

"There's no fire...," Caroline said.

"Is that good news or bad?" Jill inquired.

"I'm relieved. Maybe we can get a good night's sleep," Claire said, sighing.

The wind and rain pounded the outside of Windward Cottage with vengeance.

"We're going to need some extra blankets tonight," Caroline said, ascending the stairs. "Has anyone seen a linen closet?"

"Closets were rare in this age of house," Jill replied. "Let's see what we can find."

The second and third floors were searched but yielded no linen closet.

"Found a blanket," Diane yelled, from the second floor landing. "Look in the bureaus in your rooms."

Blankets were pulled from drawers and soon covered the beds with the women snuggled under them.

"You okay?" Jill asked Claire. "Would you like the light on?"

"I'm fine, Jill. You can turn out the light."

Claire closed her eyes and listened to the storm. Normally, she liked the sound of the rain on the roof but tonight; rather than soothe her, it set her nerves on edge. Jill started snoring. Claire put her pillow over her head, but Jill was snoring louder than the storm. Claire finally decided to get up. Feeling around for her book, and dragging her blanket, she tip-toed out of the room and down to the parlor. Ike padded silently behind her.

Once submerged in the overstuffed sofa, she opened her book and tried to read with Ike settled beside the sofa. His even breathing soon coaxed Claire into a restless sleep. She saw the little girl again. This time she seemed to be sitting on the sofa with Claire. It wasn't just any little girl, it was Betsy. Claire tossed and turned. Her tears soaked the throw pillow under her head. Betsy looked as she had in the picture, dirty and frightened. Claire reached out for her. Together they cried. Claire cradled the child in her arms and tried to comfort her.

Chapter Eight
Thursday

A loud clap of thunder woke Claire. She felt a warm body next to hers. Opening her eyes she found Ike sound asleep on the sofa with her.

"Okay, big boy, time to go out!" she whispered, patting him gently.

Ike turned his head and licked Claire's face before jumping to the floor and lumbering toward the kitchen.

Yawning, Claire stretched and looked around. *Not a bad night considering* she thought, pushing herself up and out of the sofa.

Ike was waiting for her at the back door.

It was barely dawn and the rain was coming down in buckets.

"Ike, I love you, but I'm not going out in that." Opening the door she added, "Hurry and get back here as fast as you can."

Turning back to the kitchen Claire filled the coffee maker and opened the refrigerator to retrieve bacon and eggs. A scratch at the door told her Ike was ready to come back in. Ike waited until he was in the middle of the kitchen to shake his rain soaked coat. Water flew everywhere with the final drops propelled off his tail directly at Claire.

"Oh, Ike, for crying out loud. Sit. Stay." Claire grabbed a towel and dried Ike and then the surrounding furniture and floor. Claire was on her hands and knees when Jill entered the room.

"What are you doing?"

Claire looked at her friend incredulously. "Really Jill? What does it look like? Ike decided to bring the storm inside the house."

Jill poured herself a cup of coffee. "I was worried when you weren't in your bed this morning."

"I came down here to read because you were

snoring. Ya know Jill, I would have liked to have had a fire last night. Too bad our secret visitor hadn't started one for me."

Peeling open the bacon package Jill separated the strips of bacon and laid them in a frying pan. "Frankly, I'm glad he didn't because I got a good night's sleep not worrying about someone sneaking around. How did you sleep?"

"Better than expected. I dreamed of Betsy again."

"Again? What do you mean again?"

"Oh… didn't I tell you? I had a dream a few nights ago about a little girl at the foot of my bed. It was the night I couldn't find my book. I didn't recognize her then, but after seeing the pictures I now know it was her."

Jill knitted her brows together and looked at her friend. "Claire, are you saying you saw Betsy here in the house?"

"In the house… as in my dream. It makes sense. This is her house. She knew me. I think she came to me for help."

"Claire, you're scaring me. That's morbid."

"Don't be scared. I think this house may be a 'thin place.'"

"What are you talking about? A 'thin place'?"

"A thin place is somewhere where the separation between heaven and earth is diminished and we can feel the presence of those who have lived before. I felt it my first day here but didn't recognize it. Maybe I subconsciously chose Windward House because of Betsy."

"You're really losing it."

"I read about thin places. Haven't you ever heard of it?" Claire asked.

"No. And, I'm not sure I want to."

"There's nothing to be worried about. Thin places are places of peace and tranquility, where the past meets the present. I think, Betsy is our guide. She wants our help."

Jill smelled burning bacon and turned back to the stove. "Okay, whatever you say."

"I wonder if it was Betsy starting the fires, moving my book, and crying."

"Crying? Now what are you talking about?"

Claire was seated at the kitchen table with Ike's head on her lap. "I heard crying one night. I think it was coming from Betsy's room. Don't you think it makes sense?"

Jill turned the bacon and looked back at Claire. "No, this does not make any sense. I'm worried about you."

"Don't be. Just keep an open mind. I can tell you I feel more at peace. I'm not as frightened. This feels right."

Caroline and Diane entered the kitchen at the same time. "What feels right?" Caroline asked.

Claire repeated her theory about thin places and Betsy.

"I need coffee," Caroline said, looking at Claire with wide eyes and circling her finger around her ear making the crazy sign.

Diane was intrigued. "This is interesting. Tell us more Claire."

"No!" Jill interrupted. "We're going to have breakfast in the present time and place. Claire can go into this later. How do you want your eggs?"

Seated in front of a plate of bacon and eggs Claire laid out her plan for the day to her friends. "Okay. Here's what we do. Jill and Caroline you go to the library and see what you can find about missing children. Sorry, I know this is going to be a big job. Hopefully, the library will have computers. While you're there, Diane and I will see what we can find here in the house… even though I think I have it figured out with Betsy. Let's plan to meet for lunch at Blackbeard's at one o'clock."

Diane, Caroline, and Jill looked at each other

anxiously."

Diane reached over and touched Claire's arm. "Claire, do you think you ought to call Spence and talk to him about all of this. It might make you feel better."

"Diane I'm fine. Really. Spence would only worry needlessly."

Jill had heard enough. "Claire! We're seriously concerned about you. You've always been the practical one with more common sense than anyone deserves. You need to get a grip. We'll help you with this, but I think you need some professional help."

Claire responded with assurance. "I'm fine. We only have a day to work on this and then we'll be home in our safe, little houses and this will all be a memory. Please. Just give me another day."

As promised Diane made a call to her friend, Ed, who agreed to see what he could find out about Wendell. Jill and Caroline left for the library and Claire and Diane went to the third floor.

"We may as well start up here and work our way down," Claire said.

Two hours later they had searched every nook and cranny, looked under every rug, felt walls, gone through the kitchen cabinets, and even cleaned the ash out of the fireplace using a flashlight to investigate the inside of the firebox.

Dust covered Diane's spikey hair. Claire's ponytail had failed her leaving strands of hair falling in her face that she tried to blow away with puffs of breath.

"Nothing. This is disappointing," Diane said, plopping down in the old recliner in the parlor.

"I know. I thought we would find something, even if it was only a door to the basement."

Diane stood, startling Ike who had been stretched out on the rug in front of the sofa. "Basement. That's it. There was no door. How do we get into the basement?"

Grabbing umbrellas from a brass stand by the door Claire handed one to Diane and then opened the front door. "There has to be an outside entrance."

On the side of the house opposite the driveway, they found what they were looking for. Partially covered in sand, was a metal, bulkhead door with a rusty padlock the size of a hubcap.

"Well, that's useless," Claire yelled, over the wind. Bending down, for a closer look at the lock, she gave it a hard tug. It held strong. She only succeeded in exposing her back to the wind and rain.

"Let's go back inside," Diane yelled.

Feeling defeated, they sat at the kitchen table with their hands wrapped around hot mugs of coffee.

"Claire. Do you find it interesting that the one night we don't have a fire is the night Drew is out of town?"

Claire removed the tie from her hair and shook her head letting her hair fall. "So... I'm not the only one who has questions about Drew?"

"I think I'm beginning to think like you and it scares me."

Claire fluffed her hair trying to get it to dry. "Frankly, I think it's very strange. We have plenty of time before we have to be in town. Let's take a little ride over to Drew's cottage."

"Jill is really going to be pissed," Diane said, reaching for yellow slickers on hooks beside the door.

"If he happens to be home, we'll just say we were running low on dog food."

Diane rolled her eyes. "First, we trespass and now we lie. What next?"

Pulling into Drew's drive, Claire and Diane were relieved his car was not there. The rain had eased and they ran to the porch. There was no answer to their knock so they tried the door and windows on the porch. Locked. They worked their way around the house, as they had at

Wendell's, but had no luck finding an unlocked window. There was a screened-in porch at the back of the house with windows looking into the kitchen.

Claire cupped her hands around her eyes and peered in the windows while Diane kept watch for anyone approaching the house.

"Nothing," Claire said. "Jill was right. He keeps a neat house. Dishes are even washed."

Diane shrugged her shoulders. "We may as well go meet Jill and Caroline."

"Just for the heck of it, let's drive past Wendell's."

"Why exactly would we do that?" Diane asked, incredulously.

"We should keep tabs on him. If we know where he is, he can't surprise us."

Wendell's driveway was empty. Claire was pulling the car into the drive when Diane yelled, "What are you doing? Claire, I'm not going in there again."

"Relax Diane, I'm just turning around."

Backing out, Claire turned the car toward Haworth and Diane breathed a sigh of relief.

The rain had let up a little but the day was still dark and dreary. The sidewalks of Haworth were deserted. "Looks like that depressing town where the Twilight movies were filmed, doesn't it Diane?"

Diane glanced from side to side looking around the small town. "I'm waiting for a vampire to pop out at any minute."

"How about a Chief of Police?" Claire said, sarcastically as she pointed to the right side of the street. Chief Peterson's patrol car was parked in a No Parking Zone in front of the Haworth Public Library and he was walking into the library as they passed.

"Gee," Diane said. "He doesn't seem like the reading type."

Claire continued down the street slowly. "I sure

hope Jill and Caroline are out of there."

Turning left at the next corner Claire found a parking spot half a block from Blackbeard's. "Good. There's Caroline's car. They're here."

Claire and Diane wasted no time getting into the restaurant. Leaving their slickers and umbrellas in the vestibule, they opened the interior door to the restaurant and were assaulted with noise and activity. It appeared the whole town had decided to have lunch at the same time. Claire spied Jill and Caroline sitting in a booth near the large, open hearth fireplace where a fire blazed.

"This is great," Diane said, sliding in beside Jill. "How'd you get such a good table?"

Taking a long draw on her straw Jill said, "Just luck. It's really busy in here today isn't it?"

"Did you order yet?" Claire asked.

"Only drinks," Caroline answered, who quickly gave them a rundown of the specials and soup of the day.

"Great. I'm hungry," Diane said, picking up a menu.

"What can I get you ladies to drink?" came a cheerful voice over Claire's shoulder. Claire looked up to see a perky, blond waitress smiling with her pad and pencil ready to take their orders.

"Where'd you come from?" Claire asked, surprised by her sudden appearance.

The waitress gave them a fast and furious account of how busy they were, that she liked rainy days because it meant they would be busy, it made her day go faster and her tips better, and on and on, until Diane finally spoke up. "Hot tea for me, please." Then looking at Claire, and tilting her head toward the waitress. "What do you want to drink?"

"Coffee. Cream and sugar, please."

"Got it. I'll be back for your orders in a jiffy!"

Jill smiled and rolled her eyes. "And, that's

Brittany, our server. We already know her life story so, please, don't give her any opportunity to talk. Be ready with your orders when she comes back."

"How did you make out at the library?" Claire asked, looking over the top of her menu.

Caroline answered first. "We got a lot done. We found over fifty articles on missing girls."

"We divided and conquered by state," Jill said. "We thought that was enough to start with and decided to check out the local newspaper office to see what they might have in their archives."

Diane leaned forward and with a low voice asked, "What did you find?"

Brittany returned with the beverages before Jill or Caroline could answer. "Have you decided? The clam chowder is really good today. Makes you feel nice and toasty on a day like this."

"Yes. Yes. We're ready," Claire answered.

Orders were quickly given and Brittany did her vanishing act.

Diane repeated her question. "What did you find at the newspaper?"

Caroline played with her straw and looked intently at Diane. "Absolutely nothing."

Claire blinked and frowned. "How can that be?"

"We searched the microfiche for five years around the time you thought it was. There was absolutely no mention of Betsy's disappearance."

"That's impossible," Claire said, frowning.

"We thought it quite interesting," Jill agreed.

"Did you ask anyone at the paper about it?" Diane inquired.

"No. As a cover, we told them we were doing genealogy."

"Smart thinking Jill," Claire said, forgetting she was pouring cream into her coffee until it overflowed into her saucer. "How were you treated at the library?"

"Fine. Why do you ask?" Jill said, taking a drink of iced tea.

"When we were coming into town, Chief Peterson was entering the library. That seems like a strange coincidence, doesn't it?" Diane explained. Seeing Brittany returning with their meals she stopped talking and had an idea. "Thanks Brittany this looks great. Brittany, can you tell us how late the library is open?"

"Oh, sorry, I don't read much, but you could call Mrs. Peterson and ask her?"

Claire was elbowing Caroline in the ribs. It was obvious Brittany was not a frequent visitor to the library.

"And, who would Mrs. Peterson be?" Diane pressed.

"She's the librarian. Been there forever."

"That's interesting, the chief of police's name is Peterson. Are they related?"

"Well, yeah... they're married, is that related enough?"

"Of course. Aren't small towns nice? Everyone knows everyone."

"Need anything else?" Brittany said, with a smile and pointing in the direction of the other side of the room. "Just got another table."

Caroline chirped, "We're good. Thanks. You go."

Brittany spun around and swiveled her curvy hips to the other side of the room.

"Smooth, Diane. Good thinking," Claire said. "Do you suppose Mrs. Peterson was on the phone to Mr. Peterson as soon as Jill and Caroline left the library?"

"Why would she suspect anything?" Caroline asked.

"Woman's intuition. I don't think the chief likes to get out of his car on rainy days even to visit his wife in the library. Eating donuts in a warm car watching the waves seems more his speed."

Diane looked at Jill and Caroline. "Did you do anything that would make the librarian suspicious? Did anyone see what you were researching?"

"We were very careful. We didn't say why we wanted to use the computers and sat at the side of the computer table with our backs to the wall so no one could see what was on the screens," Caroline answered.

"What about the history list on the computers?" she asked, looking at Jill.

"I buried them so deep it would take an extremely good IT guy to find them."

"Good thinking. Where are the files now?"

"We sent them to all of our home emails just in case anything happened to our iPhones or…," Jill said, not completing the sentence.

"Or what," Claire asked.

"Your paranoia is contagious Claire… in case something happened to us there would be a trail."

"You're a genius Jill."

"I'm impressed, Jill. How do you know all that?" Diane added.

"I work for an electronics firm, remember? Not really a big deal."

Diane reached into her handbag for her phone. She hit some buttons and then said to Claire, "Give me your phone."

"Why?"

"I just sent Jill and Caroline's files and my pictures from Wendell's basement to my office printer and I want to forward your pictures too. I'll have Karen, my assistant, send hard copies to us by private courier."

"Excellent," Claire said, handing over her phone.

Jill set down her coffee cup and looked at Claire. "How did you and Diane make out?"

"We struck out. Didn't find anything."

Caroline pushed her plate to the side and pulled a large envelope out of her purse. "Jill and I have more to tell you." Opening the envelope she pulled out a legal size sheet of pink paper.

"What's that?" Diane asked.

"This is a contract from the realtor to rent Windward Cottage for another week. I had decided, even before we got involved in the Wendell thing that I was not ready to go home. So…I rented the house for another week. I hope you all can re-arrange your schedules to stay longer, but if you can't I understand."

Diane was the first to respond. "Are you serious Caroline? You really want to stay another week?"

"Well, I know I don't want to go home, for obvious reasons. I'm not happy about this mess we've stumbled into, but I think we need to at least try to do something about it."

"I can work remotely, I guess," Diane said. "I'll tell Karen to keep me updated and if anything serious comes up I can always drive back to Boston."

Jill chewed her bottom lip. "Gee, I don't know. I'll have to call my boss and see if I can have some more time. I have another week of PTO but I was saving it for a rainy day."

Caroline chuckled. "Jill, in case you haven't noticed, it's raining." Then turning to Claire she asked, "What about you Claire?"

"This is very generous of you, Caroline. Thank you. Of course, I want to stay but I'll have to run it past Spence and, like Jill, I'm going to have to get approval from work."

Jill leaned toward Claire. "You have that look on your face."

"What look?" Claire said, spoon halfway to her mouth.

"That look that says your brain is working overtime."

Returning her spoon to her bowl, Claire leaned back against the back of the booth. "I was just wondering how much information we could get out of chatty Brittany. Like Diane said, people in small towns know everyone and I'm betting they know everyone's business too. Let's make sure we leave Brittany a big tip. We may need her."

"May I make a suggestion?" Diane asked.

"Of course," the other three said, in unison.

"As interesting as all of this cloak and dagger stuff is, I think we need a change of pace. Let's spend the afternoon shopping or, at the very least, window shopping. It wouldn't hurt to walk around town a little."

"I agree," Jill said. "Too much sitting this morning. Let's walk."

The foursome paid their bill, including a large tip for Brittany, and left the restaurant.

***

Jill and Caroline drove out of town first with Claire and Diane following.

"Shopping turned out to be fun, didn't it Claire?" Diane asked, looking at her friend in the driver's seat.

"Yes, it was relaxing and a nice change."

"I'm very excited about the Claire Murray rug I bought. I've always wanted one," Diane said.

Claire was silent. The rain had started again and she reduced her speed on the narrow road. Looking in the rearview mirror she slowed down even more.

"Hey Diane, don't turn around, guess who's behind us?"

"Don't make me guess, just tell me."

"It's Wendell and he's right on our bumper."

"What's his hurry? Can't he see it's raining?"

"I guess not. I think I'll slow down even more."

"Claire, are you trying to antagonize him?"

"Ya know, Diane, I believe I am," she smirked.

"Claire, you're acting like a teenager. For heaven's

sake, let's not make things worse."

Claire continued at the slow pace. "Diane, think about it. If I annoy him enough he might come after me and then we would have something to go to the police with."

"Yeah... or to the funeral director. In this rain, on this narrow road, you could get us killed."

"We're almost to the cottage. He's just going to have to wait." Claire calmly drove the short distance to Windward Cottage and turned into the driveway.

Ike ran to the car and jumped up on Claire. "Down boy. It's okay. We're home."

Jill and Caroline were waiting for them in the parlor. "What took you so long? You were behind us one minute and gone the next."

Claire went to the kitchen for a towel to dry Ike.

Diane collapsed her umbrella and dropped it in the stand beside the door. "Claire decided to try and get us killed."

"What are you talking about," Caroline asked.

As Claire dried Ike, Diane repeated the conversation they had in the car while Wendell followed them.

Jill plopped down on the closest chair. "Maybe that's not such a bad idea, but Claire, you're not his type. He likes defenseless, little girls."

"I know but, maybe, with enough pressure he'll crack."

Caroline grew impatient with the conversation. "This is crazy. Forget it. If we can compile information for the authorities, that's where this ends."

Diane moved to the fireplace and knelt down. "It's chilly in here. I think I'll beat our mysterious visitor to the fire tonight. Can someone find me some newspaper?" Just as the fire caught Diane's phone rang. "Oh geez, someone please grab that until I get up. Darn arthritis!"

Jill reached into Diane's bag and pulled out the phone. "It's Ed. Maybe he has some information for us."

"Hello," Diane said, taking the phone from Jill. "Hi. I'm good and you? You did? Great... Let me get a pencil and paper. Go on... Yes... Really? Interesting. Thank you so much, we really appreciate it... I'll explain everything later... No, I won't be home on Saturday after all. We've decided to stay another week. Yes, I'll keep you posted." Diane turned her back on her friends and talked a little longer in a quiet voice. "Goodnight, Ed."

"Hmmm... what was that all about Diane," Jill asked, with a wink.

Diane blushed. "I told him I wanted to have a long talk with him when I get home."

"Very good, Diane," Caroline said, giving her the thumbs up sign.

Diane ignored her and turned to Claire and Jill. "Ed did the check on Wendell."

"And...," Claire asked, anxiously.

"First of all, his first name isn't Wendell, it's Lloyd. He's Lloyd Wendell, Jr."

"He's a junior? Hmmm... from the age of the truck in the photo, his father must have been in the plumbing business first and then passed it to him," Claire thought, out loud.

Diane pressed on. "His mother left the area when Wendell was only six. She was never heard from again."

"Probably knocked her off too," Jill interrupted.

Diane gave Jill "the look" and continued. "Here's the really interesting thing. Wendell, I'm so used to calling him that I can't change now...is a few years younger than us, which means he would have been very young when Betsy disappeared. Do you believe a young boy could have gotten away with that and carried out all the other abductions?"

"No," Claire said. "But his dad could have." After several seconds she added, "You know, the apple doesn't fall far from the tree...."

"Oh my God," Caroline said, with a giggle. "Is pedophilia hereditary?"

"Caroline, this is no time to joke," Diane said. "If a child is raised in that kind of environment he would have a hard time knowing right from wrong."

"You're not making excuses for him are you Diane?" Jill asked.

"Certainly not. Just thinking out loud. What a horrible thing to do to your own son, not to mention those poor girls."

"Anything else?"

"Nope. Not even a parking ticket."

Jill spoke up. "Do you think Mrs. Wendell knew what was going on and that's why she left? I wonder if she's still alive."

"Two good questions, Jill," Diane said.

Caroline stood and stretched. "Is anyone getting hungry?"

"How about a good, old spaghetti dinner," Jill offered. "I got some great, Italian bread at the bakery and homemade meatballs at the deli. I think we have everything else we need, right Claire?"

"Yes, there's pasta and sauce in the cupboard."

"I'll make a salad," Caroline volunteered.

"And, I'll drink the wine," Diane said, with a grin.

Claire placed another log on the fire and followed the others into the kitchen.

Just as they were about to eat Jill's phone rang. She took the call in the parlor and then returned to the kitchen with a dejected look.

"Anything wrong, Jill?" Caroline asked, placing the freshly, sliced bread in the middle of the table.

"No. Not really. Drew isn't coming back until Sunday. Something came up and he has to stay in Boston longer than expected. He was calling to ask us to make arrangements for Ike at a kennel, but I told him we're staying another week and that we'd be happy to keep Ike." Looking around the room she added, "Was that okay?"

Claire, Diane, and Caroline all agreed it was fine. "Frankly," Claire added. "I'm really going to miss Ike when he goes home." Reaching down she slipped the dog a meatball under the table.

After the meal was finished, and the kitchen clean, the women returned to parlor.

"How about some poker?" Jill suggested.

The chips were divided, the cards dealt, and they put on their best, poker faces. Old stories of past vacations and college days filled the air, and thoughts of anything else receded into the dark corners of the old house.

"Now this is what vacations are supposed to be like," Caroline said, laughing at one of Jill's stories.

"Look at the time," Diane said. "It's nearly midnight. I'm beat. How about you all?"

Claire started stacking chips and Caroline returned the cards to their box.

"It's been a long day. Let's head upstairs. I just need to let Ike out one more time," Claire said, getting up from the table. "Come Ike."

Diane followed Claire to the kitchen to wait for Ike while Jill and Caroline locked all the doors and windows, and extinguished the fire. None of the women saw the patrol car drive slowly past the house.

Reaching the third floor Claire tried the door to Betsy's room. It was unlocked so she opened the door and whispered, "It's okay Betsy. We'll get him."

Chapter Nine
Week Two
Friday

Claire

Ike woke Claire with sloppy kisses on her hand dangling over the side of the bed.

"Ah, Ike, I was going to sleep in today," Claire whispered.

Very quietly, Claire slid from under the blankets and grabbed her clothes. Ike followed silently to the kitchen where Claire dressed. "Come on boy, let's make our getaway." Closing the back door softly, woman and dog bounded down the steps to the beach. Claire found a sturdy stick and threw it as far as she could down the beach.

It was a clear, crisp morning with a warm, yellow sun already burning off the mist. The air smelled fresh and clean from the previous day's rain, and the beach was littered with shells from the raging surf the day before.

Claire threw the stick into the water farther down the beach toward Drew's cottage. Ike ignored the stick. Instead, he ran over the dunes to the cottage and barked at the back door. When the door didn't open, he ran to the driveway and sniffed.

"Come Ike," Claire called, standing at the water's edge.

Ike raced back over the dunes to Claire and whimpered. Reaching down she patted him. "He'll be back soon. Don't worry, he would never leave you, especially with me."

Ike cocked his head and looked at her with his big innocent brown eyes as if to say, why not?

"That was supposed to be a joke, Ike. Where's your sense of humor?"

Ike found a new stick and they continued to play

fetch until they were in front of Wendell's. Claire turned and looked at the dilapidated house. Calling Ike out of the ocean she walked to the top of a dune directly in front of the house. Sitting down, she crossed her legs yoga fashion and told Ike to sit beside her. Anyone watching would have thought she was meditating. In reality, her body was positioned so that all she had to do was shift her eyes to the right without moving her head and she had a perfect view of the cottage.

"I know you can see me, Wendell. Are you up? Are you watching on your coward's cameras from your sick little room?" Claire said, softly as she scratched Ike's head. "What are you going to do about it? Do you have the guts to come out here and confront me, or am I too big for you? Maybe it's time you picked on someone your own size?"

Claire closed her eyes and enjoyed the warm sun on her face at the same time ignoring the wet sand soaking through her jeans. Still, she sat, and thought. *This is only the beginning Wendell. I'm going to find a way to break you.*

Ike, tired of sitting, lowered himself down beside Claire and chewed the stick tucked between his paws.

Spence would not be happy with me. Or would he? He would never tolerate this injustice. I wish he were here. I have to know how this evil man got away with this. I have to know what really happened to Betsy and the other children.

Claire and Ike sat on the dune for an hour. Ike chewed while Claire prayed for guidance and the strength to carry out her mission. She prayed for the lost souls whose pictures were the proof of a decayed brain. She prayed for the sorrow in the hearts of their families. "Vengeance is mine, sayeth the Lord. Could his vengeance be mine too?" Claire said, out loud.

Finally, she stood, turned, and waved at Wendell's house and then started back the way they had come. Just past Drew's cottage she looked up at the roof of Windward Cottage. There was a woman on the roof. It was broad daylight now and no darkness to distort what she saw. There was definitely someone there.

***

Caroline

"I'm going to paint a sunrise," Caroline said, with a nod to her reflection in the mirror.

Gathering her painting supplies, easel, and a new canvas she started up the steps to the roof. Her foot hit something on the first step and she put down the easel to see what it was.

"A pair of binoculars? Who found these? This is great, I'll be able to zoom in for detail."

Continuing up the steps, with her lazy man's load, she opened the door to magnificent sunshine.

Oh how different everything looks when you're happy she thought. Everything about the morning captivated her. She breathed in deeply and then went about setting up her work area. Picking up the binoculars she adjusted them to the clearest setting and scanned the beach and ocean. The feeling of that day in her bedroom when the scene in the window turned into a masterpiece came back to her. She felt like she was in a seascape painted by one of the great masters.

"There can't be anything closer to heaven than this," she said, aloud. "Is this one of the thin places Claire was talking about? Someday, I'll share this with my boys and their families. I'll paint their children playing on the beach and jumping the waves. And, I'll paint Bill with a sinister mustache and beady, little eyes... the sniveling wimp." Laughing, she pointed the binoculars down the beach. There was a woman and dog playing on the beach. Adjusting the binoculars she zoomed in. "Claire! What are you doing? For heaven's sake get back here," she called, but Claire was too far away to hear her.

Caroline set up her easel facing in Claire's direction. She would paint and keep an eye on Claire at the same time.

As she painted Caroline prayed. "Please God, keep her safe. Guide her in her quest and give her peace." Over and over she repeated her simple prayer. Each brush stroke seemed foreign. It didn't feel like her hand doing the work. There was a calming strength controlling her movements. Each time she picked up the binoculars, to make sure Claire was still in sight, when she looked back at the painting it was more beautiful than she had thought. *Was she really capable of this kind of work?* Finally, she saw Claire and Ike close to the house, she cleaned her brushes and put her paints away. Glancing back at the painting, before carrying it downstairs, she sucked in her breath sharply. There was a little girl, alone on the beach, building a sandcastle. Caroline could not remember painting the child. The hues of the colors and proportion were perfect in every aspect of the painting; the light from the sun, the shadows on the dunes, the depth of the blue water, the blond hair and rosy cheeks of the little girl.

This truly is a gift, Caroline thought, silently. *I promise not to waste it.*

***

Jill

Jill slowly opened her eyes and turned toward the other single bed. Empty.

"Darn her! I bet she took Ike by herself!"

She looked around the third floor. No Claire. On the second floor, she found Caroline's room empty and Diane's door still closed. The first floor was empty and surveying the beach from the back porch revealed no Claire, no Caroline, and no Ike. All four cars were still in the driveway.

I hope they're together. Probably just took Ike for walk Jill thought, putting her hand to her chest feeling her heart pounding.

Cooking always calmed her so she started the coffeemaker and went about making breakfast.

"If she's okay, I'm going to kill her," she said, out loud. "We made an agreement and she has no business going out alone; unless, she's with Caroline." Addressing herself she added, "Jill, calm down. Give her a break. You don't know whether she's alone or not."

As she worked, she thought about Drew. She really did miss him. *How can you miss someone you've known for less than a week? This is silly. This is the first man who has really interested me since I left Ray. Ah, heck... Drew is a rebound.*

But, is there a statute of limitations on rebounds? It's been over twenty years since I left Ray, surely that's too long for a rebound she thought, puckering her lips and cocking her head.

Trying to think about something else she forced her brain to move on to a real concern. Carrie. *What if Carrie does move away? What will I do? I can't leave my job after all this time and retirement is still ten years away. I love my little house. I don't want to move. Carrie doesn't need me anymore...I have to face that fact.* A single tear rolled down her cheek. *My baby doesn't need me anymore. I have to let her go. She has to live her own life.*

Wiping the tears away with a paper towel she forced her mind away from the painful thought and back to Drew. *Could Claire be right about Drew? Maybe I am rushing into something. Oh, but I do like him.*

We'll just take our time. There's no hurry. If he wants to see me after we leave here then that's good. If not, well if not, I'll enter a convent. That's it. A convent. Perfect. I bet they'd let me cook there she thought, setting her chin with conviction.

***
Diane

The hot water felt good streaming down Diane's body. She lathered her hair and savored the almond scent of the shampoo.

That was about the first good night's sleep I've had since we got here she thought, rinsing the bubbles out of her hair. *One could hardly call this a vacation. It seems like we've been in a state of turmoil ever since we arrived. What is it about this house? It's been controlling us ever since we arrived.*

Stepping over the side of the tub she grabbed a towel. *Gotta love this hair. No fuss. No muss* she thought, roughly towel drying her short hair.

Back in her room she sat on the side of the bed and thought about their situation. *What exactly are we doing here? We need our heads examined trying to go after a serial killer. We don't have the knowledge for this or the youth for that matter.*

Looking out the window, the house's power gripped her and the ocean waves hypnotized her. She couldn't pull her eyes away. *What if it were Deidra... or one of my friends' daughters? What if someone got this close to the answer and didn't follow through? What if...*

The beautiful day beckoned her but she couldn't move. She kept staring out the window. *Claire's right. We have to follow this as far as we can. We have Ed to help us.* Thinking of Ed she smiled. All the times he had been there when she needed him. He was her best friend. She shared everything with him; her concern for her children, the details of her business, her fear of losing her parents, even the times when she just needed to vent, Ed was there.

Diane slapped herself alongside the head. *What the hell is wrong with me? I've loved that man for years and never knew it. He deserves better.* Picking up her cell she punched speed dial. A sleepy, male voice answered.

"Hello."

"I love you, Ed. I'm sorry I've been so stupid. Will you wait for me?"

"I sure hope this is you, Diane, otherwise some wonderful, sounding woman has the wrong number."

She cried and laughed at the same time before hanging up.

***

Claire and Ike entered the delicious, smelling kitchen and were greeted by Jill's wrath. "Claire McPherson, where have you been, and why did you go out by yourself. You know the rules. You're lucky to be alive. I should kill you right now!"

Ike scurried under the kitchen table with his tail between his legs.

Claire froze, her eyes the size of dinner plates.

Jill was waving a spatula and had something yellow at the corner of her mouth.

"If you're so mad, why are you making me breakfast?"

Waving the spatula back and forth in the air Jill ranted. "Oh, this isn't for you missy. This is only for those of us who know how to obey the rules!"

Claire wanted to laugh but she knew it would make Jill madder. "Sorry. You're right."

"Jill," Claire said, meekly lowering her head. "You have something on your lip…."

"Oh damn, Claire. Can't you be serious," Jill said, running her tongue around her mouth. "It's Hollandaise sauce for Eggs Benedict and you don't get any."

"Rethink that Jill. If you really want to kill me, your vein clogging, heart stopping Eggs Benedict might just do the trick…but they are soooo worth it!"

Jill laughed and hugged her friend. "I'm just relieved you're okay. Please, don't do that again."

Claire was setting the table as Caroline and Diane walked into the kitchen.

"What is that wonderful smell," Caroline asked.

"I made us a special breakfast this morning," Jill answered. "Eggs Benedict and champagne mimosas to celebrate another week here."

Diane looked dubious. "We're celebrating walking into danger?"

"What was the name of that movie, Eyes Wide Shut?" Caroline asked. "Don't remember what it was about, but the title fits us."

Jill's breakfast was so good vocals were limited to "oohs" and "ahs." Finally, raising her mimosa, Claire said, "Here's to solving this mystery quickly and good weather for the remainder of our vacation."

Four glasses clinked in the center of the table and the women dove back into the tender poached eggs and Canadian bacon on English muffins smothered in Hollandaise sauce.

***

Caroline opened the front door to a young man in a blue and white uniform.

"Special delivery for Diane Fuller."

Hearing her name, Diane approached the front door and signed for the package. As she and Caroline both watched, Wendell drove past the house. The courier's car was parked at the side of the road with Express Courier Service printed on the door.

Tipping the young man and closing the door Diane said to Caroline, "I'd be surprised if Wendell didn't notice the courier's car. He's probably figured out what we're up to."

"I hope he has, and I hope he's scared," Caroline replied, coldly.

Claire and Jill joined them in the dining room where they spread the papers from the courier's package on the table. Diane divided the information into four separate piles. When she came to the pictures of the girls she hesitated and looked at Claire.

"It's okay," Claire said. "I have to see them sooner or later."

Jill disappeared into the kitchen where they could hear her rummaging through drawers. Returning to the dining room she started taping the pictures up on the dining room wall. Pens and paper were distributed and the women took seats around the table and started to read. One-by-one, they matched the pictures on the wall to the newspaper articles.

"Claire," Jill said, looking up from her work. "Do you realize that Betsy did not disappear from here?"

Claire looked at Jill strangely. "What do you mean?"

"The articles I'm reading, from the Bedford Gazette, say she disappeared from her hometown of New Bedford. Where were the articles in the scrapbook from?"

"I don't know. They were just clippings. The newspaper names weren't there. I just assumed, because the scrapbook was here, that the articles were from the local newspaper."

"That would explain why we didn't find anything at the newspaper office," Jill added.

Diane laid down her pen. "That might also explain why no one suspected Wendell. There was no reason to think anyone in Haworth, or The Point, had anything to do with it. They may not even have known about the abduction."

The women continued to work and, one-by-one, the pictures were removed from the wall and paper clipped to newspaper articles. Within a few hours they had fifty-three perfect matches of articles with pictures of missing girls.

"Do you think he killed the girls near their homes and kept the pictures as trophies?" Claire asked, stretching her arms over her head, and looking around the table.

"Not one body was ever recovered," Caroline pointed out.

Without warning Diane got up. "I'll be right back." They heard the front door slam and within minutes she was back with a large road map of the Eastern United States that she taped to the wall where the girls' pictures had been. Picking up her stack of articles she read each one again and with a red pen made small circles on the map.

"Look at your articles and mark the areas your victims were from on the map," she said, to the others. When they had finished Diane pulled out the picture of the map in Wendell's basement. Comparing the pins on Wendell's map to the red circles they had made, she turned and said, "They match. He marked the places where he abducted the girls."

"Does anyone see a pattern?" Diane asked, stepping back from the map.

"Not one abduction from Cape Cod. They're all on the east coast between Maine and South Carolina, and not one town is farther than twenty miles from the coast," Jill volunteered, feeling like she had just correctly answered a junior high quiz.

Caroline picked up a ruler and a red marker and drew a line from each circle to Haworth.

"It's a giant spider with dozens of legs," Jill said.

Diane started to trace each red line with her finger. "Look at this... the most direct way to get to Haworth or The Point, from any of the circled areas, is by sea."

"I'd say it's time to have lunch at Blackbeard's again," Claire said, pushing her chair back and getting up from the table.

Jill looked at her curiously. "Why do you say that?"

"Boats. I think Brittany probably knows who owns boats in Haworth."

"Let's take our bikes. We need the exercise if we're

going to eat again," Diane remarked.

Caroline left the dining room and returned with the backpack she had bought the day before, in Haworth, for her painting supplies. She removed the map from the wall and folded it carefully.

"What are you doing?" Jill asked.

"We can't leave any of this information out of our sight."

"She's right," Claire agreed, gathering up the pictures and articles and handing them to Caroline. "I'll let Ike out to take care of things while you unlock the bikes."

***

The four women on bikes looked like any group of visitors enjoying a beautiful day on Cape Cod. Their first stop was the bike rental to let them know they would be keeping the bikes for another week. From there they stopped to buy a local newspaper, out of a machine, in front of a small, grocery store. Slowly continuing down the street toward Blackbeard's, Diane who was in the lead, stretched out her arm and pointed to the police car parked in front of the real estate office that handled Windward Cottage. Anyone seeing her would have thought she was signaling to turn the corner toward Blackbeard's Tavern. At the pub, they locked the bicycles in the bike rack on the sidewalk.

Unbuckling her helmet, Claire walked closer to Diane. "What do you think Peterson was doing at the real estate office?"

"I don't know."

"Don't you find it odd that's the second time we saw him at one of the places Jill and Caroline had been."

Diane looked puzzled. "Why would he care about what we do?"

Jill and Caroline gathered around to listen.

"Maybe he makes it a habit to check in on the local businesses," Jill suggested.

"Maybe he just doesn't have anything better to do,"

Claire interrupted.

At the entrance to the dining room they were greeted by Brittany. "Hi. Nice to see you again. Would you prefer inside or outside?"

"Inside is fine," Claire answered.

Brittany showed them to a window table that overlooked a brick-lined courtyard with umbrella tables and giant clay pots overflowing with ivy and white geraniums.

"Very nice. Thank you, Brittany. Will you be our server today?" Diane asked.

"Sure will. Glad you wanted to stay inside because I'm not working the patio today. What can I get you to drink?"

"Iced tea?" Diane asked, looking at the others. They nodded and Diane confirmed. "Four iced teas, please."

When Brittany returned with the drinks, Claire inquired, "So, I imagine a lot of people around here own boats?"

"Most of the business owners do," Brittany replied. "Even my boss has a boat."

"Really? I guess they do a lot of fishing," Claire asked, with feigned curiosity.

"Oh yeah... you know men. Gotta either be on a boat or a golf course. My dad says boats are just big holes in the water you pour money into. But then, that's probably because he can't afford a boat. They're really expensive."

"Do you know anyone who takes women out fishing?" Diane piped in.

"Not personally, but if you're interested just go on down to the docks and ask around."

"Do you ever go out on boats Brittany?" Jill asked, with sincere concern.

"Not me. I get seasick. I do like to look at the names though, I think they're funny. Like my boss's boat is called Tippy Canoe. Isn't that cute?"

This gave Diane the perfect opportunity to ask more questions without being obvious. "What do some of the other owners call their boats?"

"Hmmm... well, there's True Love, Weekend Warrior, Spirit of the Sea and, of course, a lot of women's names. I think men name boats for their wives. There's a really big boat that I think is owned by a couple different men... Chief Peterson and Mr. Edwards from the newspaper, and some others. Their boat is called Swift Runner. Now that doesn't seem like a very good name for a boat does it? I mean boats don't run, they sail or float. I don't get that one."

Diane smiled and winked at her friends. "I think we're ready to order, Brittany."

As soon as Brittany had left the table Diane spoke. "I wonder if Wendell owns a boat.

"I think we need to take a walk on the docks, just like Brittany suggested and maybe even charter a boat," Claire said.

Caroline looked alarmed. "Claire, I really think that's pushing it... chartering a boat, I mean. We can take a look at the boats, but I don't think we should go out on one. If Wendell did have the cameras turned on, he knows you've been at his house and if he knows you were there, then he knows we know...oh crap, how many times did I say 'know'...anyway you know what I meant. It's too dangerous."

Claire took a long drink of iced tea and turned to Diane. "Is boat registration public record?"

"I don't know, but Ed will," Diane said, shrugging her shoulders. Looking around, to make sure no one was close enough to hear her conversation, she pulled her phone from the pocket of her jeans and called Ed. "He'll check it out," she said, returning her phone to her pocket. "He's curious about what we're up to. I won't be able to keep this from him much longer."

"I don't think you should," Jill said. "This is getting serious."

Brittany returned with their meals.

"Oh, hey, forgot to tell you. Chief Peterson was in yesterday, after you left, asking about you. Did one of you get a parking ticket or something?"

The four women looked at each other with raised eyebrows.

"No," Claire said. "We met him at the bakery one morning. He was probably just being friendly." Then just to make it interesting she added, nodding to Diane, "I think he kind of likes my friend here."

"You ladies be careful. He has a real reputation with women."

"But I thought you said he was married to the librarian?" Caroline asserted.

"Well now, you know there's married... and then there's married," Brittany replied, with an exaggerated wink before turning back toward the kitchen.

"Holy moly, that's the best over-tipping we ever did," Jill said. "She's a walking encyclopedia."

"Indeed," Claire concurred, biting into her BLT.

When Brittany returned to retrieve the check, Diane handed it to her with another big tip. "No change Brittany." Leaning close to Brittany's ear she whispered, "Just between us girls, if Chief Peterson comes in, you don't need to mention our conversation. I'd be embarrassed, if you know what I mean?"

"Oh sure," Brittany agreed, bobbing her head. "I know exactly what you mean. These lips are sealed," she promised, imitating locking her lips with an invisible key.

***

Back at Windward Cottage, the women changed into bathing suits and took Ike and Caroline's backpack down to the beach.

"Let's go over these articles again," Claire said.

"There has to be something to tie the girls together."

One by one, they reviewed the articles and compared they're previous notes.

Diane shook her head. "Nothing, there's nothing similar. The girls were between the ages of eight and sixteen, different sizes, shapes, hair color… nothing to indicate a certain type was targeted. The only similarity is they were never found."

"Wait," Jill said. "There is one thing, they all disappeared after dark when their families thought they were with friends. The disappearances were never discovered until the following day. That's plenty of time to get from any of the abduction sites to Haworth by boat."

Caroline unfolded the map and calculated the distance with the scale. "She's right. Until they got around to reporting them missing, and investigating outside their immediate areas, the girls could have been here."

Claire reached out her hand. "Let me see all the pictures."

Reluctantly, they handed them over. Claire scrutinized each picture and then handed them to the others. "Don't look at the girls. Look at the backgrounds."

A few minutes passed and Diane said, "Stone. The pictures are dark. The backdrops all look like stone walls. Claire, is this the stone wall we saw in Wendell's basement?"

"I can't be sure because the pictures are so dark, but I think the stone is the same in all the photos which would mean the girls were all taken to the same place."

***

Showered and dressed in comfy sweatpants and shirts, the women took up residence in their favorite rockers on the front porch. Each woman rocked at a pace consistent with her personality. Caroline had her eyes closed and rocked only every now and then dreaming of beautiful paintings. Claire rocked steady and fast, like her brain moved, always contemplating her next move. Diane was slow and steady, with purpose, as she was in business. Jill's rocking was erratic like her fun loving personality. Ike paced around the porch doing his sniffing act before settling down beside Claire's chair.

Claire finally broke the silence. "Anyone getting hungry?"

"I am," Caroline answered. "I saw a pizza place in town. Why don't we order for delivery, and have pizza and beer on the roof?"

Jill gaped at Caroline, "Beer? You drink beer?"

"Of course I do Jill," Caroline laughed, pushing her glasses up on her nose. "This is the new me remember. I'm actually hoping I never have to attend another country club function, or business dinner, again. I like this new life."

Diane stopped rocking. "So do we Caroline, you've come a long way."

***

On the roof, with cold beer and hot pizza, the foursome sat cross-legged around the open pizza box.

"This is great," Claire said. "We really need to do this more often."

Jill stopped chewing and said with sarcasm, "Do what? Try to get ourselves killed?"

"Oh, come on Jill, it's not that bad."

"Not yet," Caroline said. "But I have to admit I'm nervous. Wendell may be planning something bad."

"Let's just see if we can make a boat connection and, if we do, we'll turn everything over to the state police," Claire pleaded. "We're so close."

Diane pulled her phone from her pocket. "No messages from Ed. He must not have found anything yet. I agree with Caroline, this is getting too close for comfort. We make this connection and then we're done."

"You're right," Claire agreed, reluctantly. "I think we were brought here for a reason and we've done the best we can. This may be enough to convict Wendell."

Jill fanned a hot flash with a paper plate. "That's the best news I've had in days. I want to be done with this so I can concentrate on Drew."

"And, I want to concentrate on painting," Caroline said.

"I just want to concentrate on staying alive long enough to see Ed again," Diane added.

Claire stalled for time. "I want to know Betsy's at peace."

Jill threw the paper plate at Claire. "Oh, Claire, why do you always have to be so deep? Couldn't you just say something like, 'oh I don't know, like maybe you want a million dollars or something?'"

"That would be nice. I'll go with that," Claire said, laughing as she caught the plate before it blew off the roof.

Chapter Ten
Saturday

"Has anyone noticed?" Claire asked, at breakfast.

Jill turned around from the stove. "Noticed what?"

"Ike's been calmer and there have been no mysterious fires in the fireplace."

Diane sat down her coffee mug. "You're right. Why do you suppose that is?"

"I don't know, but I would like to spend some time in the house alone," Claire answered.

Jill slammed a spatula down on the counter. "That… is not going to happen! Two-by-two, remember? We are not taking any chances until Wendell is locked up."

"She's right Claire," Caroline added. "Safety first."

"You know, the lighthouse will be open for tours today. Let's take a lunch and ride out there again. I'd really like to see the view from the top." Diane said, changing the subject.

"Me too," Jill said.

Claire set her coffee mug down and played with the plastic daisies in the center of the table. "On one condition."

"And, what might that be?" Caroline eyed her.

"That tonight we have dinner at the restaurant overlooking the docks, just in case Wendell makes an appearance."

Diane swallowed a mouthful of food and asked, "Why would he do that?"

"To go night fishing," Claire replied, with a sinister look.

Jill, Diane, and Caroline looked at each other and nodded. "Okay, but this is it and then we're done sleuthing," Jill said.

Claire agreed and they finished their breakfasts.

"I wish we could take Ike," Claire said, pulling her

ponytail through the hole at the back of her ball cap and slathering sunscreen on her arms and legs.

"Me too," Jill answered. "But I think it's be too far for him. Besides, isn't it better that he stay here and guard the house?"

"Yes, of course."

Diane walked down the front steps of Windward Cottage with the bike map in her hands. "Why don't we take a different road to the lighthouse? Look here. There's a road that goes around the other side of the peninsula along the coast. It might be a little easier peddling."

Claire looked at the map. "You're right, Diane. Let's do that."

Jill secured the lunch in the basket on her handlebars. Diane tied the insulated bag with drinks in her basket. Caroline slipped her backpack with the research material over her shoulders. Claire put the bike map, a beach blanket, and sunscreen into her basket and they set off.

The good weather brought more traffic to the Cape for the weekend. People were walking on the beach or sitting on porches of the houses they passed. Pedaling was easier on this road and Claire felt herself relax into a steady cadence. Snatching glimpses of the ocean as she rode, she saw the ever-present seagulls trying to charm beachgoers out of their lunches. In the distance, black and yellow, wet-suited surfers straddling their surfboards bobbed up and down on the swells waiting for the perfect wave. The four bikers entered the lighthouse, parking area on the opposite side from their first visit and locked their bikes. A Boy Scout Troop was picking up litter while visitors snapped pictures of the lighthouse.

"Let's take the lighthouse tour," Jill said. "It looks like it's open today."

Diane tilted her head back and shaded her eyes with her hand looking up at the stately structure. "Wow! That's high. I bet the view is spectacular."

A Coast Guard Cadet greeted them at the door. "Welcome, ladies. You're just in time to join us." There were two young couples standing just inside the door. Once Jill, Caroline, Diane, and Claire entered, the cadet closed the door and started his speech. The diameter of the room they were standing in was not very large and the spiral staircase leading up to the light took up most of the space. The cadet explained the lighthouse had been built in the 1880s and originally had been manned by a lighthouse keeper and his family. Over the years, it became the property of the U.S. Coast Guard and, in the 1950s, the light was automated and there was no longer a need for a lighthouse keeper. As he slowly climbed the staircase, the cadet explained the old versus the new operation of lighthouses and the intricacies of the Fresnel lens that rotated at the top, forewarning ships of the dangers along the coastline.

Halfway up the stairs, the women were more interested in getting to see the view than the history of the lighthouse. The one thing they did hear was that there were two hundred twenty-three steps to the top. Jill audibly groaned when Caroline announced they only had ninety-seven more steps to go. Motioning the rest of the group ahead, the foursome took a break hanging onto the thin steel railing and second guessing their decision to climb to the top.

"This is far enough for me. You three go ahead. I'll sit here and wait for you," Jill wheezed.

"What did we tell you about those cigarettes," Diane laughed.

"I don't smoke and you know it Diane. You go on up. You can tell me about the view later."

Claire pushed Jill gently from behind. "You can do it. Just take your time. It'll be worth it."

Breathless, they stepped out onto the catwalk that

encircled the light. Gazing in all directions Jill exclaimed, "Holy mackerel. It was worth it! This is magnificent."

Jill jumped at the voice of the cadet behind her. "Take your time ladies. When everyone's ready, we'll descend together."

Jill batted her eye lashes trying to look young and flirty. "You will carry me down right?"

The cadet laughed and moved to answer a question from one of the young men.

Caroline removed her backpack, retrieved the binoculars, and was looking at the view when Claire asked, "Where did you get those?"

"I found them on the steps to the roof the other morning." Handing them to Claire she added, "Here, have a look."

Claire took the binoculars but gave Caroline a puzzled look. "Caroline, they were not there any of the other times we went up those stairs."

"I thought one of you set them there." Looking at the others they all shook their heads no.

Caroline stared at the others and nonchalantly shrugged. "Our guest must have left them."

Claire put the binoculars to her eyes and slowly scanned 360 degrees around the lighthouse. "This really is incredible." Looking toward the beach she zeroed in on the surfers. "I believe that's Deputy O'Reilly out there surfing," she commented. Then lowering the glasses to the beach road below, she followed it around the base of the lighthouse and down the opposite side of the point. She didn't move for quite a while and then handed the glasses to Diane and pointed. "Look at the rocks over there."

Diane did as directed and handed the glasses to Caroline to do the same thing. In turn, Caroline handed them to Jill.

"They look like the rocks in the picture in the scrapbook, don't they?" Caroline asked.

"I think they might be," Claire answered. "I'm going down there. Who wants to come?"

Jill rolled her eyes skyward. "I don't suppose we really have a choice do we?"

"Sure you do, as long as someone else wants to stay with you," Claire replied, already heading for the stairs.

Caroline took the binoculars from Jill and returned them to the backpack. "Come on Jill, we'll take our time." By the time Jill and Caroline reached the bottom of the lighthouse, Claire and Diane had the bikes unlocked and were seated waiting for them. "We're going to try to get down to the beach where the rocks are. You can meet us down there," Claire said, over her shoulder as she pushed off.

Claire and Diane followed the narrow road downhill for about a half a mile. The rocks they had seen from the lighthouse came into view, below them, along the shoreline. They slowed their speed looking for a path down to the beach. There was a pull-off but no discernable path.

"Looks like the only access to the rocks is from the beach," Diane said.

"I think you're right. It's a steep grade, but I think we can walk down without too much trouble."

Jill and Caroline pulled up beside them. Claire explained the plan and asked, "Are you game?"

Jill was hesitant but Caroline jumped right in. "Sure. Let's take our lunch down there and eat. We can lock the bikes to each other here."

Carrying their things, they carefully picked their way through the brambles and Rugosa roses.

"Ouch!" Diane yelled. "Do you see the size of the thorns on these rose bushes? Who would have ever planted roses out here?"

Claire giggled. "No one. They're wild and about the only thing that will bloom this close to the ocean." She barely finished her sentence when Jill suddenly was rolling past her down the hill.

All they could do was watch her go. Jill finally stopped spread eagle on the sand. Racing toward her the others bent down to see if she was okay.

"Are you hurt?" Claire asked.

"Who the hell's idea was this," Jill whispered. "I can hardly breathe. There's something in the middle of my back."

Carefully, Caroline rolled Jill onto her side and pulled a rock out from under her. "Oh my, that's going to bruise for sure."

Diane helped Caroline inspect the rest of Jill's body. "You'll live. Sit up and we'll get you something to drink."

Jill obeyed. "You owe me big time for this," she said, looking up at Claire.

"I'm sorry, Jill. You're right, I'll buy you lunch or a beer or something," Claire replied, trying to look serious.

"Are you laughing at me?" Jill asked, wide-eyed.

The others looked at each other and covered their mouths with their hands.

"Well," Caroline said. "You did look pretty funny. You know how it is when someone falls, it's just a natural reflex to laugh."

"Just get me something to drink will you?"

Diane handed her a bottle of water and Caroline unpacked the lunch. Claire had walked to the water's edge and was inspecting the rocks. The beach was in a sheltered cove. The rocks started fairly small but became larger as they followed the shoreline toward the lighthouse. This would be the beginning of the outcropping of rocks they had seen below the lighthouse. The lighthouse stood high above them in the distance. When Claire walked closer to the rocks, she could not see the lighthouse, which would mean nobody at the lighthouse, could see anyone standing this close to the rocks. Walking back to the water's edge she waded in up to her knees.

Jill watched her apprehensively. "What is she doing?"

"I'll go find out," Diane said, standing and walking toward Claire.

By now Claire was up to her thighs in the water.

"Claire," Diane called. "What are you doing?"

Claire motioned for Diane to join her.

"Are you kidding? The water's freezing."

"Oh, come on. It's important."

Diane took off her shoes and socks and waded out to her friend. "What is so important that we will either be swept out to sea or catch pneumonia?"

The waves hitting the women made them fight to stay on their feet. Claire was intent on studying the beach and the road above it.

"Look Diane," she said, pointing above Jill and Caroline sitting on the beach blanket. "Doesn't that look like the spot where the truck might have been parked in the picture in the scrapbook?"

"Possibly," Diane admitted. "But that was so long ago. Things change."

"Yes, of course, but that road has been here probably as long as the lighthouse."

"Okay, so can we go back now?" Diane asked, feeling her legs go numb from the cold water.

Claire slowly moved her gaze from the road to the beach and then to the rocks to her left. "Yeah, we can go back."

Diane started back toward the beach. Thinking Claire was still behind her Diane continued to the blanket and sat down. "Did anyone bring a towel?"

"What is she up to now?" Jill asked, before anyone could answer. She pointed to Claire climbing over the rocks.

"Oh, for crying out loud." Exasperated, Diane got to

her feet and went after Claire who had disappeared behind the rocks.

"Claire! Where are you?" Diane yelled, approaching the rocks.

There was no answer.

Diane found footholds and places to grip the rocks and started climbing. When she reached the top of a large rock, she could look down into a narrow space between the rocks. Claire was standing in waist deep water.

"Diane, I think there's a cave."

"Claire, come back here right now. This is dangerous."

Either Claire did not hear her or she ignored her because she walked between the rocks and disappeared.

"Claire. Stop! Come back," Diane yelled, but there was no answer. "Oh damn, now I have to come after you," she muttered, as she crawled down the other side of the rocks. Finally, she stepped into the water and looked for Claire. Fighting the waves, and the shifting sand under her feet, she walked into the opening where Claire had disappeared. The water was now chest deep and she was freezing. "Claire, where are you?"

"I'm in here, Diane. Keep walking. It gets shallow."

Diane half walked and half swam until she could feel solid ground under her feet.

Moving around a huge boulder she saw Claire standing at the mouth of a cave.

Weighed down by her wet clothes, Diane slowly made her way to Claire. "You are nuts. I swear you're certifiable."

"Diane look what we found." Pulling Diane by the arm she guided her into a cave as the waves lapped at their ankles.

"Did you know this was here?" Diane asked.

"No. If we had found this as kids, I'm sure I would have remembered."

Windward Secrets

The opening was at least twenty feet tall allowing enough sunlight in to see where they were going. The ground raised out of the water and they no longer had to fight the waves. The cave widened to about thirty feet across. The light did not reach the whole way so they stopped and waited for their eyes to adjust. Claire grabbed Diane's wrist. "Diane, what's that, over there," she said, pointing deeper into the cave.

"I can't make it out. We need to go in farther."

Holding hands they slowly proceeded and then stopped.

"Diane, are those cages?"

"I think so."

Moving closer, they reached out to make sure they didn't bump into anything. A few yards more and they touched cold steel. Their eyes adjusted somewhat to the partial darkness and they felt along the steel bars.

"These are like big, dog cages," Diane said. "Why would anyone have dogs in here?"

Claire walked along the cages and tried the doors. They were unlocked and in each cage was a pile of tattered blankets. At the end of the cages were stacked cases of bottled water and waterproof packages of food.

"Diane, look at this. There's food and water here. Any chance you brought your phone?"

"Really, Claire? How would you expect my phone to survive a dip in the ocean? It's back at the blanket. Speaking of which we better get out of here before high tide."

"The walls. Diane, look at the walls."

"What about the walls?"

"Just try to remember the walls."

The women hurried back to the cave entrance and started wading. The tide was coming in fast and in only a few seconds they were up to their chests in water. A few more waves and there was no more walking; they were swimming. The waves were coming hard. They dove under the breakers as they approached. Swimming under the water was better, but every time they came up for air they lost ground and had to swim harder.

"Try to grab a rock!" Claire yelled, to Diane.

Allowing the current to take them toward the rocks, they conserved energy but the waves rammed them hard into the rocks. They were exhausted and now being beaten against the rocks. All they could do was hang on and pray.

"Claire! Diane! Up here!"

Looking up, they saw Jill and Caroline with the beach blanket.

"We're going to throw this down. See if you can reach it."

Jill threw one end of the blanket down to Diane who grabbed for it but missed.

"Try again Diane, you can do it," Caroline yelled.

The second time Diane caught a corner of the blanket and held on with all her might. Jill and Caroline pulled and slowly Diane started to rise up out of the water using her feet to push against the rock. When Diane was safely on the top of the rock, they threw the blanket to Claire.

"Your turn Claire," Jill yelled, lowering the blanket down the side of the rock.

Claire reached as high as she could and caught the blanket. Following Diane's example she crawled up the side of the rock and collapsed.

***

Climbing up the embankment was harder than going down. As they packed the remains of lunch into the bike baskets, a biker carrying a surfboard approached from the direction of the lighthouse.

Coming to a halt among them was Kevin O'Reilly.

"Hello ladies," Kevin said. "Having a good day?"

"Hi, Kevin, how are you," Diane replied, turning

away from her bike and toward him. "I don't believe you've met our friends. Caroline and Jill, this is Deputy Kevin O'Reilly. We met him at the bakery the day Chief Peterson stopped by the cottage."

"Hi Kevin," Caroline said. "I see you're a surfer."

"Yes. The waves have been good since the storm." Looking at Claire and Diane he continued, "You're wet. Have you been in the water? "

"Yes, unfortunately," Claire admitted, sheepishly.

"I hope not down there. That's a very dangerous beach," Kevin added, with concern as he looked down towards the rocks.

Anxious not to let him know they had found the cave Diane interrupted. "Ah… we found that out. We waded out a little and got knocked down by a wave. Don't have our sea legs," she added, with a smile.

"Kevin, it must be hard to ride a bike and carry a surfboard at the same time," Caroline commented, picking up on Diane's diversion tactic.

Kevin glanced from one woman to the other suspiciously. "You just have to get it balanced right and it's fine. You ladies better head home. The water was really cold today and the temperature is dropping."

"Exactly what we plan to do," Jill said, pushing her bike closer to the road and positioning herself on the seat.

"I'm going that way. I'll ride with you," Kevin said, without giving them a chance to object.

Kevin took the lead with the ladies following. Warily, they glanced at each other as they rode.

They could hear Ike barking as they approached Windward Cottage.

Kevin stopped at the end of the driveway and waited as they turned in and dismounted. "Sounds like your dog wants out," Kevin said, with a nod toward the house.

"Poor guy, he's had a long day," Jill said, parking her bike and heading for the house.

Kevin hesitated and looked around. "Good idea to have a dog when you're out this far from town. Don't hesitate to call if you need anything." Slowly he pushed off and rode toward Haworth.

"Do you think he knows about the cave and suspects we found it?" Diane asked, when they reached the porch.

"Hard to tell," Claire replied. "He seems like a good kid and too sharp to be working for Chief Peterson."

"What young man doesn't want to be working at the beach," Caroline said, watching Kevin slowly peddle down the road.

"What the heck's wrong with Ike? He doesn't usually act up like this when we're away," Jill asked, turning to unlock the door.

As soon as the door opened Ike burst out like he was spring loaded. Claire waited for the dog to rush to her, but instead he ran to the edge of the property as if he was going to follow Kevin. Stopping at the road he barked ferociously.

"For heaven's sake what's gotten into him?" Claire asked, shaking her head.

The others shrugged and walked into the house. Claire gave a whistle and Ike charged toward her. After a fast welcome he went into his sniffing routine on the steps and porch. "Come on, buddy. We need to go inside." Ike looked back at Kevin disappearing down the road and then followed Claire into the house.

***

"But you promised," Claire exclaimed, wrapped in her bathrobe and toweling her hair.

"That was before you pulled that stunt on the rocks," Jill declared, rocking vigorously.

Caroline leaned against the porch railing. "Well, we do have to eat, and we're all too tired to cook."

Jill glared at Caroline. "Whose side are you on? She

nearly drowned herself and Diane."

"Caroline's right Jill, we do have to eat," Diane said, from the rocker on the other side of Claire. "I'm not very happy with Claire right now either, but I need a hot meal."

Defeated, Jill gave in. "Okay, then let's go because I'm beat and want to get to bed early."

Claire turned to Caroline. "Before we go, will you please get the pictures of the girls?"

Caroline entered the house and returned with backpack a/k/a filing cabinet. Pulling out the stack of articles with the pictures attached she handed them to Claire who studied them, and then handed them one-by-one to Diane. "The walls Diane. What do you think?"

Diane studied each picture. "They look like the walls in the cave."

Caroline and Jill looked at each other. "What are you talking about?"

"We found a cave in the rocks. There were large steel cages, bottled water, and food. I think the girls were taken to that cave," Claire explained.

Jill narrowed her brow. "But Claire, they couldn't have carried the girls down there without being noticed and you couldn't get a boat in there."

"Not a boat," Diane said. "But certainly a dingy."

"A dingy? From where?" Caroline asked.

"From a larger boat sitting off shore," Claire answered.

Caroline's face suddenly lost all its color. "Did you find anything else?"

Claire shook her head. "We couldn't see well and the tide was coming in so we had to get out."

"Do you think that's where he abused the girls and then hid their bodies?" Jill asked, nervously.

Diane looked at Claire and then back at Jill and Caroline.

"We have no way of knowing," she said, shaking her head slowly.

Looking defeated, Jill placed her elbows on her thighs and supported her forehead with her hands. "Go get dressed Claire. We'll lock up and wait for you in the car."

***

"Okay, here's the plan," Claire announced, sliding into the back seat beside Caroline.

Jill turned from the front passenger's seat to look at Claire. "You've got to be kidding. What plan? No more of your hair-brained ideas."

"Okay," Claire said. "Then I'll do it myself."

Diane gripped the steering wheel tighter and exhaled. "Do what Claire?"

"Check out the boats at the marina. I want to find Swift Runner? That's all. Then we can have a nice dinner and just watch to see if Wendell happens to show up and go for a boat ride."

"Oh, let's just do it. It can't take that long," Caroline suggested, as Diane pulled into the parking lot at the marina.

Claire gave Caroline the thumbs up sign and continued, "Diane and I will start at the far end of the docks and work toward the middle. Caroline, you and Jill start at this end and work your way toward us. Just walk up and down the docks and look at the names of the boats. If anyone gets curious pretend you're interested in chartering a boat. If you see Swift Runner just get a good look at it. Whoever sees it first will go into the restaurant and that will be the sign that we found her."

"Well, that can't be too dangerous," Jill sighed.

The teams split up and started walking the lengths of the docks reading the names of boats. There were a few people on boats who nodded or said hello. One particular boat caught Claire's eye. The Sea Nymph was long and sleek and, unlike the other boats, it was made of gleaming dark wood with neatly wrapped, white, canvas sails. As she stepped to the edge of the dock for a closer look, a man she hadn't noticed said, "Good evening, ladies."

"What a beautiful boat," Claire said.

"I thank ye lassie," the man responded.

"Are you Scottish," Diane asked, hearing his accent.

"Aye! That I am."

The man stood and braced himself against the brass railing that ran the perimeter of the boat's deck. He was tall and solidly built. His face was darkly tanned and wrinkled from years of exposure to the weather. His hair was black with streaks of gray. His eyes were deep pools of dark amber and he had a salt and pepper beard. He looked exactly like a storybook sailor.

"Angus Querry at your service," he said, with a mock bow.

Still interested in his boat Claire continued, "Your boat is very different from the others. The wood is gorgeous. The others look so modern."

"Aye, she's an old beauty. This is a Molich Danmark. Forty years young she is. I restored her myself."

"She's immaculate. How do you keep her so shiny?"

"Seventeen layers of varnish will do that."

"How long have you been sailing," Diane asked, now interested in both the man and the boat.

"Since a boy off the Isle of Skye where I grew up."

Claire glanced across the docks to see Jill and Caroline watching them. Caroline gave a slight nod toward a very, large yacht in front of which she and Jill where standing. Without a word they walked back the dock toward the restaurant.

"Did you sail from Scotland to here?" Diane asked.

"Not directly. I go wherever the wind carries me. Been around the world twice."

"You have the most beautiful boat in the marina,"

Claire said, then pointing toward Swift Runner she asked, "What kind of boat is that?"

"Now, that's a real fancy one, a Millennium 140 Superyacht. That type is for sailors who have lots of money and like speed. Don't see too many of those around."

"Well, The Sea Nymph is much prettier," Claire said.

The sailor smiled. "Ach, you'd be a true lover of beauty then lassie."

Diane decided it was time to head in for dinner. "Thank you for your time. Your boat is lovely and it's been very nice talking to you. Safe voyage."

"My pleasure," Angus said, returning his gaze to Claire, he smiled and touched his forehead in a salute.

Walking toward the restaurant Claire's attention was caught by seagulls circling the building. *They're everywhere*, she thought to herself. Then she noticed security cameras at each corner of the restaurant under the eaves.

Jill and Caroline were seated at a table by the window and already had a bottle of wine chilling in a floor stand and menus in front of their faces.

"Who was your friend," Caroline asked.

"A lovely Scot who took a shine to Claire," Diane answered.

Claire stared at Diane astonished. "For heaven's sake Diane, what are you talking about?"

"You were so interested in his boat that you didn't notice how interested he was in you."

"Oh, please, he just likes talking about his boat."

Caroline peeked over her menu. "She's the athletic type. He probably thought she looked like a sailor."

Grabbing a menu Claire laughed. "You're crazy, he was just being polite."

When the server came to take their orders Claire surprised the group by asking, "Why are there security cameras mounted on the restaurant?"

The waitress looked at Claire hesitantly. "Not many people notice them. There was some vandalism a few years ago so the cameras were installed. They're dusk to dawn. Any movement on the dock and they start recording. Cheaper than paying a night watchman." Glancing at the others, the server recited the specials and took their orders.

Claire leaned back in her chair and stared out the window slowly sipping her chardonnay.

"She's off and running again," Caroline said, looking at Claire. "What is it this time?"

"How would one go about getting the film from security cameras?"

Jill placed her cool glass against her forehead. "She's going to get us killed. We may as well just jump off the end of a dock and get it over with."

"Where are you going with this Claire?" Diane asked.

Claire slowly turned her focus back to her friends. "If the cameras caught Wendell taking a boat out on the dates the girls disappeared that would be the link we need."

"Well Claire, I don't know much about the law, but I do know if you steal those tapes you will land in jail," Diane said, showing her impatience.

Claire breezed past the remark. "Speaking of jail, how would a small town cop afford a boat like Swift Runner even with partners?"

"Very rich partners," Caroline said. "There are tons of rich people who buy toys like that."

"You just don't like Peterson," Diane said.

Jill, thinking of Drew, set down her glass and leaned across the table toward Claire. "Actually, Claire, you don't like anyone this trip. I'm sure you'll find something wrong with that innocent Scot you met on the dock. I hope he sails away quickly before you go after him."

Dinner passed uneventfully and the foursome delayed leaving their table as long as possible. Wendell never appeared; however, Deputy O'Reilly did.

Claire nudged Caroline. "Look there. It's O'Reilly."

As they watched he made a cursory inspection of the dock area and disappeared around the side of the restaurant.

On the way to the parking lot, Diane noticed Angus Querry leaning against one of the light posts, arms crossed over his chest, watching them. The hairs on the back of her neck stood up and she picked up the pace to the car.

***

Back at the house Jill, Caroline, and Diane went straight to their rooms. Claire took the backpack to the kitchen table and pulled out the files. Reading each file, she made a list of the dates of the abductions over the last three years.

Yawning, she reviewed the list and said to herself, 'that should cover the time since the security cameras were installed at the marina. Now, all I have to do is figure out how to get a look at those tapes.'

While she was reviewing her notes, Ike laid his head down on her lap and she stroked his head affectionately. "Do you need to go out?"

Claire leaned against the doorframe and watched Ike wander around the dunes and take care of business. When he came back to the kitchen he went straight to his water bowl and lapped noisily. Ike moved away from the bowl and Claire watched as the water splashed against the sides.

"Water... Tides... Ike, you're a genius!" Claire exclaimed, reaching down and scratching his ears. "Where the heck is the newspaper?" she wondered, as she roamed the first floor. "Trash. It must be in the trash."

Returning to the kitchen she pulled the waste can out from under the sink and started searching through wet paper towels, food wrappers, and garbage. At the very bottom she found the paper. Scanning each page, she finally found what she was looking for. "Here it is, Ike. The tide tables!" Tearing the page from the newspaper she threw the rest back into the waste can. Claire smoothed out the crinkled paper and then folded it neatly with her list of dates.

"You're a good boy, Ike. Are you ready for bed?" Repacking the backpack, she carried it up the steps and slid it under her bed.

Chapter Eleven
Sunday

The four, bathrobe-clad women sipped coffee and watched the waves break on the beach behind Windward Cottage.

Jill lowered her coffee mug to her lap. "I think this is what a vacation is supposed to be like."

Caroline wearily looked at her friend. "You mean we're not supposed to be staying in a strange house that lights its own fires and running around like mad women risking our lives?"

"Okay, so we don't have all the answers yet," Claire responded, guiltily. "But you have to admit we haven't been bored. If anything was going to happen in the house it would have done so by now. I think it's protecting us."

Diane added her two cents. "Oh no, not bored. That's for sure, but don't expect to be allowed to pick the next vacation destination."

Claire smiled. "It won't be my turn for three years which gives me time to think of someplace interesting."

"Lord help us!" Jill exclaimed. "I may not be available for that vacation."

Ike, who had been sitting quietly next to Claire suddenly bolted off the porch and raced down the beach. Claire whistled and called "Ike. Come." The dog ignored her. "Oh geez, I better get dressed and go after him."

"If anything happens to that dog, you're in big trouble," Jill yelled, behind her. "That would ruin my relationship with Drew!"

"I better go too," Jill said, to Caroline and Diane as she hurried into the house.

"I refuse to move from this spot," Diane said.

"Me too," Caroline said, taking another sip of coffee.

Before Claire and Jill returned to the porch, Ike was

Windward Secrets

running back toward the house with Drew behind him.

"Oh terrific, here comes Ralph Lauren and we're not dressed," Diane said, through a smile of welcome.

"Good morning ladies," Drew said, from the bottom of the steps.

"Morning Drew. Can I get you a cup of coffee," Caroline volunteered.

"Thanks. I'd love one. Black please."

Diane looked uncomfortable. "Well, Drew, I'm afraid you've caught us at our worst. We slept in this morning and are a little slow moving."

"Please, don't worry about me. I have a sister, an ex-wife, and a daughter; I understand perfectly."

Caroline returned to the porch and handed Drew a hot mug.

"How was your trip to Boston?" Diane asked.

"Longer than I would have liked. I'm glad to be back." Patting Ike on the head he added, "Ike looks great. Thank you for taking care of him."

"It's been our pleasure," Caroline said, with a smile. "He's been no trouble at all and we really appreciated having him around at night."

"Still having problems?" Drew asked, knitting his brows and taking a sip of coffee.

"No trouble really. We just got used to having him around." Diane said, thinking it was best not to divulge what they had been up to.

Claire and Jill came through the kitchen door letting it bang behind them.

"Well, that explains Ike's hasty exodus," Claire said, with relief. "Did you whistle or something?" she added, looking at Drew.

"No. He must have heard my car," Drew replied. Then, looking at Jill he smiled widely. "How are you?"

Jill blushed from head to toe. "I'm great and glad to see you."

"Walk on the beach? I've missed our morning strolls."

Jill was down the steps and pulling Drew toward the beach before he could put his mug down. "I'll see you all later," she called, taking his mug, dumping the coffee in the sand, and pitching the mug to Claire.

Catching the mug, Claire said to Jill and Caroline, "Hmmm... I was rather hoping this might be over."

"Why do you say that?" Caroline asked, looking up at Claire.

"I can't explain it. I think I like Drew, but there's something nagging at me."

"Claire, just don't do anything that would hurt Jill. She's a big girl and can take care of herself," Diane offered, always the voice of reason.

"I sure hope so," Claire said, thoughtfully sitting down in a rocker. "Are you two going to get dressed today?"

"If you hadn't thought you were going to have to chase Ike you wouldn't be dressed either," Caroline grinned.

"Touché," Claire laughed.

Diane stood and stretched. "I, for one, am going up and take a shower. It looks like a beautiful day."

"Put on something nice," Claire said.

Diane leaned against the porch railing. "What does that mean?"

"I think it would be nice if we went to Sunday brunch at the Marina Restaurant, don't you?"

Caroline shook her head. "She's up to something again, Diane."

Diane let out an exasperated sigh. "I'm afraid to ask but someone has to. Why are we going there Claire?"

"Go take your shower. I'll explain when Jill gets back." Turning to Caroline she continued, "You need to wear your contacts and something sexy."

"You want me to regress? Why?"

"Because, you have a special assignment today."

Claire rocked slowly waiting for Diane and Caroline to change.

***

When Jill returned from her walk, her friends were dressed and waiting on the porch for her. "Why are you dressed like that?"

"We're going to brunch," Caroline said, slowly and with a glance at Claire added, "and who knows what else."

"Caroline," Claire said. "You're going to need your painting gear."

Caroline looked curiously at Claire and went into the house to collect her things.

"You're up to something, aren't you?" Jill looked skeptically at Claire.

"Afraid so. Get dressed and I'll explain in the car."

"The suspense is killing me," Diane said, sliding behind the steering wheel.

Jill couldn't resist. "You're enjoying this too, aren't you, Diane?"

"Yes, I'm afraid so."

Claire turned to Jill. "Who in your company is an expert on security cameras?"

"I knew it. You're going after the security tapes at the marina, aren't you?"

"Not me... you!"

Jill whipped her head toward Claire. "Are you out of your mind? Don't answer that, we already know you are."

Caroline looked thoughtful. "Claire, you said yesterday was the end of it."

Claire let out a long, deep sigh. "What if one of those little girls was yours and someone could find out what happened to her? If the authorities were going to do anything it certainly would have been done by now. I believe we were brought here for a reason and this is it. We have to do everything we can to prevent any more children from disappearing, and God knows what else."

Caroline and Jill looked at Diane. "Diane?"

"I agree with Claire," Diane said, thinking of her own daughter, and not taking her eyes off the road.

Jill and Caroline looked at each other and then at Claire. "Okay. What do we need to do?"

"Is there a security camera expert at your company Jill?"

"Yes. Joe."

"Can you give him a call and see how we can get the tapes or disks or whatever it is we need?"

"It's Sunday for crying out loud. I hate to bother him... oh darn, I'll try."

The other three women listened to Jill's side of the phone conversation. "Yes. Okay. I'll call you back." Ending the call she explained, "Joe said that if we can get a look at the brand and model number of the system he can tell us what to do. Would you like to tell me exactly how we're going to do that Claire?"

"Certainly," Claire replied, with a sly grin. "Caroline is going to get the marina manager out of his office by saying she needs his permission to paint and where he wants her to do it. Caroline, you're going to have to use all those social graces you have acquired over the years to get him out of the building and keep him there as long as possible. Diane, Jill, and I will get a table and create a diversion in the restaurant. It will be busy because it's a beautiful weekend. No one will notice when Jill slips away."

"Why me?" Jill questioned, with a worried look.

"Because you know electronics better than we do. I noticed last night that the manager's office is down the same hallway as the restrooms. No one will suspect a thing when you head for the ladies room and slip into his office."

Diane pulled into the parking lot and turned off the ignition.

Claire touched Caroline's leg. "You go first. We'll give you five minutes and then we'll come in. Unfortunately, or maybe fortunately in your case, you are going to have to stay after we leave and continue painting so that no one connects you with us. We'll come back for you later."

"Okay. I think I can do this. If I learned anything from my despicable dad, it's how to lie." Caroline got out of the car and retrieved her things from the trunk of the car. The others watched as she entered the restaurant.

Diane counted down the minutes. "Okay. Let's go."

The three women were greeted by the hostess and seated at a table in the middle of the dining room. A server took their orders for drinks and explained that it was a buffet and they should help themselves when they were ready.

"Fill your plates as high as you can," Claire whispered, across the table to Diane and Jill.

"You're really making me nervous," Jill replied.

"You can do it, Jill. Don't worry, Diane has Ed to defend us."

"Oh, that's swell," Diane said. "Just when I realize I love the guy, he's going to have to get me out of jail."

"Let's get our food. Time's wasting."

The three women piled their plates with more food than they could possibly eat. Returning to their table, they found the three, large glasses of iced tea they had ordered. They were no sooner seated when Claire announced louder than necessary that she was going to the ladies room. As she got up from the table she took hold of her handbag and the tablecloth at the same time. Sliding off her chair and moving away from the table she quickly jerked the tablecloth along with her handbag. Food and iced tea flew everywhere. There was instant chaos. Claire nodded to Jill, who made a scene about the iced tea that had spilled down her blouse and headed for the ladies' room. Every server in the restaurant rushed to the table to start cleaning up the mess. Food hit several other people and Claire diligently went to work apologizing and drawing as much attention to herself as possible. Diane pretended to help the servers clean up while she kept an eye on the entrance in case the manager appeared unexpectedly.

Every eye in the dining room was on the mess in the center of the room and no one noticed Jill disappear down the hallway and into the manager's office. Locating the camera recording equipment setting on a credenza behind the manager's desk, she pulled her cell phone from her handbag and punched in Joe's number. Joe was waiting for her call and picked up immediately. Jill read off the name of the recorder and model number. "Yes. You're sure? Okay. Bye."

Disks, the system used disks not tape. She began opening the doors and drawers of the credenza. There they were, disk cases with the years clearly printed on the spines. "Holy heck! There have to be thirty or forty disks for the last three years. How will I ever get through all these?" Looking out the office window that overlooked the docks, she saw Caroline talking to the manager. "Keep him talking Caroline!"

Jill took a deep breath to steady her nerves. 'I need a system.' Pulling the first disk out she opened the case popped the disk and dropped it into her handbag and returned the empty case back to the drawer.

Open. Pop. Drop. Return.

Open. Pop. Drop. Return.

She fell into a rhythm glancing out the window every two or three disks. She was doing fine until she dropped a disk. When she bent over to look for the disk she hit her shoulder on the corner of the drawer and tore her blouse. "Ouch! Damn it!" She slammed the drawer closed and got down on her hands and knees to search for the disk. It was too dark under the credenza to see the disk so she reached back with her hand and felt around. Nothing. *It must have rolled somewhere else,* she thought looking around the floor. Jill was crawling toward the manager's desk when she heard the office door knob turn. She quickly crawled under the desk and held her breath. The door opened and someone approached the desk. There was nothing she could do but pray whoever it was wasn't planning on sitting at the desk or they would see her. Perspiration was soaking her blouse and her legs were cramping. Lowering her eyes to the space under the front of the desk she saw just the tip of a women's shoe one inch from the runaway disk. *Please leave,* thought Jill wanting to scream because her back ached from her crunched position. It felt like hours until she heard something being placed on the desk and the shoe moved out from under it. Footsteps receded toward the door and then it closed. Jill waited a few seconds and then backed out from under the desk anxious to stretch her body back to its normal shape. Wiping the sweat from her face, she tried to stand only to hit her head on the edge of the desk. "Oh, for God's sake, what next?" she mumbled, rubbing her head. She glanced out the window again, the manager was still with Caroline. In earnest she went back to work opening, popping, and dropping. Ten more disks and she was completely soaked in perspiration and as tightly stretched as a rubber band ready to break.

"This has to be enough," she said, as she dropped one last disk into her handbag. Looking out the window, the manager was no longer with Caroline. "Damn. I have to get out of here fast." Quickly she closed the drawer and left the office. She just passed the Ladies' Room when the manager rounded the corner and said, "Good afternoon."

Jill's mouth twitched with a nervous smile and she nodded.

Back in the dining room, the table was being re-set, the other diners had returned to their meals and a server was placing fresh glasses of iced tea in front of them. "Please go back to the buffet and start again."

This time the women took small amounts of food, ate quickly, and left the restaurant with apologies to the hostess.

"Please, don't worry about it," the hostess replied. "These things happen."

Claire turned to Jill. "Now what?"

"Joe said we can play the disks on a computer or disk player. Any recordings made will show with the date and time noted at the bottom of the screen. We don't have either at the house. Now what do we do?"

Diane pulled into a vacant parking lot and popped the trunk. Diane retrieved her laptop and the backpack from trunk, and handed the backpack to Claire. "Give me the dates, Claire."

Claire looked at her list and started reading off dates.

"Oh crap," Diane cried. "It's not working. There's something wrong. What do we do now Jill?"

"We'll have to get the disks to Joe. He can figure out what's wrong. I suppose I'm going to have to get those disks back into the office eventually, aren't I?"

"Not necessarily," Diane said. "Nobody knows who took them and they have no reason to look at these disks. If there had been a problem they would have used the disks at the time, not a few years later."

"I sure hope you're right," Jill answered, playing with her rings nervously. "If I go to jail Claire, you're coming with me."

Diane started the car and turned toward the road that led to Route 6. "Let's see if we can find someplace open that does FedEx or UPS." Driving south on Route 6 they found a Staples in Barnstable.

"Bingo," Claire yelled, pointing to the left.

"Won't go out until tomorrow," the young woman said, from behind the counter.

"That's okay," Diane replied. "We have no choice."

Back in the car, they returned to the Marina to pick up Caroline.

"Great job, Caroline. How did you keep him out of the restaurant so long?" Claire asked.

Caroline batted her eyelashes. "Just a little southern charm and the promise of a painting," she giggled.

"Are you sure that's all?" Jill asked, mischievously. Caroline laughed out loud.

"Would you believe I saw the SOB slip his wedding ring off and put it into his pocket? He had the gall to ask me out…like I couldn't see the tan line where his ring had been. What a jerk. Men are so stupid. Why do they think they're so irresistible? Bill probably behaves the same way. I wanted to push the jerk off the dock. Instead, I let him think he had a chance. I told him my name was Bridgett and gave him the number of the dentist's office."

Diane laughed so hard she had to pull off the road. "Oh my God, that is so good Caroline."

"Yeah, well I hope he calls Bridgett."

Tears were streaming down Jill's cheeks as she laughed. "Diane, drive. I had iced tea and you know I can't laugh with a full bladder."

Diane drove back to the house where all four tumbled out of the car still laughing.

***

The women luxuriated in the quiet afternoon. Claire and Diane read on the back porch. Caroline painted on the roof and Jill took a nap before going out to dinner with Drew.

When Drew came to pick up Jill, her posse was once again waiting on the front porch. Ike ran to Claire and tried to climb into her lap on the rocker. "Down boy. It's good to see you too."

Jill stood and gave Drew a peck on his cheek.

Claire couldn't resist. "Why don't you go to the Marina Restaurant? The food's good and the view of the boats is lovely."

Jill whirled around and gave Claire a look that would kill.

Oblivious to any hidden meaning in Claire's suggestion Drew said, "Thanks, but there's a little restaurant I wanted to try in Chatham. Is that okay, Jill?"

"Of course it is. Let's go." With one last disgruntled look at Claire, she took Drew's arm and they walked toward the car.

Diane giggled, softly. "I swear Claire, you are going to pay big time someday."

***

After a simple supper of sandwiches Caroline, Diane, and Claire climbed the stairs to the roof.

"We haven't been up here for a few nights," Diane said. Claire passed around glasses of wine. "No, we haven't. This is a nice ending to a good day. Cheers!"

Caroline led the conversation by telling them what she had been painting from the roof and how much she loved the view. "Let me show you." She disappeared down the stairs to return with the painting she had done the morning she painted the sunrise.

They propped the painting on the easel and stood back to study it. "Caroline, this is really beautiful. The colors and detail are marvelous," Diane observed.

Claire walked closer to the painting. "Caroline."

"Yes."

"Why did you paint Betsy in the picture?"

Caroline looked surprised. "What?"

Claire pointed to the little girl on the beach. "This is Betsy. Did you work from the pictures in the scrapbook?"

"No. I wasn't even thinking of Betsy when I was

painting. Claire, do you know what is really strange?"

"No."

"I don't remember painting her at all."

Diane hummed the theme from The Twilight Zone. "And, Claire thinks this house is normal."

"No... I think it's abnormally special. A thin place, remember? Something or someone is guiding us. This is another sign."

"Claire," Caroline asked, softly. "If this is a thin place and Betsy is here, does that mean she's dead?"

Claire looked sadly out to sea. "If I understand the theory of thin places correctly, then the answer is yes."

No one said anything as the bright, orange sun slowly slid behind the horizon and the moon steadily made its climb to join the stars.

In an effort to lift the mood Caroline got the binoculars and handed them to Claire. "Let's look at the stars and see how many constellations we can identify."

Claire scanned the sky and then the sea, and, finally, up and down the beach. Standing up from her green and white lawn chair she walked to the edge of the roof that faced Wendell's. "There's a light moving over there!"

Diane and Caroline joined her at the railing and she handed the binoculars to Diane. "I see it. It appears to be going back and forth from the house to the driveway." She handed the binoculars to Caroline.

"It looks like a flashlight, doesn't it?"

Suddenly, Claire turned for the stairs. "Get your things. He's moving the evidence."

Running through the house they grabbed jackets, handbags, and phones."

"Caroline, you drive. Drop us at the end of Wendell's drive and then wait up the road for us to call you."

"Oh crap, here we go again," Diane mumbled.

Hunkering down, Claire and Diane stealthily moved

through the tall grass and bushes toward Wendell's house. When they were close enough to see the house, they crawled under the shelter of low, hanging branches of a pine tree. Wendell came out of the house carrying a box and loaded it into the back of his truck. Before he finished, the door to the house opened and another man came out carrying a computer monitor.

Claire and Diane looked at each other and shook their heads. It was too dark to see who the other man was. The men each made two more trips from the house to the truck and then got into the truck and slowly drove out of the driveway.

Claire hit speed dial. "Caroline, come get us. Quickly. They're leaving." She and Diane left the hiding place and ran toward the road. Just as they reached the road Caroline pulled up and they got into the car.

"Did you see which way they went?" Diane asked.

"Yes," Caroline replied. "They're headed for town."

"Turn off the headlights, Caroline. We don't want them to know they're being followed," Claire directed.

Caroline did as she was told and slowly followed the pickup. They could just barely see the tail lights in front of them.

"This is dangerous. I can hardly see the edge of the road," Caroline said, with a quiver in her voice.

"It's okay. They're not going fast. Take your time," Diane encouraged.

They passed Windward Cottage and were half way to town when Caroline exclaimed, "Oh hell! There's a cop behind us with his light blinking."

"Oh damn!" Claire swore. "Pull over, Caroline."

Caroline carefully maneuvered the car to the side of the road and rolled down her window waiting to see who would exit the patrol car behind them.

"Good evening ladies," Deputy O'Reilly said.

Caroline turned on her southern charm. "Hi, Kevin.

How are you?"

"Ma'am, do you realize you were driving without your lights?"

"Really?" Caroline looked in front of the car and then at the dashboard. "Gosh, you know what? I didn't. The moonlight's so bright I forgot to turn them on."

The deputy aimed his flashlight into the car at Claire and then at Diane in the back seat. He moved the light over the back seat. Diane's handbag containing her gun was in full view on the seat beside her. Beads of sweat began to form on her upper lip and it took all she had not to reach for the purse.

"Where exactly are you headed?"

There was an uncomfortable pause until Claire leaned toward Caroline's window. "We thought we'd check out Blackbeard's for a little nightlife."

"Ladies. It's Sunday night, off season; there's no nightlife anywhere in Haworth."

"Oh," Caroline said, innocently. "Can you suggest somewhere else?"

O'Reilly lowered his flashlight. "No, I can't. If you turn around and go home, we'll call this a warning and there won't be a citation."

"Yes, of course. We'll go right home officer. Thank you," Caroline said, appropriately humble.

"Go a little farther and there's an area where you can turn around. Turn on your lights and be careful! I'll follow you back to the house," the deputy said, before returning to his car.

"Geez, I feel like I've been scolded by one of my sons," Caroline said, looking over her glasses for the headlight control.

"What the heck is he doing out here?" Diane asked. "You'd think there would be more to do in town than out in the middle of nowhere."

Claire was provoked. "I think it's one, strange

coincidence that he was out here the night Wendell was cleaning out his secret room. Do you think he was standing watch for them?"

"If he was, do you think he would have let us off so easily?" Diane asked.

Claire thought for a moment. "No, you're right, if he had seen us coming out of Wendell's drive, I don't think he would have let us go." Then turning to Caroline, "did you notice exactly when he started to follow us?"

"I didn't see his light until we were past Windward Cottage and I didn't see him while I was waiting for you. He must have come along the shore road after I picked you up. Hopefully, he just thinks I'm a dumb, woman driver."

Caroline pulled the car into the drive at Windward Cottage. Deputy O'Reilly pulled in behind her, backed out, and turned toward Haworth.

"I wonder who the man was with Wendell and where they were taking the stuff." Claire thought out loud, walking toward the house,

Opening the front door, they were greeted by Ike and a warm fire.

"Drew's back and we have a fire again. How interesting," Claire said.

"Really Claire? How can he be with Jill, and here starting a fire at the same time?" Diane responded.

Caroline sunk down into the sofa and looked thoughtfully at the fire. "It's the house."

Claire and Diane looked at her curiously.

"There's nothing menacing about the fire. Whoever, or whatever, could burn the house down around us if it wanted. It's trying to comfort us."

Diane sat down beside Caroline. "I think you're right. All of the unusual things like the beds that weren't supposed to be made, the coffee was started and the table set for breakfast, and the locked room becoming unlocked. These aren't things that could harm us. Caroline's right, they're signs of hospitality."

Claire opened the door for Ike to come in and then turned back to her friends. "I'm glad you're finally seeing the light. Now do you believe me about the house?"

Ike followed Claire as she slowly walked around the room. Stopping in front of the fireplace, she touched the smooth wood of the mantle and the rough surface of the stone. Next, she fingered the stair balusters like a harp and ran her hand down the banister.

Claire turned toward her friends. "All of these strange things are a woman's touch. Right?"

Caroline and Diane nodded in agreement.

"Where are you going with this Claire," Diane asked.

"Well, I don't think a little girl would think to make beds, start fires, and especially place binoculars where we could find them."

"And?" Jill encouraged Claire to go on.

"If you were a mother of a lost child, what would you do?"

"Never give up trying to find her," Diane answered, sadly.

Claire pointed at Diane. "Exactly! I think Mrs. Carter is here too. She's the one trying to help us. I bet she's the woman we've seen on the widow's walk."

Caroline and Diane watched as Claire continued her inspection. She touched different objects and finally stopped in front of the bookcases containing the games. When she turned, she had a Monopoly game in her hands. Setting it down on the table, she removed the game board and placed it in the center of the table. She lifted the Chance cards, shuffled them and placed them face down in the Chance rectangle on the board. She did the same thing with the Community Chest cards.

Caroline and Diane got up from the sofa and joined Claire at the table. "What are you doing?" Diane asked.

"We used to play Monopoly on rainy days," Claire replied, softly. She picked up the little, silver, players' pieces and cradled them in her hand. Picking up the racecar, she placed it on the corner of the board that said 'GO.' "Will was always the racecar. He loved speed." Next she placed the top hat on 'GO.' "David liked the top hat because he thought he was debonair," she smiled. "Patty liked the iron because she said she could hit David over the head with it. I was the thimble because Mom was always trying to teach me to sew; she never succeeded." Another grin and Claire continued. "Betsy was the shoe. She hated it because it was a baby shoe, and she said she wasn't a baby." A tear trickled down Claire's cheek as she placed the tiny shoe on the corner of the board. "How could I have forgotten this? We played for hours. We would even leave a game in progress for several days."

Pushing herself up out of the soft sofa cushions, Caroline walked across the room to Claire and placed her arm around Claire's shoulders.

Claire reached across the board and drew a Chance card. She turned it over and laughed. Holding it up to show the others she said, "We're safe. This is a get out of jail free card."

Chapter Twelve
Monday

Claire and Caroline were sitting at the kitchen table when Jill entered looking radiant.

Caroline smiled. "You had a good night didn't you Jill?"

"Yes. We had a lovely time."

Claire sat with one elbow resting on the table and her chin in her palm as Jill poured herself a cup of coffee.

Diane was next at the coffee pot. "What's on the agenda for today?" she asked, turning toward the others.

"Well, I'm going to walk with Drew," Jill said, with a dreamy look on her face.

"Geez Jill, you're acting like a teenager," Claire said.

"I feel like a teenager," Jill replied. "And, I like it!"

Claire shook her head. "When you take Ike back to Drew today, I think you should take his bowls and food."

Hearing his name, Ike's ears perked up and he tilted his head looking at Claire.

Jill was surprised. "What do you mean Claire? He's not coming back tonight?"

Claire looked at Diane and Caroline. "Tell her about last night," she said, nodding toward Jill.

Diane and Caroline took turns telling Jill how they felt about the strange happenings in the house. "We think we're safe. It's been very generous of Drew to let us have Ike at night, but it's time to cut the apron strings… or rather leash… and let him go home where he belongs," Diane concluded.

Jill still looked puzzled. "What about Wendell?"

"Wendell would be a fool to try anything. He may have even left town. We saw him taking what we think was the evidence out of his house last night."

"Well, if you're sure," Jill said, bending down to

pick up Ike's bowls. She washed them and put them into the canvas bag along with his food.

Claire leaned over to Ike and buried her face in his neck. "Good bye, sweet boy." When she finally let go and sat up her eyes were full. "Oh damn, all I seem to do any more is cry." Reaching for a tissue she said to Jill without looking at her. "Please, go."

Jill opened the door and called Ike. "Come on, boy. Your dad misses you." Ike slowly walked out the door hanging his head. Jill looked back at Claire and tried to smile, but the lump in her throat forced her to swallow instead.

Caroline reached over and patted Claire's hand. "It'll be okay. You have a few more days to see him again."

Diane cleared her throat and blinked several times. "And, you don't even like dogs."

***

"This might actually be fun," Claire said, as they drove toward Barnstable. "The GPS says it's three hundred feet ahead on your right."

Diane pulled into a mini mall and looked for the scuba shop. The parking lot was nearly empty and she was able to park right in front of the store.

"You want what?" the young man said, at the counter.

"We would like to rent snorkeling gear and wetsuits," Claire repeated.

"You realize this is not exactly snorkeling weather?" The young man looked, up and down, at the two women standing in front of him.

"Well, of course," Diane said. "We just want to do a little bit. We'll have your gear back before closing."

"Now listen, Aaron, you don't need to worry. We've done it before and we're good swimmers even though we may not look like it," Claire added, looking at the name embroidered on his shirt.

"Okay. If you're sure." Stepping from behind the counter, Aaron gathered everything they would need and packed it into a large box. Taking their drivers licenses for ID he wrote up rental slips and had them each sign a release of responsibility for the shop and then charged their deposits. "I need everything back no later than five o'clock today."

"No problem," Diane said, as she lifted the box off the counter.

Claire held the door for Diane who winked as she passed.

Back in the car Claire needed to vent. "Why do young people think that after the age of forty you can't tie your own shoe strings? Wait until they reach our age, they'll see. There's still lots of life in these bodies."

"Speak for yourself," Jill said. "I certainly feel my age some days."

Diane laughed. "It's a good thing you're not going in the water Jill."

"Darn good thing," Jill agreed.

Diane drove directly to the rocky cove where they had found the cave. They hauled the equipment down to the beach where Claire and Diane stripped to their bathing suits and squeezed into the wetsuits.

"Talk about a muffin top! This is a whole Bundt cake," Diane laughed.

Claire pulled flashlights wrapped in plastic bags out of the beach bag and handed one to Diane. "Zip this under your suit."

Caroline couldn't hold her tongue any longer. "Claire, really, I don't think you should be doing this. Please, let's just return the gear and go back to the house."

"Relax, Caroline. I checked the tide tables; it's low tide. It will be easier swimming in and out this time."

"You have Ed's number. If we're not out in an hour, call him," Diane added.

"Oh, that's encouraging!" Jill said.

Claire and Diane looked down at their bodies. Each had a small, rectangular lump where their cell phones were and a cylindrical shape from the flashlights. Pulling up the hoods of the wetsuits and adding the masks and snorkels completed their ensembles. They picked up their flippers and walked toward the water.

Jill looked at Caroline. "If I wasn't so worried I'd laugh. They look ridiculous."

Claire and Diane waded into the water until it reached their waists and then slipped the flippers over their feet. Adjusting their masks they waved at Caroline and Jill and slowly disappeared under the water. The water was murky, but the swimming was much easier than the last time. With the exertion of energy the suits warmed up and it was not unpleasant as they swam around the large rocks toward the cave.

Claire raised her head above the water at the cave entrance. Giving Diane the okay signal she pointed to the cave and swam in. Pulling off their flippers they threw them onto the sand and walked out of the water.

"Not bad," Diane said, removing her mask. "Actually, if the water were clearer this would be fun."

Claire pulled her flashlight out of her wetsuit and turned it on. Diane did the same and they moved the beams around the interior of the cave. Nothing appeared to have changed since they had been here before. Moving deeper into the cave they found a smaller cavern behind the first. It was barely high enough to stand and was empty except for mounds of sand around the sides.

Diane looked at Claire nervously and pointed to the mounds. "Do we dig?"

Claire gulped and nodded. "This is what we came for."

Kneeling down they crawled into the small cave and started to dig with their hands. Finding nothing they moved to different spots and dug more holes. Nothing.

"I can't believe there's nothing here," Claire said. "I was really hoping we would find something."

Diane stared at her friend. "You were really hoping to find something? What exactly did you think we would find? The only thing we would find buried in a cave would be bad! I'm relieved we didn't find anything. Let's get out of here."

Claire started to smooth the sand as close to its original shape as she could.

"What are you doing?"

"We don't want anyone to know we were here?"

"Claire stop. That's ridiculous. What does it matter? We have everything we need and we're going to turn it over to the State Police tomorrow. Who cares if someone figures out we were here."

Claire sat back on her heels. "You're right. Let's go."

Back in the main cave they took out their phones and snapped photos of the interior of the cave and everything it contained.

Caroline and Jill ran to the water's edge with relief when they saw the snorkels appear around the rocks like miniature, submarine periscopes.

"Thank God," Jill said. "I couldn't have waited much longer."

Claire and Diane swam close to shore and removed their flippers. Standing up they walked to the beach.

Jill and Caroline stared in amazement and then burst out laughing.

Claire removed her mask. "What's so funny?"

Caroline could hardly talk. "How can two post-menopausal women go swimming and come out pregnant?"

Diane and Claire looked down at their fat abdomens and patted them as they had when they carried their babies. "Miracles never cease," Diane said, raising her chin in an aloof attitude.

The foursome walked to the beach bag containing towels and dry clothes. As Caroline and Jill watched Claire and Diane slowly unzipped their suits and removed large round plastic bags.

"What in the world is in those?" Jill asked.

"Blankets from the cages," Claire answered. "We're hoping there might be some DNA that can be retrieved.

Caroline gazed at her friends in awe. "You two really do think of everything, don't you?"

Getting out of the wetsuits when they were wet was even harder than getting into them. Quickly they dried and pulled on jeans and sweatshirts.

"Let's head for home. There's nothing more we can do," Claire said.

"Do you really mean that Claire," Jill asked.

"Yup. The party's over. Elvis has left the building. There's nothing left to do but give the information to the police."

***

Back at Windward Cottage, they settled in for a quiet afternoon reading on the back porch each in her favorite rocker.

Caroline broke the silence. "Somehow it seems unnatural to actually be relaxing."

She no sooner said the words than Diane's phone rang. "Hello. Hey Ed," she said, with a huge smile and left her chair for the privacy of the kitchen. Ten minutes later she returned looking a little flushed.

"Is that a blush we see on your face?" Jill asked.

Diane grinned and nodded. "Wow. This does feel good doesn't Jill?"

"Sure does. Welcome to the club."

Caroline kept her head down reading her book.

"Sorry Caroline," Diane said. "We really don't mean to rub salt in your wound."

Caroline looked up, sadly. "Please. Be happy. It's okay."

Claire brought them back down to earth. "Did Ed say anything about tracing Swift Runner's registration?"

Diane nodded. "The yacht is registered to a corporate conglomerate and not to individuals. Ed says he's digging into it, but it will take a while to get to the individual names."

"So, Peterson doesn't own it?" Claire confirmed.

"Not unless he is the CEO of a huge corporation. He must know someone important who loans him the boat."

Claire looked disappointed. "Well, darn. I thought for sure we'd find some dirt on him if he could afford a boat like that."

"Afraid not," Diane said. "He just has a wealthy friend."

"You're just going to have to dislike him because he's a jerk, Claire. Isn't that enough?" Caroline said.

Jill couldn't resist. "Yeah, Claire. It's not like you need a good reason to dislike people."

"Oh, come on you guys. I just have exceptionally, sensitive intuition."

Everyone laughed and went back to their books.

An hour later Jill went into the kitchen and returned with iced tea and snacks. "So, where do we go from here?"

Caroline was the first to respond. "I'm still not ready to go home. I'm going to stay the rest of the week and paint. I have some serious decisions to make. Anyone want to join me?"

"I'm in," Jill volunteered. "I took the time off so I may as well use it."

"Did you really think we expected anything less considering Drew is here?" Claire asked, leaning forward in her rocker looking at Jill.

Jill ignored her and looked at Diane. "What about

you, Diane?"

Diane hesitated. "As much as I love being with you all, I'd really like to see Ed and spend some time with him. Would you be terribly upset if I went back to Boston?"

"Hey," Claire said. "Why don't you have him come out here for a few days? We promise to leave you alone... well, that is, once we get to know Ed."

"Now, that scares me," Diane returned. "If you decide you don't like him Claire, you'll make his life miserable."

"Diane. How could I not like someone who has loved and taken care of you for how many years... and never asked for anything in return?"

Diane gave her a wary look. "With you, Claire, one never knows, but I'll think about it."

All heads turned to Claire.

"What about you Claire? Are you going to stay?" Jill asked.

Claire looked down at her lap and then slowly looked up. "I want to play Monopoly."

Diane's phone rang again. A sheepish smile crossed her face and she returned to the kitchen.

Caroline stood up and stretched her arms over her head and bent slightly to the left and right. "I think I'll go up to the roof and paint. Would anyone care to join me?"

"No thanks," Claire and Jill uttered, in unison.

Jill lowered her head back to her book and Claire gazed out at the ocean. Movement to the right caught her eye. Drew and Ike were walking up the beach toward Windward Cottage. Claire reached over and tapped Jill lightly on the arm. When Jill looked up Claire tilted her head toward the man and dog. Jill smiled in appreciation and laid her book on the porch floor.

Claire watched as Jill ran to Drew. He picked her up and swung her around with Ike barking and jumping beside them. Hand-in-hand, they walked toward Drew's cottage.

Ike stopped and looked back at Claire, and then followed his master.

The wind blew lifting little dust storms across the tops of the dunes. The sea grass bent slightly waltzing with the wind. Claire's eyes scanned the beach and the breakers in wonder of the beauty before her. Closing her eyes she rocked gently. When she opened her eyes there were five children on the beach; two boys and three girls. The boys had built a mountain of sand and were playing King of the Hill. The girls were trying to fly kites that kept crashing back to earth. Finally, the boys gave up their battle and helped the girls until all three kites were high in the sky. The smallest girl's kite was the highest. She laughed and squealed with excitement pointing to her kite.

Claire watched for quite a while before the kites were pulled in. The children ran into the surf, jumped waves and kicked water at each other. Smiling at their joy, Claire continued to watch as the children worked their way down the beach and disappeared.

Funny thought Claire. *Those are the first children we've seen since we've been here.*

Claire woke to a touch on her shoulder. "Time for supper Claire," Jill said, softly.

Claire shook the sedation of sleep away and looked up at Jill. "Did you see the children on the beach?"

"What children, Claire?" Jill looked at her friend with a furrowed brow.

"There were five of them. They were flying kites and playing. They went in the direction of Drew's cottage, I thought you might have seen them?"

"Claire…we were sitting on a dune the whole time. There were no children," Jill said, very slowly and softly.

Claire shrugged. "Must have been a dream."

Jill returned to the house and Claire looked down the beach. Lifting her hand she gave a tiny wave and whispered, "Goodbye."

Chapter Thirteen
Tuesday

Claire yawned and rubbed her eyes. Turning over she saw Jill was already up and gone. *Probably off with Drew* she thought, as she sat up and looked around the room. It was strange not to have Ike beside her. The sun beckoned through the windows and Claire headed for the shower. Betsy's room had been left open since they found the scrapbook and Claire paused and leaned against the door frame. They had cleaned the room and opened the windows to air it out. No longer musty and forlorn, the room now looked like any other little girl's room from years gone by.

Diane and Caroline's doors were still closed when Claire passed them. Jill had started coffee, but was nowhere to be seen. *Hmmm… it's such a beautiful day I think I'll ride into town and get some cinnamon buns.* Leaving a note, telling the others where she was going, she unlocked her bike, strapped on her helmet, and peddled toward Haworth. She felt invigorated. The morning was clear and crisp; not a cloud in the sky. The ocean to her right was a brilliant blue with frothy, white caps. She and her friends had gathered enough evidence to put Wendell away. And, she had found memories of her childhood. Life was good. She felt great.

The sound of a car drew her attention and she looked up to see a white panel truck in the opposite lane. It was coming fast and started to cross the center line.

What the heck is wrong with that driver? Surely he sees me? Claire could see two men clearly in the front seats as the truck headed directly at her. She looked to the right, it was a sheer drop to the ocean below. Her only option was to cut left and try to get to the other side of the road. She jerked the handlebars to the left and pumped as hard as she could.

***

Jill walked up the beach alone to find Diane and Caroline rocking on the back porch.

"Did you have a good walk?" Caroline asked.

Looking dejected Jill replied, "No. Drew wasn't there. His car was gone and so was Ike."

"Did he mention he wasn't going to be home this morning?" Caroline asked.

"No, he didn't," Jill said. "I'll call him later." Looking around Jill asked, "Where's Claire?"

"She rode into the bakery for pastries," Caroline replied. "She should be back soon."

Diane looked at her watch. "You know we've been talking for over an hour and Claire's still not back. Don't you think she should have been here by now?"

"Sure do," Jill commented. "My stomach's growling."

Caroline rose from her chair. "I'll give her a call on her cell."

Moving into the kitchen Jill and Diane set the table in anticipation of breakfast. They could see Caroline through the doorway tapping her phone and instantly heard a phone ringing in the parlor.

"Oh great," Caroline called out. "She didn't take her phone with her."

Diane went to the cupboard and took out several boxes of cereal. "I'm not waiting any longer. She probably decided to ride longer since it's such a beautiful morning. We can always make room for pastries later."

Caroline looked back at her phone checking for messages. There were at least a dozen from Bill. Turning off her phone she held it up with her thumb and index finger like a dirty sock and let it fall back into her bag.

Another hour passed, the kitchen was cleaned up, and there was still no sign of Claire.

Jill went to the front porch and looked up and down

the road. Returning to the kitchen she said, "I'm getting worried. Claire should have been back by now. What if she fell off that stupid bike?"

"That's a good point," Diane agreed. "Let's go look for her."

Jill hesitated. "Caroline, why don't you stay here in case she comes back. You can paint on the roof and call us when she returns."

It was agreed and Jill and Diane went to the car. They're first destination was Haworth. Diane pulled up in front of the bakery and Jill went inside to ask if Claire had been there. The only woman working assured her she had not had any customers matching Claire description. Diane drove up and down every street, but there was no sign of Claire. From Haworth, they took the beach road around the peninsula past the lighthouse. They stopped at the cove where they had found the cave and searched the hillside and beach.

"You don't think she would have gone back into the cave do you?" Jill asked Diane, concerned.

Diane shook her head. "I really don't think so. There was no reason to. She seemed satisfied with our search yesterday."

One last look around and they climbed back up to the road. Instead of continuing along the coast road, they wound inland on narrow, back roads. They checked fields and ditches. They stopped at roadside, gift shops and farm stands, but no one had seen a woman on a bicycle.

Caroline called several times to see if they had had any luck, and to tell them Claire had not returned to the house. After several hours Jill and Diane returned to the cottage.

Jill was starting to show her concern with her habitual pacing. "I'm worried. Something must have happened to her. She's been gone since, since when? Do either of you know what time she left the house?"

Caroline and Diane compared their times. They had gotten up between eight-thirty and nine o'clock.

"Jill, what time did you go to walk with Drew?"

"About seven-thirty."

"That means she left here sometime between seven-thirty and eight-thirty," explained Diane. "It's almost two o'clock. She's been gone nearly six hours. This is serious."

"I'm going to call Spence," Caroline said. "Maybe she decided to go home."

"Go ahead, but she wouldn't have gone home without telling us."

Caroline made the call and while she was talking to Spence, Diane said to Jill, "I think we should go to town and report her missing to Chief Peterson."

Jill's eyes widened. "Do you really think he'll do anything?"

"This is pretty serious. He can't be so incompetent that he wouldn't follow-up."

Caroline returned from speaking with Spence. "He hasn't heard from her. He did say that she sometimes rides for hours, but agrees that we should be concerned. If we don't hear from her in an hour or two, he wants me to call him back and he's going to drive up."

Diane looked at Jill. "How about asking Drew to bring Ike up to see if he can follow her scent?"

"Great idea. I'll call him right now."

Diane got her handbag and car keys. "Caroline, why don't you come with me to town to find Peterson."

***

Haworth was fairly empty and in a few minutes they were parked in front of the police station. Diane and Caroline entered the building to find a young secretary filing her nails. The name plate on her desk read Christy Blake.

"We'd like to speak with Chief Peterson please," Diane said.

"He's not here," Christy said, putting down her nail file and looking annoyed.

"Where is he?" Diane asked, impatiently.

"Out," the secretary said, with a smirk.

That was all it took. Diane strode across the room and slammed her hands down on the desk. With her face two inches away from Christy's she said, "Find him. Now."

Christy pulled back and put her hands up as if to ward off a blow from Diane.

Diane picked up the phone on Christy's desk and handed it to her. "I told you to find him."

Christy meekly took the phone and hit speed dial. "There are two women here to see you." There was silence while she listened. Looking up at Diane she asked, "What's your name?"

Diane told her and waited as Christy repeated it into the phone. "He wants to know what you want."

"We're here to report a missing person."

"They say someone's missing," Christy repeated. "Yes, sir. Goodbye."

Replacing the phone on her desk Christy looked up at Diane. "He'll be here in a few minutes."

Caroline sat down in one of the orange plastic and chrome chairs that lined the front wall of the office. Diane paced back and forth, casting glances out the windows, anticipating the arrival of Chief Peterson. Fifteen minutes passed and Diane had had it. Once again, she approached the secretary's desk. This time she reached across the desk and grabbed the front of Christy's tight, red sweater and yanked her out of her seat. "Where is he?"

"Heeeee's... attttt... Bllllackbeeeeard's," Christy stuttered.

Diane shoved Christy into her seat so hard it sent her rolling backwards into the empty desk behind her.

"Come on Caroline," Diane said, as she pushed the station door open so hard it nearly came off its hinges.

Caroline had to wait for the door to close to keep from being hit. Quickly re-opening the door she ran to the car where Diane already had it started.

Diane whirled the car in a U-turn squealing the tires on the pavement. At Blackbeard's she was out of the car and in the tavern so fast Caroline had to run to keep up.

Peterson was sitting at a round table near the windows with two other men. Diane strode up to the table and shoved the beer in front of Peterson so hard it flew off the table.

"What the hell do you think you're doing?" Peterson yelled.

"I'm forcing you to do your job, that's what the hell I'm doing," Diane replied.

The other two men pushed their chairs away from the table and waited to see if Diane was going to come after them.

Peterson stood, taking a defensive stance and glaring at Diane. She wasn't fazed, she walked to within inches of him. "You were called and told there is a missing person to report and you refused to come to the office." Then, reaching into her bag, she pulled out her cell phone. "I'm one touch away from the State Attorney General's office. If you want to keep your lazy ass job you're going to accompany us back to your pathetic little office, fill out the appropriate paperwork, and organize a search party. Do I make myself clear?"

Peterson scooped up his hat that had been lying on the table and, without looking at the other men, he walked toward the door with Diane on his heels.

Caroline looked at the two men still seated at the table. The man on the left looked familiar. Pointing her finger at him she asked, "Where do I know you from?"

"No clue, lady."

Following Diane's example she placed her hands on the table and looked at him closely. "I never forget a face.

It'll come to me."

Then in her deepest southern drawl she said, "Good afternoon gentlemen," and walked away.

Back at the police station Christy started to complain about Diane's treatment of her when Diane said, "Shut up and sit down." Christy quickly took her seat and tried to look busy.

Peterson removed his hat, hung it on a hook, and strode into his office. Diane and Caroline followed.

"What's this about a missing person," he said, sitting down and leaning back in his chair with his arms crossed over his fat belly.

Diane explained the details of Claire's disappearance and waited.

Peterson was obviously stalling to annoy her. "Well now. It's my guess your friend just found someone of interest she wanted to visit. We get a lot of that from ladies on vacation by themselves."

Diane glared. "If you are inferring that Claire is having some kind of illicit affair, then you're even dumber than you look."

Peterson's face glowed red with anger and his nose looked like it would explode. "Listen here lady..."

"It's Ms. Fuller to you," Diane quickly interrupted.

"I was about to say," Peterson said, clearing his throat, "that we don't consider an adult a missing person until they haven't been heard from for three days."

"We're not going to wait three days," Diane said, reaching into her handbag and pulling out her phone.

Chief Peterson quickly held up his hands. "Wait. There's no need to be hasty." Getting up and walking to the filing cabinets on the other side of the room he pulled out a piece of paper. Returning to his desk, he sat down and started asking questions. With the form complete, he slid it across the desk. "Read it and sign it."

Diane did as she was told and passed the paper

back. "When will you start a search?"

Peterson looked bored. "Ya know, your friend probably is already back. Why don't you girls hustle on back there and see?"

Diane, not liking his attitude responded quickly. "Just what is it that makes you so lazy?"

Peterson was out of his chair and leaning over his desk in the blink of an eye. "Now, wait just one God damned minute. Who the hell do you think you are?"

Diane was on him like a dog on bone. Nose to nose she said in a calm, but strong, voice, "I am a taxpaying, law abiding citizen whom you are sworn to serve, and you are not serving! Another taxpaying, law abiding citizen has been missing since seven thirty this morning and you sat on your fat ass and drank beer, not only while on duty, but after you had been informed of the disappearance of that person. You sir, are in deep shit!" With that Diane turned and left the office.

Caroline looked at Peterson and added, again in her sweetest southern accent, "I'd be worried about that pension if I were you... asshole."

Peterson sat down hard in his chair and waited until he heard the outside door to the station close. Picking up the form lying on his desk, he crushed it into a ball and hurled it into the waste can beside his desk.

***

Diane's phone rang. It was Jill. "What's going on? I thought you would be back by now."

"Peterson was not cooperating. Did you call Drew?"

"Yes, but he still didn't answer."

Caroline was beginning to feel like a fifth wheel. Diane sure didn't need any help. Caroline guessed Diane didn't need much help with anything else either.

When she hung up Diane turned to Caroline. "Drew didn't answer. I wonder where he is."

Caroline turned to look out the passenger's window.

Where was Claire? Was she safe? And... where was Drew?
"Why didn't you tell Peterson what you found at Wendell's? Wendell could have taken Claire," she asked, turning back to Diane.

"Because I don't trust Peterson. I think if he thought we suspected Wendell, he would protect Wendell before he would help us. I also don't want him hindering an investigation into Wendell. We'll let the State Police handle that."

"Diane, let's make one more stop."

Diane took her eyes off the road for a second to look at Caroline. "What did we miss?"

"The marina."

"Caroline, you're right. How could I have forgotten that? Did something happen when you were painting to make you suspicious?"

"Not really. I just noticed how easily boats slipped in and out and nobody paid any attention because that's what happens at a marina. People are having parties and inviting guests onto their boats all the time. And...."

"And what?" Diane asked, skeptically.

"There was that Scot that Claire liked. Maybe she was riding around the marina and wanted to take another look at that boat. He could have invited her onto his boat and...."

Diane pulled into the marina parking lot. Both women got out of the car and quickly walked toward the docks. Diane located the dock where they had met Angus Querry and walked to his slip. The Sea Nymph was gone. Diane and Caroline exchanged worried looks.

As they walked toward their car, they saw a young man trimming bushes along the side of the parking lot.

"Excuse me," Caroline said, approaching the young man.

The young man stopped what he was doing and turned to address Caroline, "Yes ma'am, what can I do for you?"

"I was just wondering, when a boat leaves the marina does the captain have to report where he's going? You know, like pilots do at airports."

"No, ma'am. They come and go as they please."

"Well, how does the marina keep track of what boats are in what slips?"

The young man took his cap off and wiped perspiration off his brow with his sleeve. "Forms are filled out when the slips are rented so the marina knows who to charge."

"What if the boat is not going to be here for a long time?"

The young man was getting curious. "Do you want to rent a slip?"

"No. I was just wondering how a marina operates," Caroline said, smiling up at the young man.

"If there is a slip available, all you have to do is fill out the paperwork and pay in advance."

"Thank you. I appreciate your help."

Back in the car Caroline looked at Diane. "Well, we can find out who the Scot is, but not where he was headed when he left. I guess that's up to the Coast Guard."

Diane thought for a moment and then said, "I think we better get back to the house and see if Jill has heard from Claire or Drew."

***

Claire

Claire opened her eyes but she couldn't see anything; there was something covering her face. She was lying on a flat, rocking surface. The movement made her nauseous. She couldn't move her right arm or leg without stabbing pain. There was something heavy on top of her. She wiggled the fingers of her left hand to see if they moved. Feeling around, there was something warm and sticky under her left hip and side. She reached up to feel the weight on her body. Tracing the object she realized it was her bike. Claire moved her hand to her face and smelled blood. She couldn't feel her face because her head was covered with cloth. When she pulled at it, two strong hands grabbed her arm and held it to the floor. She tried to move away but it was no use. The arms holding her were much stronger and the pain so intense she had to stop. The next thing she felt was a needle sliding into a vein in her arm.

***

The kitchen at Windward Cottage was overflowing with food. There was fried chicken, potato salad, a carrot cake and brownies cooling on top of the stove, and a fruit salad in the refrigerator.

"What the heck is all this?" Diane asked Jill surveying the kitchen.

Turning from the sink Jill wiped her wet hands on a tea towel. "I cook when I'm nervous," Jill answered. "Did you find her?"

"No," Diane said. "How about you? Any news?"

"Nothing." The more Jill wiped her hands the faster she paced around the kitchen. "Where is she? I can't understand why we haven't heard from her. And, where's Drew? Why isn't he answering his phone?"

Diane and Caroline were bringing Jill up-to-date on their activities when there was a knock at the front door. All three arrived at the door at the same time.

A uniformed, Overnight Express, delivery man stood on the porch. "Special delivery for Ms. Jill Stone," he said, holding up a large envelope. Caroline ran for a tip while Jill signed for the envelope and started opening it.

Jill quickly fanned through the contents. "It's pictures from Joe. He was able to open the disks from the security cameras and print the frames that showed activity." Suddenly, all but one picture slipped from her hands and she turned white.

Caroline bent to pick up the photos and Diane grabbed the one in Jill's hand. "What is it?"

Jill slumped down into the nearest chair. "Look closely at the men in the photo."

Diane and Caroline sat down on the sofa next to Jill and studied the picture.

The picture showed four men walking along the dock that ran parallel to the Marina Restaurant in the direction of Swift Runner. The image was excellent because they had not yet turned onto the dock that led to the slip where Swift Runner was berthed.

The faces of three of the men could be seen clearly. They recognized two of them. Wendell and Peterson. The third man's head was turned looking at the water.

Caroline pointed to the fourth man. "Jill look at this man. He was at the restaurant today with Peterson. I know him from somewhere."

Jill looked more closely. "We saw him at the newspaper office. Remember. I think he's the owner."

"Who's the third man?" Diane asked.

Jill and Caroline shrugged their shoulders and shook their heads.

Diane looked at Caroline. "Where's the backpack. We need to look at dates."

Caroline ran to the third floor and pulled the back pack out from under Claire's bed. Back in the parlor, she started reading off dates when girls had gone missing while Caroline and Jill searched through the stack of photos for matching dates in the lower left corner of each photo. They only needed to match three or four dates before Diane exclaimed, "Oh my God! Peterson and Wendell. What have I done? I just turned Peterson loose on Claire. He may be involved in her disappearance. We have to find her before he does."

The words were barely out of her mouth when they heard Ike barking in the distance. It was more of a soulful wail.

Jill raced to the door hoping to see Drew with Ike.

Ike was racing out of the woods on the other side of the road toward the house. He didn't wait for the door to be opened but burst through the screen and directly toward Jill. Grabbing her pant leg with his teeth he started pulling her toward the door.

"Something's wrong. We have to follow him," Jill said, trying to calm Ike.

Faster than what seemed humanly possible Diane ran to the kitchen and grabbed flashlights and jackets. Returning to the parlor she threw one of each to Jill, opened her handbag and pulled out her gun. "Caroline, you stay here to take calls. If Spence, or anyone else for that matter calls, tell them which way we've headed; that is, anyone other than Peterson and O'Reilly."

Ike let go of Jill's jeans and ran back through the hole in the screen door barking frantically. Jill and Diane followed him.

Diane stopped on the porch and looked back at Caroline. "Lock all the doors and windows. We'll call you if we find anything."

***

Ike led Diane and Jill through trees and brambles up the hill that overlooked Windward Cottage. At one point they trudged through a stream in knee deep water. Ike would race ahead and then return to urge the women on. As they climbed higher Ike barked less.

"We must be getting close to whatever he wants to show us," Jill said. "He's not barking as much."

Diane stopped to catch her breath and called Ike to her side. Patting his head she said, "It's okay Ike. Take it easy."

The dog seemed to understand and continued more slowly and without barking.

After an hour of steady climbing they came across a

dirt road and Ike once again hurried ahead of them. Within minutes he was back tugging at Jill's pant leg pulling her toward the side of the road.

"I think he wants us off the road," Jill said. "Let's stay where there's cover."

Even Ike was treading carefully and making very little noise. Twenty more minutes and Ike stopped and stood perfectly still. Peeking from behind trees, the women saw a dilapidated shack with two vehicles parked in front. One was a white van backed up to the shack and the other was a black Mercedes with a Massachusetts license plate.

Jill stared at the black Mercedes with an expression Diane couldn't read. Diane carefully walked to Jill and whispered, "You stay here with Ike. I'm going to see if I can see inside the shack."

Jill nodded and watched as Diane carefully made her way to the back of the ramshackled structure. Dusk was upon them making it difficult for Diane to pick her way quietly to the shed. There was only one window at the back where Diane could see in through a ragged curtain.

Claire lay on the floor in a heap like a disjointed doll. Her face was turned in the opposite direction. Diane couldn't tell whether she was breathing. There was a large, dark stain on her shirt.

Three men stood looking down at her. Diane could not see their faces. The man closest to Claire pushed her shoulder with his foot and she flopped onto her back.

"You idiots," he snarled. "You got the wrong one."

The other two stepped closer to Claire and looked down at her. "What do ya mean? She fits your description better than any of the others."

"You morons. I never should have entrusted you with this." Then to himself he added, "If you want something done right, you have to do it yourself."

"What are you going to do?" one of the other men asked.

"I'm going to finish what you started?" he said, turning toward the door.

The other men followed.

Diane slipped around the side of the building to see where the men had gone. Peeking around the front corner of the shack she saw the man, who had rolled Claire over, open the trunk of the Mercedes and remove a large, red, gasoline can.

"Hey man," called one of the other two who were now standing near the white van. "We want our money."

"You'll get it when the job's done and not before."

From nowhere, Ike burst past Diane and went for the man holding the gas can. The man saw him coming and was ready for him. Holding the can with both hands, he swung the can toward Ike's head just as Ike leaped. The can hit Ike squarely in the head and knocked him into the Mercedes. Ike slid down the side of the car and lay motionless on the ground.

Diane stepped around the corner of the building with her gun grasped in both hands and pointed it directly at the man with the gas can. Taking a police stance she called out, "drop the can and don't move."

"Oh, come on lady," the man yelled. "Who do you think you're kidding?"

With practiced precision Diane slipped the safety off, pulled the trigger, and took out his right knee. Screaming, the man dropped the can and collapsed.

"Now, does that look like I'm kidding?" Turning quickly, she aimed at the other two men.

"Don't shoot. Don't shoot," they yelled, and raised their hands above their heads.

Jill was now beside Diane.

"Jill, go into the shed and see if Claire's alive."

Diane motioned to the two men beside the van to walk closer to the man at the Mercedes. "Move over there and if you try anything you're dead."

Jill did as she was told and returned shortly. "She's breathing, but barely."

"Look in the van, and car, to see if you can find a blanket."

"Diane, is that Drew?" Jill asked, nodding toward the man near the Mercedes.

"I don't know, I didn't get a good look at his face. Take care of Claire."

Jill found a blanket in the van and went back inside the shack.

Holding the gun in one hand, pointed at the men, Diane pulled her phone from her pocket and hit speed dial. "Ed. It's me. We found Claire and she's hurt. We need an air ambulance and the State Police. We're on a hill above the house we rented. It looks like there's a field big enough for landing. Yes. Serious. Three of them. Track me by the GPS on my phone. We'll turn on the headlights of two vehicles. Ed, bring a vet too, please. Yes, I said a vet." Her next call was to Caroline to update her.

Diane switched off her phone and called for Jill. "Turn on the car lights. Did you see any rope anywhere?"

"No, but I wasn't looking." Going back to the van she returned with bailing twine.

"Hog tie them as tight as you can. Do your best to cut off the circulation," Diane said. "I don't want them to move an inch."

Both women walked closer to the three men. When Jill reached for the first man's arms he made a move toward her and Diane shot him in the foot. "I warned you."

"You bitch," he yelled, falling to the ground.

Jill proceeded to tie his hands behind his back and then his feet, and connected the two so that his body was shaped like a C.

The first man Diane shot was still writhing in pain so Diane turned the gun toward the third man. "Come on. Make a move. I need the practice."

The man slowly lowered his arms behind his back and let Jill tie his hands. "You're nuts, lady."

"On the ground," Jill instructed. "And don't talk to my friend like that."

Once down, she hog tied him as she had the first man.

Cautiously, Jill walked to the man near the Mercedes. As she bent down to look at his face he reached out and grabbed her ankle. Yanking hard he brought Jill to the ground.

Jill hit hard and rolled away from him as quickly as she could.

Diane fired. One clean shot and his thumb was gone.

"Damn, men. They just won't listen," Diane said, shaking her head.

Jill scrambled to her feet. "It's not Drew."

"Thank goodness," Diane said. "Do you recognize him?"

"No," Jill replied.

Ike hadn't moved. Jill knelt down and patted him gently. "Hang on boy. Help's on the way." Then she ran to the van and pulled out another blanket. After covering Ike with the blanket she went back inside the shack to stay with Claire.

Diane walked closer to the man beside the Mercedes and looked down at him. She didn't recognize him. "Who are you?"

The man just stared up at her.

"Oh come on… like we're not going to find out."

The man said nothing. He tried to put pressure on both his thumb and knee to stop the bleeding.

What seemed like an eternity ended with the sound of a chopper and search lights overhead.

Chapter Fourteen
Wednesday

Ed was the first off the helicopter and ran to Diane who lowered her gun to her side and hugged him fiercely. Two men and a woman in hospital scrubs carrying medical kits were headed for the wounded men when Jill stopped them and led them into the shack to take care of Claire. A casually, dressed man was on his knees beside Ike. Claire was brought out of the shack on a stretcher with her right arm and leg splinted, a neck collar in place, and an IV bag being held by the nurse as the two men carried the stretcher toward the helicopter.

The chopper pilot walked to Ed. "We can't take everyone at the same time."

"Take the woman and the dog," Ed said, without hesitation. "Have the doc do what he can for the other two and we'll transport them by cruiser."

"You want us to take a dog before a human?" The pilot looked at Ed in disbelief.

"That's right," Ed said. "The dog is more valuable than these scumbags."

It was another hour before three Massachusetts State Police cars slowly drove up the dirt road.

The troopers swarmed like bees and to Diane's dismay confiscated her gun. Ed took charge answering as many questions as he could. The three men were taken into custody, placed in two of the cars, and taken down the dirt road. Diane, concerned because Jill was showing signs of shock, covered her with a blanket and kept her talking. One of the troopers produced a thermos of hot coffee, which Diane convinced Jill to drink.

It was nearly dawn when Diane, Jill, and Ed were driven by one of the troopers to Windward Cottage.

Jill's cooking had not gone to waste. There was a state police cruiser in the driveway and Caroline had kept busy feeding two state troopers. The three women collapsed into each other's arms finally releasing their pent up emotions. When they separated and dried their tears, Caroline told them the State Police had intercepted Spence on his way to the Cape and escorted him to Massachusetts General Hospital where Claire was in surgery.

"Did he say how she is?" Diane asked.

Caroline eyes filled and she bit her lip trying to maintain control before answering. "It's very serious. We'll be lucky if she makes it through the surgery."

Jill started to cry again and reached for her handbag and jacket. "We have to go, right now!"

Ed gently placed his hand on her arm. "Jill, wait. There's nothing we can do until she's out of surgery. You all need to get some sleep and then we'll go in a few hours."

Diane nodded her head as she swallowed the lump in her throat. "He's right. Let's get some sleep. Just a few hours and then we'll go."

Jill wasn't done yet. She frantically looked around and began to babble, "Where's Drew? Has anyone heard from Drew? I don't understand, where is he? Why wasn't he with Ike? Was that his car up there?"

Caroline walked over to Jill and took her by her shoulders. "Stop, Jill. Listen to me. Drew was here. Ike ran away yesterday morning about the same time Claire disappeared. He thinks Ike knew she was in trouble. Drew spent all day driving around trying to find him and then came here. When we learned where the vet had taken Ike, Drew left to be with him. You will see Drew later today."

Jill stared at Caroline with a blank look. It was too much to take in. She just stood there and then started to shake.

Ed turned to one of the troopers who had been standing by. "Get a doctor."

Diane led Jill to the sofa where she got her to lie

down and covered her with a blanket. "Caroline, get her some water please."

A doctor arrived with an ambulance and after checking her over decided all Jill needed was a sedative and some sleep. "Keep an eye on her, but I'm sure she'll be fine once she gets some rest."

Diane and Caroline helped Jill up the stairs to bed.

"What the hell's going on here?" the doctor asked, turning to Ed.

***

After settling Jill into her bed, Caroline and Diane returned to the first floor with the backpack and bags of blankets from the cave.

"You two need some sleep too," Ed said.

"Not yet, Ed," Diane said. "We have to show you something first."

In the dining room, they reconstructed their investigation into the missing girls including the map on the wall and the pictures from the security cameras at the marina.

"Holy Hell," Ed whistled. "This is major."

Ed made a phone call to someone who, from Ed's side of the conversation, was not happy about being awakened at dawn. Then he called the troopers into the room. "You are to guard this house and this information with your life. The FBI is on their way."

Fatigue hit Diane and Caroline like death itself and, with the evidence in safe hands, they laid their heads down on the table and fell asleep. A smile crept across Ed's face. Diane was going to hate it when he told her she fell asleep on a dining room table in front of state troopers. He motioned for one of the troopers to carry Caroline to her bedroom. He then lifted Diane in his arms and carried her to her room and laid her gently on the bed. He slipped off her shoes and covered her with a blanket and then took off his own shoes and lay down beside her. Taking her in his arms he whispered in her ear, "Thank God you're okay. If it had been you, I don't know what I would have done." His eyes closed and for the first time in many years he was exactly where he wanted to be.

Four hours later Diane, Jill, and Caroline were getting caffeine kicks with black coffee in the kitchen surrounded by state police and FBI agents.

"Ed, will you drive us to Mass General?" Diane asked.

"Not just yet Diane. We have time for breakfast."

"Ed! We need to get to the hospital."

"Trust me Diane there's time. Claire is out of surgery but in ICU. She's heavily sedated so there's no need to hurry."

That was all Jill needed to hear; she was up and pulling frying pans from everywhere. "Okay. How does everyone like their eggs?"

Caroline and Diane looked at each other and laughed.

"She's back," Caroline said.

After breakfast, Ed spent an hour in seclusion in the dining room with the agents while the women cleaned up the kitchen and then took their posts in the rocking chairs on the back porch. They heard the sound of a helicopter, in the distance, and turned their attention to watch as it flew low along the shore line toward them. The chopper slowly lowered to the beach in front of them spraying them with sand that felt like millions of needles piercing their skin.

Ed stepped out the back door. "Come on, ladies. You wanted to go to the hospital didn't you?"

Jill and Caroline looked at Diane. "How does he do all this Diane?" Caroline asked.

"I told you he's the Attorney General."

Jill jumped up. "No, you didn't. You said he was 'AN ATTORNEY,' not THE Attorney General."

"Well," Diane said. "Minor difference."

"Really?" Caroline said, collecting her handbag. "Just a minor difference?"

***

The chopper landed on the helicopter pad at Mass General and they were escorted to the ICU. Standing at the glass wall that separated them from Claire, they watched as a doctor and nurse administered to her. Claire's face was black and blue, her right arm was in a cast from hand to shoulder, her left leg was casted and in traction, and there were tubes it seemed in every orifice of her body. Spence was fast asleep in a chair with his head on the side of the bed. His left hand was holding her hand with the IV and his right hand rested on her cheek.

Jill wiped her eyes and looked at Caroline who put her arm around her waist. Ed took Diane's hand and gave it a squeeze.

The doctor, seeing them, made one last check and then left Claire's room to speak with them.

"How bad is she?" Diane asked.

"You're Mrs. McPherson's friends who were with her on the Cape?" the doctor asked.

"Yes, Diane replied, introducing the women and Ed."

"It's bad. Besides the obvious broken bones, there are serious internal injuries. Luckily she had a helmet on or I'm sure she would have died. It was a long and intricate surgery. We repaired all the fractures and stopped the bleeding. She's on a respirator to help her breathe. Now it's up to her."

"How long until we can see her?" Caroline asked.

"She should start coming out of the sedation in a few hours. We'll check her then and let you know."

The doctor started to walk away and then came back. "Who's Betsy?"

Diane, Caroline, and Jill looked at each other and then back at the doctor. "Why do you ask?" replied Jill.

"Mrs. McPherson, talked to her through everything."

When they did not respond, the doctor looked confused and continued. "Well, she must be her guardian angel or Mrs. McPherson would never have survived. I'm still not sure she will, but most people wouldn't have made it this far. She's going to be setting off a lot of metal detectors with all the screws and pins we had to put in her."

A nurse directed them to a waiting room where they found Amy and Beth, Claire's daughters. The girls rushed into the women's arms. Once everyone was calm Amy and Beth wanted to know what happened. Diane, Jill, and Caroline did their best to explain what they knew and then there was nothing to do but wait. Eventually, a nurse came to the waiting room to tell Amy and Beth they could visit their mother for a few minutes. Addressing the others, she explained that until Claire was conscious and stable they would only be permitted to take turns visiting for fifteen minutes every hour. The day progressed, slowly, with a rotation of visitations to Claire's side.

Jill tried Drew's cell phone to let him know how Claire was and get news on Ike. Again, there was no answer. "What is wrong with him? Why isn't he answering?" Frustrated she threw the phone in her purse.

Ed was busy making calls and finally called the three women into a private room used for family conferences with doctors.

With a serious look on his face, he asked them to be seated and then proceeded to ask them why they had started their investigation of Wendell.

Diane became the spokesperson and explained about Claire finding the clipping in the scrapbook, how she had known Betsy as a child and was compelled to find out what happened to her.

Ed listened quietly, at times looking down thoughtfully at his hands folded on the table in front of him.

When Diane finished her story he looked up. "You ladies have no idea how dangerous this was. That being said... I have to tell you how brave and courageous you are. The four of you have exposed the largest, human trafficking ring in history."

"What?" Jill said, starting to tremble. "Human trafficking? You mean those girls were kidnapped and sold."

"Yes. Exactly. All over the world."

"Have any of them ever returned home?" Caroline quietly, asked.

Looking directly at her, Ed slowly shook his head from side to side. "None that we have been able to determine."

The women sucked in their breath and prayed Ed was wrong.

"The FBI has been working on some of the individual cases for years, but they never made the connection with the man you call Wendell. As it turns out, thanks to you, they have cracked the case wide open."

"I don't understand, Ed," Diane said. "If the FBI has been working on the same cases, why didn't they make the connection?"

"There was no evidence pointing to The Cape until you found it. The trafficking began on a small scale over fifty years ago and grew to this horrible monster. You were right, Wendell's father was involved early on and slowly brought in a few people, but it was still a small enterprise until they found the perfect piece to the puzzle."

"And what was that," Diane asked.

"Actually, it was two pieces. One was protection from suspicion, and that was Chief Peterson. He ran a tight little town where nothing ever happened because he extorted money from the business owners to guarantee their silence in return for the safety of their families and businesses."

Jill slammed her hand down on the table. "Claire was right about him all the time. The good-for-nothing...."

Ed continued. "The second major piece of the puzzle was Swift Runner, the yacht."

"Really," Caroline asked. "How does that tie in?"

Ed stood up to stretch his legs and continued. "As I told you originally, the yacht is owned by a corporate conglomerate. We finally dug deep enough to locate the owners in the Middle East. They're the other half of the equation. You got the pictures of the four Americans operating from Haworth. Wendell, Peterson, Johnson, and a man named Jeffries who captains the yacht. They abducted the girls and then turned them over to the Middle East connection. We believe the girls were held in the cave until they could make the transfer at sea. The forensics on the blankets will not be back for a while. We're currently gathering as much DNA from the missing girls' families as possible."

Diane held up her hand to interrupt. "Ed, what happened to the children after they left here?"

Ed, who was looking out the window, turned to Diane. "They were sold to the highest bidders. Human trafficking is one of the fastest growing and most heinous crimes in the world. This was a huge ring, but there are many more out there."

Jill was folding and unfolding a tissue in her lap. "Is there any chance of getting any of the children back?"

Ed looked at Jill with sad eyes. "It's doubtful Jill, but we're trying."

Jill crossed her arms on the table in front of her and rested her head on her arms. Silent sobs shock her shoulders.

"I know how compassionate you women are," Ed continued. "If nothing else, you can be assured you have prevented more girls from facing the same peril."

"Where are the four men from Haworth now?"

Diane asked.

"They're in custody and the boat has been impounded," Ed replied.

"And, what about the evidence from Wendell's basement?" Jill inquired, dabbing at her eyes with her tissue.

"The night you saw them removing items from the house, they took it to the basement of the newspaper building. It's all been recovered and will put these men away for a very, long time."

Caroline who had been sitting quietly listening stood and walked around the table. "Okay," she said, holding up her hands and ticking off the pieces of the puzzle. "But there's one thing I don't understand."

Ed got a very strange look on his face and glanced at Diane who met his look with concern. "What's that Caroline?"

"Who were the men who abducted Claire? How were they involved? Were they trying to get rid of her because she was getting to close to the trafficking?"

Ed walked back to the table and pulled a chair out for Caroline. "You better sit down."

Taking her seat Caroline's eyes searched Ed's face. "What is it?"

Ed swallowed and looked at Diane and Jill. "The men who took Claire thought they were taking you, Caroline."

"What!" Caroline exclaimed. "Why would they want me?"

"The man with the black Mercedes, whom Diane shot in the knee, is your husband, Bill."

Caroline could only stare in disbelief. "This is ridiculous. You're mistaken."

Ed leaned over and placed a hand on her shoulder. "I wish we were, but it's a positive ID. He hired the two men in the van to kill you."

Diane got to Caroline just as she passed out. Lowering her to the floor, Diane asked Jill to get a nurse.

When Caroline came too, she looked around dazed. "Diane, what's he talking about?"

Diane looked at Ed and nodded for him to continue. "Bill wanted to run off with his mistress and he needed to get you out of the way so there would be no monetary settlement through a divorce."

"This is crazy. We were having problems, but you're talking murder."

"Apparently, your husband is a very, greedy man. He wanted everything," Ed explained.

"But why did they take Claire instead of me?" Caroline asked, bewildered.

Jill answered before anyone else, "I know, I know... your appearance. You changed your hair, your style, and got rid of the contacts. Bill would have given a description of the way you used to look. The two goons thought Claire was you. Isn't that it Ed?"

"That's exactly right, Jill."

"Claire is in there fighting for her life because of me?" Caroline asked, shaking her head. "This is insane. Where is he now?"

"He's in the infirmary at the prison in Boston. He'll be in prison for a very long time."

"Do the boys know?" she asked.

Again, Ed looked at Diane and then back at Caroline. "Yes. They've been notified and are probably on their way here."

Caroline slumped back in her chair. "Is it too late to stop them?"

"I can try," Ed said. "But why?"

"They don't need to be dragged through this. It's between Bill and me. Please see if you can turn them around. Tell them I'll be in touch when things are sorted."

Ed left the room and the old friends sat and held

hands without saying anything.

Finally, Jill broke the silence. "Well, I still hope the Marina Restaurant manager calls Bridgett."

Diane cracked a smile and looked at Caroline.

"Leave it to Bill to come to kill me in a Mercedes. He always has to show off...," Caroline said, with disgust.

***

Returning to the main waiting area, they found Drew. He was disheveled and looked exhausted with two days' beard growth.

Jill ran to him and he took her in his arms. "How's Claire?"

"Not good," Jill replied. Pushing Drew back slightly, Jill looked up into his eyes. "Where have you been? I've been so worried."

"I've been with Ike." Drew put his face into Jill's neck and wept. "He didn't make it."

To give them privacy, the others went to the cafeteria.

Caroline surprised them by getting a huge ice cream sundae.

"Caroline what are you doing?" Diane asked.

"Celebrating."

"Celebrating what?"

"Not having to make the hard decision about divorcing Bill. He made it for me."

Chapter Fifteen
Thursday

Diane, Caroline, and Jill returned to the hospital early to find Spence still at Claire's bedside and two nurses working in the room. Claire didn't look much better. Caroline tapped lightly on the glass wall. The two nurses turned around; one of them smiled and joined them outside the room.

"Carrie," Jill whispered, in surprise. "What are you doing here?"

Carrie gave her mom a hug and then pointed to Caroline. "Caroline hired me as a private duty nurse for Claire as long as she needs me."

Jill and Diane both looked at Caroline for an explanation.

"It's the least I can do, I should be the one in that bed."

"Spence is exhausted. Why don't you see if you can persuade him to get some rest?" Carrie suggested.

Diane followed Carrie into Claire's room and touched Spence on the shoulder. "Spence, Amy and Beth are staying at my house. When they get here, why don't you take a break and go there for some sleep? We'll let you know if anything changes."

Spence looked at her not seeming to understand. "Spence, it's okay. You can come back as soon as you're rested."

Amy and Beth had entered the room without Diane hearing them. "Come on Dad," Amy said, gently guiding her father out of the room. "Beth and I will take care of him, Diane. We'll be back later."

The vigil of rotating visits with Claire continued for the second day. When it was Caroline's turn, she sat beside her friend and took her hand. "Oh, sweet Claire, I'm so sorry for this. I don't know how, but I'll make it up to you."

While Carrie cared for Claire's every need, Caroline stroked Claire's arm and reminisced about their years of friendship. Carrie smiled at the stories she had never heard before and swallowed hard when Caroline re-visited the hard times the four friends had faced together.

The minutes stretched into hours and there was still no change in Claire's condition.

Drew arrived and entered the waiting room where Diane, Jill, and Caroline were waiting their next turn to visit with Claire. "How is she?"

Jill slowly shook her head. "No change."

"Can I take a turn with her?" he asked.

They hesitated, remembering how Claire had not been completely comfortable with Drew.

"I know she isn't crazy about me, but I promise I won't upset her," he added, understanding their concern.

Jill took his hand and led him to Claire's room. Together they stood beside her bed and Drew leaned over and whispered in her ear. "Come on, Claire, you can beat this. I know you, you're the toughest woman I ever met. We all need you, and that includes me."

Jill walked to the window and looked down into the parking lot. While she watched the cars driving in and out, and strangers going about their daily business, Drew lifted Claire's good hand off the bed. Turning it over, he placed something in her palm and then closed her fingers around it and laid her hand back down on the bed.

Drew walked to Jill at the window and from behind put his arms around her and rocked her gently. She turned and laid her head on his chest.

***

Shortly after Drew left, Carrie hurried to the waiting room.

"She's starting to come out of it. Please call Spence and let him know."

Diane and Caroline rushed to Claire's room while

Jill called Spence to tell him the good news.

By early afternoon Spence and the girls returned, and Claire's brother, Will, had arrived.

Everyone hurried to Claire's room where Spence and the girls entered. While they watched from outside the glass, Claire opened her eyes and looked at her family. She was only awake long enough to blink a few times and then fell back to sleep.

Carrie and another nurse went about checking the monitors and Claire's vitals until the doctor arrived.

Back in the waiting room everyone was nervous with anticipation. The doctor finally left Claire's room. "This is good. We're going to attempt to wean her off the respirator to see if she can breathe on her own. If that's successful, then we'll try her on some liquids and see how she does."

Diane, Caroline, and Jill spent the afternoon bringing Will up-to-date on the past two weeks. He shook his head. "I didn't know about Betsy either. It doesn't surprise me that Claire was so determined to find out what happened to her. You know how stubborn she can be." Then turning to Caroline he said, "Caroline, I'm really sorry about all of this and your situation. You can't blame yourself. If Claire had known what was coming, she wouldn't have changed a thing. She would have willingly taken your place on that bike, so there's no need for you to feel guilty about what happened."

Caroline took his hands in hers. "Thank you, Will, but I'll never forgive myself for exposing Claire to this. I should have stayed home and faced Bill and our problems. I was too anxious to get away from it all."

"Caroline you really need to let it go. You had no way of knowing Bill would do anything this drastic. I'm sure Claire wouldn't blame you," Diane interrupted.

Jill cut in. "Will, what do you remember about the vacations you spent at The Point? Did you ever run into

Wendell?"

Will went back in his memory as far as he could and told them what he remembered. "We loved The Point. The Carters owned that big house you rented and our family rented a cottage a little farther up the beach. Claire and I were really disappointed when we stopped going there. When I think back, the summer Betsy disappeared must have been our last. There was never an explanation and, as kids, we didn't question it."

"Do you think your parents knew about it, and that's why they never took you back?" Diane asked.

Will shrugged his shoulders. "That's certainly plausible. They never said. They're gone now, so we can't ask them."

"What about Wendell?" Jill asked.

"I remember a shy kid we would run into on the beach occasionally. We asked him if he wanted to play a few times, but he never did. There were lots of families around, so one more kid wasn't anything out of the ordinary."

Caroline spoke up. "Did you ever go to the beach near the lighthouse where Claire discovered the cave?"

"We rode our bikes out there fairly often, but I don't remember that particular beach and certainly not a cave. We were always exploring new places and new beaches. We were totally unaware of any danger."

As the day wore on they continued taking turns visiting Claire. She was able to stay awake a little longer with each visit, but was still exhausted and the pain medication kept her in a semi-sedated state.

To everyone's surprise, Ed and Deputy Kevin O'Reilly stepped off the elevator and walked down the hall toward them.

"Ed, what's he doing here," Diane asked, pointing at Kevin.

Ed held up his hand in a calming gesture and

replied, "We need to explain some things. Let's go into the conference room."

With everyone seated Ed explained, "Kevin is not a deputy sheriff. He's an FBI agent who was on assignment in Haworth."

Glancing around the table he waited for a response, but none came. "Isn't anyone going to say anything?" he asked.

"Nothing is going to surprise us at this point, Ed. Go on," Diane responded.

"He was investigating Peterson for suspicion of extorting funds from the local business people." Looking at Diane he continued. "When you called about the boat, we realized there was something bigger."

Deputy O'Reilly spoke up. "I knew from things that Peterson said in the office that you ladies had found something. He was never specific, but he increased the pressure on the business owners and Wendell was on the phone or in the office more than usual."

"Had you suspected Wendell of anything?" Jill asked.

"No. I thought Wendell was one of the people Peterson was threatening and that he couldn't make his payments."

"When did you realize we were onto something?" Diane continued.

"When you met us for the first time, at the bakery, Peterson's attitude was all wrong for your complaint. Instead of being concerned, he tried to make me think you ladies were overreacting. He refused to let me look into it. That was the first clue. I tried to keep an eye on you during my shift. I'm pretty sure it was Wendell who was on your porch that morning, but Peterson refused to investigate. I could tell then that he was protecting Wendell for some reason."

"Did you follow us to the Marina Restaurant one

night?" Jill inquired.

"Yes."

"And, the night on the road when we didn't have the headlights on?" Caroline asked.

O'Reilly smiled. "That was actually an accident. I just happened to be driving the shore road when I caught you."

Diane was more inquisitive. "Did you know Wendell was moving things out of his house that night?"

"I suspected something was going on because I heard Peterson talking on the phone to him when I came on duty. He made reference to 'tonight' so I figured I'd hang around out there. I thought Peterson was going to Wendell's to pick up his payment."

"You just missed them. It wasn't about extortion money. It was about getting rid of the trafficking evidence in Wendell's basement," Diane said.

"Yes, we know that now. They moved everything into the basement at the newspaper. What I can't understand is why they didn't destroy everything."

"So, why are you here?" Diane asked, still apprehensive.

Sincerity emanated from Kevin's dark brown eyes. "I wanted to see how Mrs. McPherson is, and I want you all to know I'm one of the good guys."

Diane glanced at Jill and Caroline. "What do you think?"

"I always liked him," Jill said, with a smile and a chuckle. "He's too clean looking to be bad."

Caroline leaned back in her chair and grinned. "I'm just happy not to have a traffic violation for driving without headlights at night."

Ed looked at the three of them and held up his hands in surrender. "I don't even want to know what that means."

"Do you think I could see Mrs. McPherson?" Kevin

asked.

Diane rose from her chair. "I need to ask the doctor and Spence. I'll be right back."

***

With the others watching, Kevin entered Claire's room. Spence stood up and shook his hand. They had a few words and then Spence gently woke Claire. When she saw Kevin, Claire was frightened and tried to move away. Spence quickly took her hand and leaned down to reassure her she was safe.

Spence stepped away from the bed and Kevin sat down in the chair he had vacated. Kevin took Claire's hand and spoke to her softly. He explained who he was and assured her that the FBI was diligently working on the case.

"You're a remarkable woman. Thanks to you, we have enough evidence to put these creeps away for good, and we're working with Interpol to unravel the operation internationally."

Claire tried to speak but was only capable of a raspy whisper. "Are any of the girls alive?"

Kevin nodded his head and smiled. "I just received word that we have been able to rescue thirty-one girls. They'll be back with their families in a few days. Our agents overseas are working as fast as they can, we hope to find more."

Claire breathed a deep sigh and closed her eyes. For the first time since regaining consciousness a look of peace crossed her face and she fell asleep.

Kevin gently caressed her hand and left the room. Saying goodbye to Diane, Caroline, and Jill he winked and said, "Try to stay out of trouble will you? And, no more snorkeling in dangerous caves!"

The women exchanged glances and feigned innocence.

Kevin laughed. "It's no good. Aaron's a friend of mine. He called me shortly after you rented the gear. I was keeping an eye on you that day too."

"Well, I'll be darned," Jill exclaimed.

"Did you know about the cave?" Diane inquired.

"Nope. I figured you were up to something, but we didn't find the cave until Ed brought us in on the case."

Caroline walked over to Kevin and gave him a hug. "Thank you, but I sure wish we had known sooner so that my nerves wouldn't have been so frayed with all of Claire's antics. You would make any mother proud."

Ed placed his hand on Kevin's shoulder. "Time to go, Kevin. We have work to do."

Watching the two men walk toward the elevator, Jill couldn't help noticing Amy and Beth giving Kevin the once over. "Go for it girls," she said. "He's a good catch!"

Chapter Sixteen
Three Months Later

  Claire had never been to The Cape in the winter, let alone on New Year's Eve. As Spence drove toward The Point she found herself becoming tense. There had been snow earlier and, in the dark, it was hard to see if the road was slick. Halfway between Haworth and Windward Cottage she strained against her seatbelt and pointed out the windshield. She didn't have to say anything; Spence knew she was showing him where she had been hit. She started to tremble and had trouble catching her breath.

  "It's okay, Claire. The road is fine. There's no need to worry," Spence said. "We're almost there."

  As they broke the crest of the hill, Claire could see the glow of Windward Cottage. There she was, the grand old lady, in all her glory, windows ablaze with lights while the wind whipped snow around her like a gossamer veil. Claire inhaled deeply to absorb as much of the scene as she could. Spence continued slowly, turned into the driveway, and shut off the engine. Claire reached over and touched his arm.

  "Can we sit for just a moment?" Her eyes followed the lines of the house that she loved so much, from the widow's walk down to the porch where she spent that first afternoon watching the seagulls. It had never looked more beautiful. The snow, frozen to the shingles and gingerbread trim outlined every detail with sparkling crystals that reflected the moonlight. This was a special place, a thin place, she was sure.

  "You okay?" Spence asked.

  "Yes. This house just takes my breath away and, especially tonight, with the snow. Isn't it something?"

  "Sure is. We better go in. Everyone's waiting."

  Spence walked to Claire's side of the car and opened the door. Handing him her cane, she slowly maneuvered herself around until she could get both feet on the ground. With Spence's help she stood and reached for her cane.

"Now, be extra careful," Spence said. "The ground is slippery."

Claire slowly made her way to the porch. Before she could place her foot on the first step the door opened and Jill appeared.

"Happy New Year! Welcome! Welcome! We're so glad you could make it. Here let me help you. Drew and Ed, get out here and help Claire," Jill said, in one breath.

Claire laughed out loud. "You'll never change, Jill!"

In one swift and sure movement the three men swept Claire up the steps and through the front door.

The parlor was glowing with lights, a fire, and a tall Christmas tree occupied the corner beside the fireplace. Delicious smells were coming from the kitchen and soft music enveloped the room.

Diane and Caroline waited patiently for Claire to remove her coat and get her balance.

Claire smiled at her friends. "What are you waiting for? Come give me a hug. I promise I won't break."

***

The dining room looked like a holiday photo shoot from Victoria magazine. The table was set with fine china and crystal that glistened from the flames of a dozen candles scattered down the center of the table. Fresh, cut greens mixed with red, holly berries and white mistletoe intertwined between the candles.

Diane directed Claire and Spence to the side of the table facing the windows and pulled out a chair for Claire. Claire laid her hand on top of Diane's on the back of the chair and gave her a sad smile acknowledging Diane's effort to keep Claire from having to face the wall where they had taped the pictures of the girls. It was a kind and thoughtful gesture but Claire didn't need to see the wall to see the tortured faces...they would live in her brain forever.

Jill served an incredible meal of Caesar salad, broiled lobster, baked potatoes, steamed vegetables, and cold aspic salad. This time, there really was baked Alaska for dessert.

"Oh, Jill, this is incredible. You really out did yourself," Claire complimented.

"As much as I would like to take all the credit, I can't. Everyone helped."

Diane pushed her chair back and picked up her wine glass. "Let's go into the parlor and let the dishes wait."

"Don't worry about the dishes," Drew announced. "That's all taken care of."

Jill looked at him curiously. "Are you going to do them?"

"No. I have some help coming in so that you don't have to do them. You worked hard all day and I want you to relax and enjoy yourself."

Jill kissed the tip of his nose.

Claire smiled and thought, *Jill may have found the right man this time.*

Settled in the parlor, the conversation revolved around everyone's Christmas with their families.

"Speaking of Christmas," Caroline said. "I have a gift for you Claire." Walking to the Christmas tree she bent down and picked up a large, red envelope. Returning to Claire she handed it to her and said, "Something for your New Year."

Bewildered, Claire opened the envelope and pulled out legal-size papers. Slowly, she studied the papers and looked up at Caroline. "Caroline, I don't understand. What is this?"

"That is the deed to the abandoned, sweater factory in your town."

Claire turned to Spence. "Did you know about

Windward Secrets

this?"

Spence looked as bewildered as Claire. "No. I had no idea."

Handing the papers back to Caroline, Claire said, "Thank you Caroline, but we can't afford this."

"You own it free and clear. Let's just say it's a little something from Bill."

Everyone laughed and Caroline continued. "Of course you all know we were not exactly poor...." Another laugh erupted from the others.

"That's an understatement," Diane said.

Caroline made a motion with her hand as if brushing Diane away. "You're a good one to talk. At any rate, Bill purchased your dream for you Claire without even knowing it. Divorce settlements are even bigger when your spouse is convicted of attempted murder. Call it retribution, justice, whatever… it's yours."

"We can't accept; it's too much." Claire tried, again, to give the papers back to her.

Jill spoke up. "Actually Claire, it's irrevocable because we are all depending on you."

Diane stood and walked to the tree to retrieve another envelope. Handing it to Claire she said, "Ed drew up the papers to incorporate. Drew has a business plan ready and waiting when you decide what you want to do with the factory." Looking at Jill, Diane chuckled. "Jill has a few ideas for you and, of course, they involve food. I will take care of advertising and marketing with Caroline's help with the artwork. We have all chipped in seed money. And, your board of directors are all sitting in this room with you right now."

Claire looked around the room incredulously.

"What? You don't think we're qualified?" Ed asked, pretending to be offended.

Claire just shook her head.

Jill spoke up. "Oh, come on Claire, you've never

been speechless as long as we've known you."

More laughs and Claire wiped at her cheeks. "My gifts will certainly pale in comparison to this."

With Spence's help Claire stood up and he handed her a gift bag. Slowly she made her way around the room. To each of her friends, she handed a small jeweler's box and waited for them to be opened.

"Oh Claire," Caroline exclaimed, as she slowly drew a gold chain out of the box. "A mustard seed necklace. How incredibly appropriate. I've always wanted one."

In turn, Caroline, Diane, and Jill stood and hugged Claire. After they were seated, Claire walked to Drew. "I am returning your gift to me... it was my mustard seed." She picked up his hand, opened his palm, and then closed it around a small object. "Why didn't you tell us?"

Drew looked at the tiny object in his hand and then back at Claire. "Sit down and I'll explain."

Claire hobbled back to sit beside Spence and looked at Jill who nodded and smiled.

Drew opened his hand to show the others what Claire had given him. It was the tiny, silver, top hat from the Monopoly game. "Jill knows, but I haven't told the rest of you. My name is not Drew Carson."

The faces in the room had become sullen not knowing what to expect.

"My real name is David Carter. Betsy was my sister, and this is my house."

The silence was deafening.

Finally, Diane asked, "Why?"

"I started coming back to The Point, after college, whenever I could. I used an alias and never stayed in this house because I didn't want any publicity. I just wanted to grieve and honor Betsy's memory privately."

Caroline looked at him with compassion. "That's understandable Drew or rather David... this will be hard because we're so used to calling you Drew." Looking at the others she added, "How does everyone else feel about it?"

Diane answered first, "I think we have to respect Dr... er... David's decision. He had no obligation to us. I can understand completely."

"I like him no matter what his name is," Jill said, smiling, from ear to ear.

Diane couldn't resist. "That too, is an understatement."

Everyone laughed and Jill moved over to sit on David's lap.

David looked at Claire. "You were unconscious when I gave you the top hat. How did you know it was me?"

Claire swallowed hard. "SHE told me."

No one said anything for a very long time. They needed time to digest what Claire had said.

"David."

"Yes, Claire."

"When did you recognize me?"

"Shorty after you all arrived. Young men never forget the long-legged beauties of their youth. You were the most beautiful girl I had ever seen. I was smitten. Of course, I didn't figure it out until that last summer. It was 'puppy love' for sure... that time," he finished with a glance at Jill.

The women all laughed. Ed and Spence looked at each other realizing they were on the outside of an inside joke.

Claire blushed. "Oh come on David, I didn't recognize you."

"No, you didn't, but you knew something was off and that's why you were so hostile... at times, no offense, but you were. Besides, you never had a crush on me and that's the difference."

"And, a darn good thing she didn't have a crush on

you!" Jill blurted out.

The laughter was back.

Caroline was still curious. "David, surely you couldn't have been sure about Claire's identity?"

"Well, first of all Claire is not that common a name so I was pretty sure but, when I went to Boston, when you kept Ike, I did a little research and confirmed it."

It was Claire's turn to ask a question. "Why didn't you say anything? It certainly would have made things easier."

"Another understatement," Diane declared.

"Because I suspected you were on to something regarding Betsy's disappearance and I wanted to see what you would turn up."

"Well, David, it's nice to see you again after all these years," Claire said. "I apologize for being rude. However, if you hurt my friend, I'll have to kill you."

David laughed and pushed Jill off his lap. "Actually Claire, you don't need to worry about that. He stood and then lowered himself to one knee. Taking Jill's hands in his, he looked up at her and said, "Jill Stone, would you do me the honor of being my wife?"

Jill looked as if she was going to start her trembling.

"You better say yes or Claire's going to hurt me." Letting go of Jill's hands he pulled a diamond ring from his pocket and held it up. "What'll it be?"

Jill bent down and took his face between her hands. "You are the kindest, most thoughtful man I have ever known. I love you more than I knew was possible. It would be my honor to share the rest of my life with you."

David slipped the ring on her left ring finger and everyone clapped.

"Okay, now help me up! I have a bum knee."

Jill gave him a hand up and said, "I'm only doing this to save your life you know."

Ed laughed. "I think it's Diane you have to worry

about. She's the one with the Beretta."

More laughter and Caroline brought champagne from the kitchen. The friends gathered in front of the fireplace to toast the couple. As they drank Claire closed her eyes and thought of Betsy.

"What a wonderful ending to a rather rough year," Diane said.

Ed put his arm around her and pulling her close whispered in her ear, "I love you."

Everyone returned to their seats and David held up his hand for quiet. "There's one more gift." He went into the kitchen and returned with a large box that he placed at Claire's feet. "Belated Merry Christmas, Claire."

Claire wrinkled her brow. "For heaven's sake David, you didn't have to get me anything."

"Go ahead. Open it."

Claire leaned over in her chair and removed the lid from the box. Reaching in, she lifted out a wiggling, black, Labrador puppy. As she held him close to her face to smell his sweet puppy scent, he licked the tears from her cheeks. All she could do was look at David and nod.

"Has anyone noticed the time?" Jill asked. "It's nearly midnight. We need to toast in the New Year." Standing up she resumed her role as tour director. "Caroline, more champagne please. Grab your coats everyone. David and Spence you help Claire up the stairs."

"Up the stairs?" Spence questioned.

David patted Spence on the back. "Oh yes, it's their tradition to have nightcaps on the roof."

Spence became seriously concerned. "The roof? Are you kidding? We'll get blown away and Claire's not up to it."

"Oh yes I am," Claire declared. "I wouldn't miss this for the world. It's too cold for 'Ike' so I'm going to lock him in the kitchen until we come down."

David looked at Claire. "So, it's Ike, is it?"

Claire smiled. "What else? Will you help me get him settled in the kitchen?"

Ed and Diane took the lead up the stairs followed by Caroline and Jill. David and Spence took Claire under her arms and with very little effort she hopped up the stairs on her good leg.

"The Confessional" on the roof once again released it's magic. The snow and wind had stopped. It was quiet, calm, bright from a full moon, and eerily warm for December 31st.

The men walked the perimeter of the roof to make sure it was safe and marveled at the view. Returning to the women gathered at the railing, facing the ocean, they counted down the seconds. "Five, four, three, two, one…Happy New Year!" Their glasses were raised and clinked together. They drank and then threw the glasses toward the ocean.

As the others moved toward the door to the house Claire called out, "David, will you wait with me?"

"Of course, Claire, what do you need?"

Claire motioned for the others to go down the stairs and close the door. Then she took David's hand. "Just wait."

Mystified, David did as he was told. He and Claire stood near the door to the house and waited.

"There," Claire whispered, pointing to the far side of the widow's walk near the railing.

David turned in the direction she was pointing and squinted his eyes. Shaking his head he whispered in return, "It can't be."

"But it is…," Claire said, quietly watching the tall woman and blond, curly-haired, little girl smiling at them peacefully.

Matthew 17:20

And Jesus said unto them, Because of your unbelief: for verily I say unto you, If ye have faith as a grain of mustard seed, ye shall say unto this mountain, Remove hence to yonder place; and it shall remove; and nothing shall be impossible unto you.
- King James Bible "Authorized Version," Cambridge Edition

About the Author:

After a long and varied business career, Kathleen Andrews Davis turned to writing as a way to leave a legacy for her grandchildren. During her career Mrs. Davis wrote everything from press releases to policy and procedure manuals, and was managing editor of a corporate newspaper. Creative writing was never a consideration until grandchildren became the catalyst to becoming a storyteller. Several short story awards encouraged Mrs. Davis to write Emerson's Attic, a time-travel series for middle-grade readers. While writing, Smoke and Mirrors, the second in the Emerson's Attic series, the characters of Windward Secrets invaded her brain and refused to leave. Writing Windward Secrets was like visiting with friends. Davis is currently working on the third Emerson's Attic and plans to continue with adult fiction as well. Encouraging young people to read is her passion, writing is her joy.

Acknowledgements:

"Some people come in your life as blessings. Some come in your life as lessons." - Mother Teresa.

This message is never truer than in an author's life. Every person we meet has a story, an experience or a trait that influences us, some good and some bad. I have been blessed by both and wish to thank those who have played valuable roles in my journey as an author.

Thank you, to my wonderful husband, Denny, for his encouragement and giving me the space to be me. Thank you to our daughters for being the unique and incredible people they are; Kelly, my rock, whose humor keeps us laughing and who's always there for me without being asked; and Kristin, who humbles me with her success and has given us the ultimate gift of grandchildren.

Thank you to my selfless friends who never say no when I need input, especially Diane Meling and Sandy Geimer on whom I tested the first draft of Windward Secrets when it was only half written to see if they thought it had merit. Their enthusiasm was overwhelming and gave me the confidence to keep going.

Special thanks to my dad, who never knew how important his common sense and "can do" attitude was to me. He never drew the invisible line that girls weren't supposed to cross. And to Mom, the extrovert of the family, whose wanderlust and stubborn independence taught me to never limit myself.

This year has brought many new author friends, Chantal Jauvin, Bette Stevens, Kathryn Jones, Deanie Humphreys-Dunne, and Fia Essen, all of whom I thank for sharing their knowledge and experience. Also, a big thank you to Judi Slogoff, my little terrier friend, who never lets me give up.

Special thanks to Carolyn Sparks, my soulmate, who is a constant source of ideas and encouragement. And to her husband, Jack, who puts up with me interrupting his quiet time.

Finally, my gratitude to God, for answering my prayers time and time again, and blessing me with loving family and friends.

Social Media Links:

Website: www.kathleenandrewsdavis.com

Blog: http://dollhousesmemoriesandmore.com

Facebook:

Kathleen Andrews Davis:
https://www.facebook.com/Kathleen-Andrews-Davis-323632201162944/timeline/

Emerson's Attic: https://www.facebook.com/Emersons-Attic-Series-574120916052537/timeline/

Twitter: https://twitter.com/DavKathleen

Made in the USA
Middletown, DE
17 February 2016